BEAC
BLONI

To Marilyn —

JOHN LAWRENCE REYNOLDS

With every good wish!

BEACH BLONDE

AT BAY
press

WINNIPEG

Design by M. C. Joudrey and Matthew Stevens.
Layout by Matthew Stevens and M. C. Joudrey.

Published by At Bay Press November 2021.

Library and Archives Canada cataloguing in publication is available upon request.

ISBN 978-1-988168-54-8

Printed and bound in Canada.

This book is printed on acid free paper that is 100% recycled ancient forest friendly (100% post-consumer recycled).

First Edition

10 9 8 7 6 5 4 3 2 1

atbaypress.com

For
Wombat and Mo

Just another B-flat blues…

Men, unlike women, are able to trust one another,
knowing the exact degree of dishonesty
they are entitled to expect.

– STEPHEN LEACOCK

1

They got along well in Millhaven, Arden with his cool attitude and class, Slip with his street smarts, both feeling like high society compared with the guys they ate and worked out with, most of them two-bit heisters and general scum.

Four months before Slip's release and a year before Arden scored parole, Slip told him about strings he'd been pulling, strings that would open doors for an ex-con like him who played by the rules. Arden wasn't sure at first what the rules were and who set them, but they became clear when Slip agreed to share them.

"Where you gonna go, you get out of here?" Slip asked, and Arden said he had no idea.

"Okay," Slip said. "I can help you with that," saying he'd been talking about Arden to a friend, the same guy on the outside who was helping Slip pull those strings. Meaning the Russian. "He likes what you did, what got you in here," Slip said. "Thinks you're a hero. Might have a job for you soon's you're out."

They were in the workout room, Arden doing arm curls with ten-pound weights, Slip lying back and talking. "Who's gonna hire an ex-con, his first day back on the street?" Arden said.

"My guy will. Viktor Khrenov. You heard of him? Runs a bunch of companies called Odachni. It means good luck or somethin' in Russian. Odachni Construction, Odachni Wholesale, Odachni Property Management, bunch of others. This guy's something. Got here twenty years ago without a pot to piss in. His old man was a commissar back in Russia, a big shot before the country fell apart. Tells his son, 'Go to the States, Canada, nothing here anymore,' and Viktor did. The States wouldn't let him in, didn't like the old man's history. So he tries Canada. Lands in Toronto, gets a job in construction, figures out that you don't get rich with a hammer in your hand unless you're using it on the guys who've got what you want, and now he's worth, what? Forty million? Maybe fifty million easy."

Arden kept nodding his head, trying to show he was impressed. He hadn't thought about a job when he got out, hadn't thought about anything except surviving. He arrived at Millhaven planning only to keep his head down, then stay as far away from the place as possible. By the sound of things, he shouldn't think about messing around with a guy like Viktor Khrenov.

Then, walking with Arden in the yard a week later, Slip said, "I got word about that job waiting for me, just like Viktor promised. See, soon's I got sent up here Viktor said, 'First day out, you got job with me. Good job too. No shovelling shit. I find something you like, you deserve.'"

Slip lowered his voice and guided Arden away from the other cons. "Viktor comes through for guys if they, you know, go to the wall for him. He's doin' it for me. Sent word this morning. Listen to this. He's gonna have me running a restaurant and a bar for him when I get out. He just bought the place and he's got plans for it. He even signed me up for lessons, a correspondence course on bookkeeping. It's all basic shit but I'll be able to watch things for him, the money comin' in and goin' out. He's got his own people, accountants and all, at his offices in Toronto but I'm gonna be sixty klicks away, down the lake on this beach. I was always good with numbers, you know. I get out of here, work for Viktor a while and I'll be doin' something besides driving trucks and roofing. Had enough of that crap."

Arden asked what the prison people thought about him taking a correspondence course in bookkeeping.

"People here, the parole assholes," Slip said, "they love it when you tell them that stuff, how you plan on improving yourself."

Arden looked away so Slip wouldn't see him smile and maybe ask what was so damn funny. Guy in the pen taking a correspondence course on bookkeeping? Didn't that raise eyebrows, make somebody suspicious?

"You think, puttin' all them numbers down and keepin' track of money, you think it's gonna be hard," Slip went on. "I looked at some of the stuff they sent to get me started. I figure, after you pick up a few things, there's nothin' to it. Somethin' I shoulda learned long ago. It'll give me the perfect job. I mean, who the hell wouldn't want a job runnin' a bar and a restaurant, free food, cop a few drinks, pinch a waitress's ass now and then?"

Arden wondered what Slip had done to make the Russian so grateful. He figured keeping his mouth shut about whatever put Slip in Millhaven for three-to-five probably qualified.

Over the months before Slip was released, he and Arden hung together in the yard and in the workout room, Arden preferring Slip's company because, while Slip was no prize, he knew how to do time and told stories with an edge to them. Like the way he picked up his nickname.

"My old lady named me William," Winegarden said. "She'd call me that. 'Will-yum' she'd yell out the door to get me home. One day, I was ten years old, I had three cops chasing me down Parliament Street. I'd been grabbin' bikes off porches and backyards, sellin' them to a guy on Queen Street who'd slip me ten, twenty bucks for them. The cops see me grab a bike and take off down Sherbourne and they send two cruisers after me. Cruisers are behind me, blue lights flashing, sirens going, all that crap, and I pedal my ass down an alley, going between houses, tearing right through a couple of back yards and I lose 'em. Ditch the bike and haul back home. 'He gave 'em the slip,' one of the neighbours said to my old lady. He'd seen me take off from them, then get home. 'Five whistles and two cruisers and your boy gave 'em all the slip'. My ma, who'd pulled a few games in her day, thought it was funny as hell. She started calling me Slip and it stuck."

Slip told Arden stories about Khrenov too, like the one about Viktor's construction company pitching for a job renovating an office building on Yonge Street.

The owner of the building advertised for tenders, and eight companies wanted to bid on it. Or they did until they heard about the Russian planning his bid. He's the one who told them, calling them up, telling them who he was, and saying, "We all in race and best company win, okay?" Before the other guy could reply, the Russian would say, "Who's best company, huh?" He didn't have to say that. He said it because he wanted to. They knew what was going down. Within a week, six of the outfits backed out, saying they'd prefer to bid on other jobs or they were too busy or made some other excuse. The only outfit left in the running besides Odachni was a new operation, couple of young guys trying to get started, never went up against the Russian before.

The Russian finds out who they are, and three days before the tender is due he sends his quote sheet to them by fax, sends it to these guys who aren't used to dealing with Viktor and don't know what he can do when he's going head to head with somebody. Sends them the whole thing, the details, the schedule and the bottom-line estimate, to the guys bidding against him. Viktor waits two, maybe three hours, then calls the construction outfit and asks to speak to the president. "I am such idiot," he tells him, laughing. "I spend week, maybe two weeks on tender and I make mistake, send to you, not to owner. I am sorry, but makes no difference because your tender, your price, is higher than mine, right? Is right?" Then lowering his voice he says in a voice like wet gravel, "I know is right." The next day the new outfit, having asked around the city "Who is this guy?", meaning Viktor, withdraws their tender. When he gets the word, Viktor sends the partners a bottle of cognac.

Slip laughed when he told Arden about it in the yard at Millhaven, leaning back and giggling while Arden nodded his head, getting the story, understanding it.

"Guess you don't screw around with him," Arden said, meaning the Russian.

"You good with him, he's good with you," Slip said.

"You ever try to cross him?"

Slip shook his head and looked away. "Don't know anybody ever tried to cross Viktor and is still walking around," Slip said.

The day he was released Slip handed Arden a piece of paper with a Toronto address and telephone number on it. "It's Viktor's," he said. "He wants to meet you. He likes heroes."

Eight months later Arden was on a bus heading to Toronto, released early for staying out of trouble, carrying his clothes stuffed in a plastic suitcase with room to spare.

Slip had written Arden to remind him about looking up Viktor. He included a map showing the bus stop nearest to Viktor's office, and another map showing a place called Tuffy's on the beach strip at the west end of Lake Ontario.

Viktor's office was in a former candy factory. Three stories high, the place still smelled of vanilla, an old brick building with steel-framed windows, except on the top floor where oversized picture windows were shaded with drapes. "He lives on the top floor," Slip wrote. "Supposed to have a goddamn palace up there. Haven't seen it myself. I hear it's got a shower that'll hold six people or, as Viktor puts it, 'Five pussies and me'."

The sign at the entrance said *ODACHNI INDUSTRIES – OFFICE SECOND FLOOR*. Arden climbed the stairs and gave his name to the first person he saw, a guy standing at an open file drawer, saying his name and that Slip Winegarden had sent him to meet Viktor Khrenov. The guy turned from the files and looked toward the open door of a big office at the far end of the room, one entire wall of it windows. The Russian was coming out of his office, having heard his name and Arden's. He walked through the place like a general inspecting his troops, looking around at other people, some working at desks, some standing and watching.

"Hero is here," the Russian barked, pointing at Arden. Everybody in the room paid attention, looked to where the Russian was pointing. "Real hero. Man does what is right, he breaks neck of *mudak* who raped his sister. That's hero, eh? You guys, come look at Arden Hero, he's here."

The Russian stopped in front of Arden, offered his hand and shook Arden's. To Arden, Khrenov looked more Mexican than Russian, his skin dark, his black moustache untrimmed and his chest heavy. He wore a stained white shirt and baggy trousers with cuffs, but the Rolex on his wrist, shining with diamond inserts on its face, and the gold chain around his neck said he could afford to dress any damn way he pleased.

"Goose," the Russian called over his shoulder, still gripping Arden's hand. "Come meet Slip's friend, real hero."

"I'm not," Arden began.

Khrenov said, "You meet Goose, he needs friends like you."

Arden wanted to say he didn't want any friends, especially didn't want friends who looked like the guy walking toward them, six-two, maybe six-four, two hundred and fifty at least, with a shaved head and dead eyes. The hand extended by the bald guy was soft and pink. Arden withdrew his hand from the Russian's and took Goose's hand.

Arden said, "How you doing?"

"Mick Googins," the guy said.

"Is Goose, eh?" the Russian said, slapping Googins on the side of the head and laughing, Googins smiling and showing a gold tooth in front. Turning to Arden the Russian said, "You, you are Arden Hero, eh?" Arden was about to say his last name, but before he could speak the Russian said, "Wallet." Arden didn't know what he meant until the Russian stuck out a hand that looked like a fielder's mitt, palm up.

"He wants your wallet," Goose said. "I'd give it to him, I was you."

Arden took his wallet from his pocket and placed it in the Russian's hand.

Looking up at Arden from time to time the Russian flipped through the wallet, grinning a little. He raised his eyebrows at the picture of Arden's sister Donna Lee. There wasn't much else in there. His parole officer's business card, pictures of Arden's parents and one of Sally, his dog when he was a kid. The bus ticket from Millhaven, his health and social insurance cards, the map to Tuffy's that Slip had sent, and five twenty-dollar bills given to him when he left prison that morning. Viktor took out four of the bills, handed them to Goose and gave the wallet back to Arden.

"What you think?" the Russian asked Arden. "Is fair?"

"For what?" Others around him were watching with their arms folded or looking around and grinning, ready for a show.

"Job fee. I find you job, you pay me."

"What's the job?"

"You pour beer, wash glasses, stuff like that. Easy. Fun too."

Holding the bills in his hand, Goose said, "Slip got you a job at Tuffy's on the beach strip, down the lake. He tell you how to get there?"

Arden said, "He sent me a map."

"Viktor's paying you six a week plus private room and board. You can help yourself to a beer now and then, and there's more if you do a good job."

The Russian was watching, nodding and grinning. When Arden looked at him, Viktor waved a hand toward the door and said, "Go."

"You're leaving me with twenty bucks," Arden said. "How the hell do I get there?"

The Russian shrugged and kept grinning, and Goose said, "Nobody gets anything for nothing around here."

Before Arden could speak the Russian asked, "After guy rape your sister, you really break guy's neck, like Slip say?"

Arden stood silently as though considering whether to answer or make a move to get back his money. Answering was safer. "Yes, in a way I did."

Goose hadn't moved. The men who had been watching, waiting for Viktor to put on his show, never sure what the Russian would do in front of an audience, grew serious. No more grins, no elbowing the guy next to them.

"Shouldn't be in prison, you do that," the Russian said with a hint of compassion. "Should be hero, like I call you. I call you hero, right?"

Arden wanted to say it wasn't like that, what everybody said he had done and why he had done it. It got him time in prison and respect from people like Slip while he was there, and maybe from people like the Russian now that he was out. What happened three years ago wasn't like everybody thought it was, but it was better to let them think what they wanted rather than try to explain the complicated truth.

Viktor started walking away.

"When do I get my eighty bucks back?" Arden asked the Russian's back.

The Russian's response was to keep walking and raise a hand, waving it in a gesture that said he really didn't give a damn.

Arden looked at Goose, who shrugged his shoulders. The other men went back to doing whatever they had been doing when Arden arrived.

The hell. Arden turned and rode the elevator downstairs, trying to work out what had just happened. Crossing the parking lot he grew angry about the Russian handing his money to Goose and daring Arden to take it back, daring him to even *ask* for it back. Wondering what the best way of getting to the beach strip was, and if twenty bucks would get him there, he heard the Russian call, "Hey, hero."

He looked back to see Khrenov leaning from an open window, Goose behind him, watching. "Refund. You get refund. See what happens, you impress me?" The Russian tossed the twenty-dollar bills out the window and Arden stood watching them float down, the air calm, no wind to scatter them. He walked around the parking lot, bending to pick them up, knowing Viktor was watching. The son of a bitch is humiliating me, he realized. He's watching me bend to pick my own money off the ground. Maybe it was a test to see if I would take his crap and be a good soldier. If it was a test, Arden told himself, he had passed it.

Arden flattened the bills, replaced them in his wallet, and walked away without looking up at the window where the Russian had been watching, Arden not caring if he was still there or not.

2

There was nothing like Tuffy's on the beach strip, and the beach strip was nothing like Arden had seen before. Two, maybe three miles of sand sometimes only a hundred yards wide, the lake on one side, the city and bay on the other. A canal cutting across the strip with a freakin' high bridge above it carrying an endless stream of trucks, buses and cars three hundred feet over the canal. At ground level an iron lift bridge, the bridge going up and down every half hour so lake boats and ocean freighters and rich guys in yachts could sail in and out of the bay, to and from the city with its factories and warehouses.

Arden watched all this through the bus window, marvelling at how his life had changed over the years from hot-shot military man to ex-con, and wondering where the next turn would take him, probably away from this strange place.

Tuffy's had opened as Tiffany's a hundred years earlier, an upscale restaurant and guest house back when the beach strip was the summer destination for wealthy families who moved from the city into ten-room turreted houses facing the lake, mini-mansions they called cottages. The families and servants were there for the sand and water and especially for the cooling effect of the lake. When the air temperature back in the city was stifling hot, the beach strip was several degrees lower.

By the fifties, air conditioning made summers on the beach strip unnecessary and unfashionable. The rich families stayed in the city, leaving the strip to factory workers and their families. Tiffany's became a roadhouse named Tuffy's, with young women in short skirts slinging beer and burgers and the management renting upstairs rooms for a couple of bucks a night. Or an hour.

Tuffy's had started moving back to being the kind of place it used to be. Not a stodgy joint with velvet furniture and crystal chandeliers, but a comfortable spot where you could get a good steak and a bottle of decent wine, maybe have a martini before dinner in the bar. You could sit looking out at the lake, listening to a small jazz group in the corner and telling yourself you were sampling the good life.

This lasted until the guy who had fixed up the place sold it to Viktor Khrenov within a month of it reopening. That was pretty hasty. In fact, the only thing faster than him deciding to sell the place was how fast he disappeared after closing the deal. Some people thought he went south, maybe to the Turks and Caicos, one of those places in the Caribbean where rich guys spend their days checking out the topless beaches and their nights in the casinos. Others weren't so sure.

The day after closing the deal, Viktor arrived at Tuffy's like a thunderstorm through an open window. His first move was to fire the jazz group. Viktor disliked almost any music except the kind that inspires Russian men to dance while sitting down. He replaced the guy who had managed the place for the previous owner with the newly released Slip Winegarden, just as he promised.

The guy who had sank millions into the place before vanishing knew the beach strip was about to change back to an upscale destination. Everybody's home and doghouse was air-conditioned, so it wasn't the cooling effect of the lake that appealed to people who wanted to live there. It was the lake itself, and the shoreline that could almost stand in for northern Malibu in summer. Winter was a different matter, but the people who were willing to pay top dollar just to look at a lake in summer escaped it by jetting off to Florida or the Bahamas when snow arrived.

Many people were ready to spend a million dollars or two on a condo the size of a double garage if its windows faced the lake. You spend that much on a place to live, you look for a classy place to eat and hang out, not a dive where the customers have more tattoos than teeth.

Slip explained all this after greeting Arden with slaps on the back and while showing Arden his room on the second floor. The room had a double bed, a four-drawer dresser, a couple of chairs, a table, a washroom with a shower, and two windows facing the lake.

"Did you see those new places for sale, up near the canal?" Slip said. "You wanta live there, you gotta get your hands on at least a million, some of them go for two, three million. And whaddaya get? Two bedrooms, one big room that's all windows facing the lake, a couple of crappers, and a place to park your Porsche. You got young hotshots working in Toronto, comin' over here because the same place in Toronto, right on the lake, sets 'em back twice as much, easy."

Arden was putting his clothes into the dresser drawers, listening to Slip.

"But see, there's a limit to how many people will lay out that much for a view," Slip went on. "So there's places up and down the strip here, some neat houses but a lot of 'em dumps held together with baling wire and hope. Some of them people, this is the only place they've lived, only place they *want* to live, just so they can see the sun rise over the water every morning, if they get up early enough. Some are on welfare, livin' in rooming houses next to rich big shots who ride the train or drive their Benz into Toronto and back every day. They're drinkin' single malt scotch, eat nothin' but good steak, people next door are dinin' on bologna, and they're all neighbours. Hell of a mix, eh?"

Arden said, "Yeah, I guess so."

Slip was still talking. "You got yourself a million-dollar view here," pulling the drapes open, showing the lake shining as blue as the Caribbean in the summer afternoon light. Then, turning back to face Arden, he said, "When're you supposed to go and see your parole guy?"

Arden told him in a week at an office down the strip, he could walk there.

"Not gonna be happy knowin' you're workin' with me," Slip said.

Arden said the people back at Millhaven weren't happy about it either, two parolees working together. They made an exception for his good record before being convicted, and because it was important for him to have a steady job. Even in a bar.

Slip said when his parole officer objected to him getting a job in a bar, Viktor's lawyer took care of things. Viktor's lawyer took care of a lot of things, Slip added, and once again Arden wondered just what Slip had done to earn Viktor's gratitude.

"You're about my size, right?" Slip said. "Sixteen and a half collar, thirty-four arm? I'll give you a couple of my white shirts to get started. Pick up some of your own in town after you get your first paycheque. I'll bring some down from my room for you." He headed for the door. "After you get changed we'll go to the bar and I'll show you how to use the register, take the credit cards."

Before Slip could leave, his phone rang. Slip looked down at it, said "Aw, shit," then brought it to his ear and said, "Yeah, Viktor," walking away quickly so Arden couldn't hear.

Arden discovered that the Russian called Slip two, sometimes three times a day, Arden never hearing anything more than "Yeah, Viktor," before Slip headed for some place where Arden couldn't hear him.

An hour later Arden was in the bar wearing one of Slip's shirts and tying a white apron around his waist, Slip checking the bar receipts.

"Can I ask you a question?" Arden said. When Slip said sure, go ahead, Arden told him about Viktor and Goose taking the eighty bucks out of his wallet, then throwing it back at him out the third-floor window. "Why's he do that?" Arden said. "He didn't need the eighty bucks. Not like I did."

"'Cause he wants you under his foot," Slip said. "If you'd tried to get it back, he'd've had Goose throw *you* out the window and kept the eighty bucks."

"Why does he act that way?"

"I told you. His father was a fuckin' commissar. Runs in the blood, those Russians. They're all either dictators or, whattaya call it, people back four, five hundred years, did what they were told and had no rights."

"Serfs."

"Yeah, them. Viktor's no serf, that's for sure. Did he tell everybody you're a hero?"

Arden nodded. "Yeah, never asked my full name. Just called me Arden Hero."

"That's what got him interested in you. I told him about you from Millhaven. It impressed the hell out of him. Anybody who does what you did for your sister, settle the score on the spot and screw the consequences, that's his kinda guy. Grab a glass, I'll show you the right way to pour a draft."

"What's Goose, his muscle?" Arden asked, getting a glass down from a shelf.

"Googins keeps an eye on construction for Viktor." Slip started filling the glass, moving the lever like a maestro. "Used to be a project manager for one of the big companies, doing business in Europe, Asia. The company got caught bribing governments, and Goose got caught coming through customs with half a key of blow. He's back on the street a year later and nobody'll hire him except Viktor. Goose checks the construction projects, keeps Viktor informed. Viktor doesn't like going to construction sites. He needs Goose because Goose knows how to get a building up and finished. But his real job is being Viktor's muscle, working with a little shit named Heckle."

Slip finished pouring the beer and held it up to admire the head, an artist showing off his work. "Whatever you do, keep away from Heckle." He handed the glass to Arden. "That's how you pour a beer. Drink up. You get two a day on the house."

Arden learned Tuffy's was a serious money-maker for the Russian and an upscale meet-market for everybody else. The clientele was young, almost nobody over forty, lots of them singles. He was happy to stay in one place for a while, tend the bar like he had been told to do. Slip, on the other hand, was a man in motion. He kept moving around the place, surveying the dining room, walking through the kitchen, scanning the receipts at the bar, and chatting up women everywhere, or trying to.

Slip wasn't a bad-looking guy, Arden admitted. And he seemed pretty good at making women laugh, telling them stories, hearing them giggle. Arden couldn't get over the change. Couple of months ago, Slip had been on a bunk at Millhaven talking big, another bullshitting loser. Now he was mixing martinis, sometimes finding women to take home on Saturday nights. The Russian gave him the chance for that, Arden knew. He still didn't know why. But he could guess.

After closing that night, Arden watched Slip collect the cash and total the credit card receipts, making notes on a scrap of paper. "He makes a lot of money from this place," Arden said, meaning the Russian.

"Bet your ass he does," Slip said. "Viktor never loses money on a deal. Never. But it's not the money. You think he bought this place just for the money?" Slip was looking at the bar receipts, counting the beer bottles. He stopped to look around, make sure they were alone in the bar. "Viktor's got his hands in a lotta places they shouldn't be, okay? Runs the cash from here through the books back in Toronto. Makes it ten, twenty times more than it is and he can wash all his money clean. The guy's fuckin' brilliant that way." Then, looking at Arden and grinning, he said, "Bought it for the women, too. You'll see when he shows up here some day. He won't tell us he's coming. Never does. He gets here and he'll let everybody know he owns the place. He'll chat up some broad, get her laughing, next thing you know she's writing something on a piece of paper and handing it to him, and it ain't a recipe for borscht. He gets rich in Toronto and gets laid here. How's that for a good deal? I'll tell you something else. You work with the guy, with Viktor, you're playing chess with him, right? You gotta know that going in. He's a Russian, they all play chess. Play chess, drink vodka, screw women. It's what they do, what Viktor does. You gotta remember, Viktor's always a couple moves ahead of you, right?"

"I don't play chess," Arden said. "I'll bet you don't either."

"Don't be a wise guy, okay? What I know about chess is, you win by thinking ahead of the other guy. When you're workin' with Viktor and he does something, anything, it's something he planned to do two, maybe three moves ago. So you want to keep up with him, you gotta know he was gonna do it, *capice?* You want to play Viktor's game his way, you gotta remember that he's always thinking ahead. Like he did with this place. Look around. You like this place?"

Arden looked at the panelled walls, the lighting, the furniture. It wasn't Buckingham Palace but it looked good enough to be in a Hilton somewhere, not on the beach strip. "He must've sunk a lot of money fixing this place up," Arden said. "Or at least the guy he bought it from did. Must've put, what? Couple of million in it."

"Guess who bankrolled most of it, off the books?"

Arden nodded, getting the picture. "What happened to him, the guy who did all the work with Viktor's money?"

"Depends." Slip stood up, folded the piece of paper he had been making notes on and stuffed it into his pocket. "Ask Viktor, he'll say the guy retired to Mexico, he's sitting on his ass by the ocean, drinking tequila. Ask Goose and he'll say the guy isn't *by* the water, he's *in* the water and he ain't comin' up. Let's go, I'll show you the booze invoices, how to handle them."

"How do you feel, working with the Russian, him doing things like that?" Arden asked, both of them walking toward the office.

"Like I should see him as little as I can. The less I see of Viktor, the better I feel." Slip paused at the office door. "Go see Charm Darby," he said, meaning the Caribbean woman who ran the kitchen, "get us some coffees, cream with no sugar for me. I'll be out in a couple of minutes," shutting the door behind him.

Two nights later Viktor arrived at Tuffy's, walking in and smiling at everyone, Goose a couple of steps behind. In the bar, Viktor waved Slip over and the three men entered the office, closing the door behind them. Ten minutes later they emerged, Goose carrying a metal box, Slip and Viktor smiling. Viktor looked over at Arden as though seeing him for the first time. "Arden Hero," he said, walking toward him. He slapped Arden's back and said, "Slip telling me you doing good job, maybe do his job yourself some day, eh?"

Arden shrugged and muttered that he wasn't so sure about that, just as Goose walked past, looking at Arden with one raised eyebrow. Viktor just laughed and walked away, his voice booming goodbye, and waving as he headed out the door.

"I have to tell you, I don't like this setup."

Arden's parole officer was a guy named Albert Renton who spoke with a Scot's accent, like he was ordering haggis or had a set of bagpipes in his filing cabinet. Renton had called Arden at Tuffy's, telling Arden to be in Renton's office the next day at two o'clock. Not asking if it was convenient or even if Arden knew where Renton's office was. Just an order to be there, as though Arden was still back in Millhaven and the warden wanted to see him.

Renton didn't say hello when Arden arrived, didn't even offer to shake hands. He gestured at the only chair in his office, the size of a gas station's bathroom. He turned to open a file folder and started flipping through it, his expression saying he liked nothing he saw. Arden sat quietly, telling himself this guy could send him back to Millhaven with a snap of his fingers.

"Let's put it on the record," Renton finally said, closing the file and looking up from it. "I'm not comfortable with you working down there, not a bit. I had my way, you'd've spent a few months in a halfway house to familiarize yourself with the community. We waived that on special appeal because you had a job and a residence of sorts. Plus you're not far from my office. I can keep an eye on you." His voice dropped a tone or two. "And I will. But I am still not happy about this arrangement. Not happy at all."

Arden asked what Renton was worried about.

Renton said, "Get it clear. I'm not worried. You're the one who should be worried. You're working in close conjunction with a former inmate, you're serving alcohol, and your employer Mr. Khrenov is well-known to law enforcement officials."

"Never been convicted, I understand."

"True enough."

"So he's innocent before the law."

Renton tilted his head and looked at Arden as though Arden had just told him the world was flat. "Don't be naïve."

"Look," Arden said, "there is no way I'm going to do anything that might put my ass back behind bars. Ever."

Renton said, "You want to guess how many people have sat in that chair and told me the same thing?"

"How'd things go with your parole officer?" Slip asked Arden when he returned.

Arden said they were all right. He didn't want to discuss it with Slip. He planned to be careful about anything he'd discuss with anyone until he had a better idea about whose side everyone was on.

Arden soon realized that Winegarden didn't run Tuffy's as much as watch over it for the Russian. A grey-haired guy named Carter ran things in the kitchen, working with Charm. Together they set the menu, bought the goods, supervised the chefs, and showed Slip what they planned to do two or three days in advance. Slip would nod and say yeah, yeah, bored with it all. Christine was the head waitress in the dining room. She had a working-class earthy look that Arden liked. Sarah, tall and slim with a voice an octave lower than you might expect, was the dining hostess; she helped out the wait staff when needed. Everyone knew their jobs, and it became clear to Arden that all of them were damn good at it.

There were no major decisions to be made. Some outfit in Toronto chose the wine and sent shipments every two weeks. The beer reps knew when to fill the cooler with bottled beer, charge the draft kegs, keep the inventory up, all of it scheduled and automatic, almost no input from Slip needed. The staff was paid with bank deposits out of Toronto; Slip didn't touch their paycheques.

Slip's biggest chore, besides walk around like he owned the place, was to work with Charm totalling the receipts every night. Charm processed the credit card charges and Slip handled the cash, writing the daily amount on a piece of paper and putting it into the safe with each day's take.

The place took in a lot of cash, especially on weekends, sometimes two thousand or more a night. "How come we get so much cash?" Arden asked, and Slip said because a lot of people didn't want to leave a trail of credit card receipts, especially in the bar. Others on the beach, not the ones in the million-plus condos, didn't have credit cards. Slip did the cash privately, taking the money into the office, doing the counting there before putting the cash in an envelope and locking it in the safe.

Every Monday before noon Goose arrived with a metal box to be filled with the previous week's cash. Viktor almost never came along for that, Slip explained. The cash wasn't big enough to interest him. Besides, Viktor wasn't a morning guy, and he had other things to do on Mondays.

"You see the deal?" Slip said to Arden. "You see how he worked things out? Construction company handles millions, tens of millions of dollars. Easy to hide a fortune there, but it's not cash, right? This place," meaning Tuffy's, "does nothing in comparison but as long as there's cash he can boost it, the cash. It gives him two ways to hide the money, get it?"

Arden didn't get it entirely.

Slip just shook his head and said, "Guy's a fuckin' genius."

Slip explained he totalled the cash each night, kept a copy for him and Charm, and entered the figure on a private computer site, the figures encoded so nobody else could read them but Viktor. "This way, nobody can take any cash after I count it, right?"

Carter, the guy in the kitchen, did things Slip might have been expected to do, including opening the place up in the morning, getting things started. Slip never got out of bed before ten a.m., sometimes later.

Slip and Arden fell into something of an employer and employee relationship after Viktor's visit to Tuffy's, with Slip speaking to Arden only when he wanted to point out something that Arden was doing wrong or could do better. It's not that he was acting pissed at Arden, only that he had become more like a boss than the guy who got Arden the job in the first place. Which encouraged Arden to get close to the other people at Tuffy's, people he dealt with day to day. Like Charm, who ran things in the kitchen and brought lunch and dinner to Arden. She started setting aside dishes for him he liked—cold pasta salad with chunks of white tuna, and pork schnitzels with sauerkraut. A couple of dining room waitresses found ways to throw Arden a smile or two. Arden would smile back, say they looked good, comment on their hair and all. But nothing more than that. Not right away. He didn't want to cross some unmarked line, break some rule that would get him fired and out on the street. If that happened, Renton would move his ass to some halfway house in the back end of Toronto, some place where Arden would come home every night to a crowded dining room table and an empty bed.

Slip seemed careful dealing with women, especially the staff at Tuffy's, never taking any of them home or inviting them up to his room, although he'd talk a good line. One night Arden was busy cleaning glasses at the bar, polishing the beer tap levers, doing housekeeping. At the far end of the bar two women on the sunny side of forty were putting away vodka martinis, both in silky blouses and pencil skirts, one with short hair, deep mahogany red, the other with hair the colour of lemons, down to her shoulders.

Slip and Arden watched while a bald guy in a cheap tweed jacket wandered over and asked how the women were doing, having no better line than that. They smiled, said they were fine, turned their backs to him, and he got the message.

Slip laughed and said, "You need a damn good line to pick up women like them."

Arden looked over and said, "So what's a good line? You got any?"

"You know what works for me? It's 'You look as good as a twenty-five dollar cinnamon roll'."

"You're kidding me."

"Nope. I'll tell you why it works. Because it's fun and they don't expect it. You make her laugh, hit her with a line she hasn't heard before, maybe needs to think about it, and you're not dangerous anymore. Some guys in here, they figure women are like fish, a trout or something, and all you need to hook them is the right bait."

"Like what?"

"Guy comes in here one night, says to one of the regulars at the bar, 'Have you been sitting on sugar?' She can't figure it out, so she says, 'No, why?' and he says, 'Because you've got one sweet ass'."

"And that worked?"

"Must have. She kept talking to him."

"Was her ass that sweet?"

"Don't know. I missed the view." Slip leaned closer to Arden, lowered his voice. "Did you ever think when we were in Millhaven, all that time we were up there dreaming about women and booze, that it would all be here for the taking?"

"How much've you took?"

Arden meant the women. That's all. Just the women, talking guy to guy, nothing more.

But Slip blinked, caught his breath, and walked away, heading back to his office, closing the door behind him harder than necessary.

Slip knew most of the regulars, especially the women. He'd tease and flirt with them, playing the jovial host, flattering them. Some teased back, enjoying the attention, women in their thirties and forties pretending to be bad, hanging out at an upscale roadhouse, drinking rum and coke, or margaritas, daiquiris, whatever.

Slip tried to impress Arden as much as the women. Slip may not have broken the neck of his sister's rapist, but he could show his buddy from Millhaven a thing or two, maybe build up Slip's opinion of himself, his own ego, along the way.

Arden had his own chances to talk to women, some asking where he was from, and he'd say he'd been away, on the road and on the move. If they'd ask where he'd been, he'd say "here and there," a way of telling them to mind their own business. He kept reminding himself he'd get serious about meeting women only after he got used to being out of prison, when he no longer jumped at the sound of a dropped pot or a broken glass. He'd look for a low-maintenance woman, somebody who wouldn't cling to him, somebody who knew what she wanted and wasn't desperate; he'd had it with desperate women. A woman who knew who she was, maybe have a bit of edge to her, not bitchy, just toying. Like the forty-something blonde who came in a couple of nights a week and sat alone in the far corner. She'd talk to Slip a little, and twice Slip told Arden to watch things for him, he'd be back in half an hour, giving the woman his arm and opening the door for her.

"You got something going with her?" Arden asked one night when Slip returned, and Slip frowned and said it was none of Arden's goddamn business.

One night the blonde came in and sat at the bar instead of the far table. Slip was in the office, telling Arden before he left that he had things to do and not to disturb him. Arden brought her the Bacardi and Coke she always ordered. Handing it to her he smiled and said, "I'm Arden," and she said, "I know." He asked how she knew, thinking she had asked around about him, and she said she could read, picking up the sales receipt he had handed her and turning it to show his name printed on it by the sales computer.

He said, "Since I don't get sales slips from you, I gotta ask. What's your name?"

She said, "Josie."

"Josie? What, is that some short form of a name? What's it short for?" And she said, "Susan," looking down at her drink.

Smart-ass broad, Arden thought. He walked away and left her, thinking he'd bet she was no natural blonde. Well, the hell with her.

3

Josie short-for-Susan was in the bar the night Viktor called Arden and told him to come with Slip to a meeting at eleven o'clock. Viktor had been in Tuffy's that afternoon, striding into the place alone. Grabbing a handful of peanuts from the bar he tossed them in his mouth and walked around the dining room talking to people with his mouth full.

In the kitchen he hugged and planted kisses on the cheeks of Charm Darby and two of the lunch-hour waitresses, the women smiling as they walked away, looking for a tissue to dry their cheeks.

The Russian came into the bar and shook Arden's hand, asked how the hero was doing. Then he turned to Slip and said, "Let's go," and the two men went into the small office off the kitchen, closing the door and remaining there five, ten minutes before coming out, the Russian doing all the talking, Slip looking down at his feet and nodding.

Viktor pointed a finger at Slip and said something before leaving Tuffy's by the beach entrance. Through the windows in the bar Arden watched the Russian walk north toward the canal along the paved trail, wearing a shapeless cotton hat on his head, nodding and smiling at people he passed. How's he getting home? Arden wondered, but it was none of his business.

"Jesus, I'm glad he's gone," Slip said, coming up behind Arden. "You glad he's gone?" he said to Charm as she walked past. Charm smiled and said nothing, heading for the kitchen.

Slip remained tense after the Russian left, walking in and out of the office several times, talking to nobody. Just before the dinner crowd arrived Josie short-for-Susan showed up and sat at a table in the back. Arden set a Bacardi and Coke in front of her and smiled tightly. She muttered "thanks," and he walked away.

A few minutes later Charm leaned in through the door from the dining room and told Arden to pick up the phone, Viktor wanted to speak to him.

"You come with Slip tonight," the Russian said, not even a hello. "Okay, Arden hero?" Arden could hear traffic in the background and wind noise. Viktor was in a car somewhere on the highway. The Russian hung up without another word.

Arden knocked on the office door. Slip pulled the lock aside and looked through the partially opened door. "Viktor called," Arden said, "wants me to come with you tonight. What's this about anyway?"

Slip frowned and turned away. "Told me he's thinking of buying some property down the lake," his voice and expression telling Arden he was thinking of something else as he spoke. "Said I should look at it with him."

"What, he wants your opinion?"

Slip nodded. "I'm supposed to be meeting him somewhere at eleven," Slip said. "I don't know where. He'll let me know later. Never told me you'd be coming along. That's how he does things, keeps you guessing." He closed the door and slid the lock back in place.

Half an hour later Slip entered the bar and sat next to Josie, Slip doing the talking and the blonde shrugging and nodding, looking as bored as Slip looked anxious.

Arden didn't care what they were talking about. He was still pissed at her. Hell, he'd known Josie was short for Josephine, something like that. Just making conversation, that's all, and she cuts him up? Who needs a bitch like that?

At about ten-thirty Charm came in and said, "Viktor's on the phone again, wants to talk to you," and Arden picked up the receiver in the bar.

"Tell Slip I'm at Esso station on Lakeshore," the Russian said. Arden could tell he was in a car again, on the move. "Make sure he brings cellphone."

Arden said okay, and the Russian asked if Arden had a cellphone. When Arden said he didn't, Viktor told him to get one. "You don't have one, how I reach you when I need you?" Which made Arden wonder why Viktor would want to talk to him at all, and also wonder why the Russian hadn't called Slip on his own phone instead of having Arden pass the message on to Slip, like he did.

Arden waved at Slip from behind the bar, calling him over and telling him what Viktor had said about picking him up at the Esso station.

"I'll have Charm watch over things, the bar and stuff, until we get back," Slip said, checking his cellphone. He looked at his wristwatch. "Should be back here by closing. Might as well go now." Slip took his car keys from behind the bar. He looked back at Josie short-for-Susan and waved at her. She smiled tightly in return and drained her Bacardi and Coke.

Slip drove a dull-green Toyota, smelled like a delicatessen inside but it seemed to run well. He swung the car out of Tuffy's parking lot onto Beach Boulevard about twenty minutes to eleven, the lake a dark presence to their right, highway traffic on the high-level bridge to their left.

Arden was thinking about something his parole officer had said to him the day before, "Some day I want you to tell me why Viktor Khrenov gave you such a good deal," Renton had said, adding, "Because I still can't figure it out." Arden didn't say anything then, but he'd been wondering about the same, about the deal Viktor had given Slip. So he asked Slip now.

"Told you," Slip not taking his eyes off the road. "Worked for him. He owed me."

"I know you told me, but he gave you a hell of a deal here, right? He's gotta trust you too, handling all that cash. Gotta trust you a lot. And me too, I guess."

"The hell you mean by that?" Slip looked across at him, then back at the road.

"Well, we both got records, you right out of Millhaven, me out a day when I started, and he's got us handling liquor and money? How many guys're going to go that far? How's that work?"

"It works because Viktor wants it to work," Slip's tone saying he didn't want to talk about this.

Arden said nothing. Driving over the lift bridge on the canal, getting ready to turn onto Lakeshore Road, Slip looked across at Arden, this time with no edge in his voice. "You don't need to know details, okay? You don't need to know nothin' because Viktor don't want anybody knowin', but I did that time for him, okay? In Millhaven. I did it for him."

Arden shrugged. He'd figured this out for himself.

After telling Arden he didn't need to know details, Slip told him details anyway. "There was some stuff, some material, a special kind of Italian marble, hard as hell to get over here and expensive. One of the companies was using it in a new bank downtown, and Viktor wanted it for his job, a head office we were doing up in Don Mills." Slip looked around, like he was checking for somebody watching or listening before pulling onto the highway.

"He sends me to the job site downtown at night, big truck with a lift on it," Slip said. "Promises if I pull this off he'll cover for me, make it worth my while. He's treating it like it's nothin', like it's somethin' he's doing and everybody does it, no big deal. That's what he tells me. I know better, but Viktor keeps sayin' it's all right. Me and two other guys, we go in and tell the watchman on the job site that we need to move twenty-five square metres somewhere. We've got papers and all, a requisition order from the builder. He says he's gotta check and I tell him there's no goddamn time to check, if he does anything to hold us up I bury his ass under a ton of the goddamn marble, so he stands back and we load the crap on the truck. I hand him a couple hundred in cash to keep his mouth shut and not get his legs broke, and we leave."

Arden said, "You had to know he'd report it, the watchman."

"Yeah. And I heard something happened to the watchman too.

Maybe, maybe not. I hear a lotta stuff over there, Viktor's office. You'd be amazed. Anyway, two days later the place downtown goes to use the marble, they're five hundred feet short, track it down to Viktor's company, and the watchman I.D.'s me."

"You tell the police it was all your idea, Viktor knew nothing about it."

"Something like that, yeah."

"The marble was already down when they came after you, right? Installed in the project, the one Viktor was doing?"

"No flies on you."

"Viktor gets you a lawyer, tells you to take the fall and he'll look after you when you're out."

"Cash in my pocket and an easy job when I get out." Another look at Arden.

"I'll bet you didn't have much of a choice. You take the fall, everything's cool. You implicate him, he breaks your legs."

"Breaks whatever the hell he wants."

"What'd you tell me you got, three years? Maybe Viktor didn't get you such a good lawyer. Or maybe you had a record, not your first conviction."

"And maybe you should shut up about stuff you don't know nothin' about." Slip bit his lip, looked out the side window for a moment. "I got a record. Before that stuff with the Italian marble. Nothing big. Couple of probations, sixty days in Milton. Nothing like Millhaven."

"Figured that," Arden said. Then: "Was it worth it? The time in Millhaven for Viktor?"

Slip's tone changed again. "None of your fuckin' business. There's the gas station. Where the hell's Viktor?"

The gas station was lit like a small town, a restaurant to one side and a dozen pumps filling the space in front of it. Three cars and a pickup truck were at the pumps, and maybe half a dozen cars in front of the restaurant. Slip wheeled the Toyota into the station, looking around, then swung the car toward the restaurant.

"There he is," Arden said, pointing to the far side of the restaurant where the Russian emerged from the shadows wearing a black leather jacket and a Blue Jays baseball cap.

"The hell's with the cap?" Slip said. "He's never talked baseball with me."

Arden watched the Russian walk toward the car, head down. When he reached the Toyota he opened the passenger door and said "In back," to Arden, who stepped past Viktor, inhaling the Russian's citrus-scented cologne, and climbed into the back seat, behind Slip.

"We will go," the Russian said, pointing down the highway. "You turn when I tell you." He opened the car's glove compartment and began looking through the papers in there, shuffling them without reading them.

"What're you looking for?" Slip asked when they were on the highway again.

Instead of answering Viktor looked around the car's interior as though he were thinking of buying it.

"What'd you need Arden along for?" Slip said, his voice higher in pitch now, the nervousness coming back.

Viktor laughed, more a bark than a laugh, and turned in his seat to look back at Arden and smile. "I like this guy," he said. "Good man. Hero. Arden Hero, that's his name, eh? Breaks guy's neck for other guy *nasiluya* his sister? You know that?"

Slip said, "Yeah, yeah," waving away the Russian's words with his hand. "I'm the guy told you about it, remember?"

Viktor straightened himself in the seat, looking out the windshield again. "Show respect. Should show respect to heroes. Big orange light up there. Turn there. Got your phone?"

Slip nodded and slowed down the Toyota, turned where the Russian had told him, into a lane made of interlocking stone set between lines of cedars, past a sign that said NO TRESPASSING and another sign saying FOR SALE over the name of a real estate company and ZONED FOR COMMERCIAL. The lane led about a hundred feet to an empty concrete block foundation, ending at a slab of concrete that had been the floor of the garage. Beyond it, the shoreline sloped to the lake. Clouds had moved in. There were no stars, no moon to be seen. Just lights from the road behind them, lights from the shore to the right of them where the canal cut through the beach strip, and strange light off the clouds, reflected from the steel companies along the bay.

The Russian held up his hand for Slip to stop before they reached the concrete slab where the garage had been, looking around, checking out the land. The grass remained uncut; the garden was weedy and sad. "Idiot owner doesn't sell when he is alive," Viktor said. "Million easy, he could make. He dies, kids dump it cheap." He looked at Slip. "Good place for restaurant, eh? Viktor's restaurant?" He frowned. "Is that song, old song? Something like that? Get everything you want at Viktor's restaurant?"

Slip was fumbling with his phone, looking back at Arden, making sure he was still there. "Yeah, nice spot. What'd you need my phone for?"

"Give me." The Russian held out his hand and Slip gave it to him, Viktor starting to enter numbers in it, dialling. "How much you take?" Viktor said, his eyes on the phone.

Slip smiled, frowned, shrugged. "How much what?"

"Money. From me. How much?" He set the phone on the dashboard, watching it like it might explode, not caring if the number he dialled was answered.

"I don't…" Slip swallowed hard. "The hell're you talking about, Viktor? I took nothin' from you. Nothin'."

From the back seat Arden saw Slip's hand move toward the door handle. The Russian saw it too and his left hand seized Slip's right arm, gripped the bicep hard enough to make Slip wince.

"Jesus, Viktor," Slip said. He was beginning to cry. Arden moved back in the seat, into the far corner, not wanting to know what was coming but knowing anyway. "I didn't take nothin' from you."

"You insult me twice?" the Russian said, sounding more tired than angry. "No, three times." He turned in the seat to look back at Arden, his hand still a vice on Slip's arm. "Three times this piece of *dermo*, this turd, pisses on me, eh? Three times. He steal from me, he lie about it, and he talk, eh? Three times, I can count. Viktor can count." Looking at Slip. "He talk to people about me, people he shouldn't talk to about me, what I do, things I do…"

Arden didn't know what the hell the Russian was talking about, but Slip seemed to know. He turned to face Viktor, his eyes wide, looking at the Russian's face, then looking down, Arden not knowing at what until Viktor's right hand came up holding a small revolver. The sight of it was enough for Slip to find new strength. He managed to pull his arm from Viktor's grip, his arm upright and his body twisting away as Viktor fired and the bullet tore through Slip's upper right arm with a flash and a sound inside the closed car that sent Arden deeper into the corner of the back seat.

Slip screamed in pain and in fear, dropping his arm now and turning to face Viktor, his expression like a punished child, crying and saying "Viktor, please, you owed me, *you owed*…!" until the Russian put the muzzle of the gun against Slip's head and fired again.

Arden looked away before Viktor fired the second time. He opened his eyes to see the back of Slip's head against the seat and the passenger window with a hole in it, blood running down to the sill along with something Arden didn't want to think about.

The Russian frowned, looked back at Arden. "He used right hand always, eh? Didn't he? Should have watched."

Arden's throat was full of stones but he managed to say yeah, Slip had been right-handed, wondering if he should open the door and try to run.

The Russian nodded, then did something that astonished Arden. He handed him the revolver he had just used to kill Slip. "Wipe off," Viktor said. He reached into a jacket pocket and withdrew a handkerchief, the old-fashioned kind, red with white patterns, tossing it at Arden and saying, "use this."

Arden thought, I could shoot him with this or take it and run. But Viktor hadn't given him the gun by mistake, he wouldn't take a chance like that. Now he sat watching Arden, waiting for him to do what the Russian told him to do. When Arden started wiping down the gun Viktor turned and took Slip's phone from the dashboard and tossed it back at Arden, saying, "This too." Then he reached inside Slip's jacket, removed his wallet, and took a key from the wallet. Arden had seen Slip take the key from there several times. Obviously so had Viktor.

Now Viktor sat smiling at Arden, watching him run the handkerchief over the gun and phone. "Big adventure, eh?" he said. "Go for drive, nice night, look what happens." He gestured at Slip's body, looked back at Arden and said, "Okay, now put gun in his lap, anywhere."

Arden had to rise and lean forward to drop the weapon on the seat next to Slip.

"Now phone. On floor." He snapped his fingers, extended his hand to Arden. "Rag. And go. Out."

Slip hadn't turned off the engine. After Arden passed the kerchief to the Russian, he opened the rear passenger door and saw Viktor use the rag in his hand to grip the button and lower the window on his side a little, then slip the car into Drive. As the car began to creep forward, he opened the door still with the rag in his hand, leaving no prints on the handle. He stepped out of the car to stand near Arden, watching the car move onto the concrete garage pad before waving to Arden to help him, and the two men put their shoulders to the back of the car, easing it along the pad and past some dead shrubs to the lip of the rise, tilting it over the edge and down.

Watching the Toyota roll into the water, Arden realized he hadn't wiped his prints from the door handles or from anything inside the car, which had enough momentum to carry it out into the water where it started to sink beneath a canopy of bubbles. What happens to fingerprints under water?

Viktor looked at his watch. "Come," he said, and began walking along the lane back to the highway. "You think I did bad, Arden hero?" Viktor said, Arden glad to be walking away.

"You did something," Arden said, almost relaxed now, knowing the Russian was not going to shoot him like he did Slip.

"You help somebody, you good to him and he steal from you and lie to you, try to get people after you, what can you do, eh? What, you say 'Okay, my friend, I am like Jesus, I forgive you, we kiss and make up, eh?' You think I can do that?"

Arden said no, he didn't think anybody he knew could do that.

"You ever see that before, see man shot?"

"In Somalia. I was there with the army."

"How many you see?"

"Dozen. I don't know. All of them Somalis anyway. After the first couple of times, a lot of things don't matter anymore."

"That is right. You are right. After time, nothing matters. Move on. We move on, you and me. People see you go with Slip tonight, right? Leave Tuffy's, just you and him?"

Arden, knowing where this was going, said, "Yeah, some people did, I guess."

"And nobody see me with you or him."

"Nobody did." Arden had a good idea who Viktor had called from Slip's phone and why, but he didn't see any benefit in telling the Russian what he had figured out. "What the hell do I say?"

"To who?"

"To the police. To anybody who says, 'You left with Slip in his car and he winds up dead.' I'm the guy they'll think shot him."

The Russian was grinning. "Maybe. But you did not. What, no faith in justice system? You don't kill him, you don't go back to prison."

"So what do I say happened?" Meaning something besides the truth, the truth being that he witnessed the Russian execute Slip right in front of him.

"You tell them this," Viktor said, not slowing down or looking at Arden. "You tell them Slip say, 'Come with me, see what Viktor buys, wants land for new restaurant,' and you go but then you see gun, Slip shows you gun in car and you don't like idea. You tell Slip, you say, 'Let me off at restaurant, pick me up later,' something like that, and he does. You wait, have beer maybe, he doesn't come back, you take cab back to Tuffy's.' All figured out, eh?" And the Russian touched the side of his head with his forefinger.

Arden said, "Where are you supposed to be when all this went down?"

"I am home." Viktor stopped, waited for Arden to stop and look at him. "Is true. I am home, Slip calls me on cellphone, I tell him fuck off, I am busy and hang up, Slip shoots himself maybe." He put his arm around Arden's shoulder and smiled. "Not to worry, eh? You my hero. You good man, I can tell. I do not hurt good men, ask anybody. You are safe, for sure." He handed Arden the key from Slip's wallet. "You know his job?"

Arden nodded, avoiding Viktor's eyes.

"Good you do it now, eh? Bad news, Slip's gone. Good news, you got new job."

At Lakeshore Road Viktor looked left and raised an arm. A pair of headlights came on from a car parked on the shoulder maybe a hundred feet away. The car began moving toward them. "You were not here, eh?" Viktor said, both men watching the car approach, Arden seeing it was a Chrysler 300S, black it looked like. "And I was not here. Get in back," Viktor said as the big Chrysler pulled up, Viktor already opening the front door and stepping in. Arden could see a young woman behind the wheel, her dark hair in a short pixy cut, showing off big gold earrings. With both doors closed she swung the car in a one-eighty heading back toward the gas station and restaurant, saying nothing to either man. Arden guessed her age at twenty tops, keeping his mind busy wondering about her age so he wouldn't remember, wouldn't think about what he had just seen.

"How did it go?" the woman asked without looking away from the road.

"Good," Viktor said, like somebody had asked what kind of day he'd had, getting home from work, thinking about dinner. "We had good talk, and Slip's happy, happy man now." Turning to look at Arden in the back seat, he said, "Good talk, eh?" and Arden kept staring straight ahead through the windshield, watching them approach the gas station and restaurant they'd left maybe twenty minutes ago.

"Go in, have beer, maybe two. Stay, wait, let people see you, then take taxi back, close up shop, okay?" Talking like Arden didn't have a choice.

"Why?" Arden said. The pixie wheeled the car behind the restaurant where the Russian had been when Slip picked him up.

"Why what?" The Russian not looking around.

"Why am I doing all this? What the hell? You tell me to ride here with Slip and now..."

The Russian turned to look at Arden. "Why? I tell you to. Is enough, okay?" Then, with a smile, "Hey, you new manager at Tuffy's. Get more money, new apartment, get to meet women, maybe *yebat* different one every night, eh?"

"I don't know anything about running a restaurant, a bar."

"Don't need to know. Carter, the black woman Charm, the others over there, they all know. Got problem, you call me, okay?"

"What about the books, the cash and stuff?"

Viktor waved it away. "You know how. Slip said he teach you. Cash in safe, write down cash, keep for Goose to come on Monday." He turned to face forward again. The car was stopped, the engine purring, the dark-haired pixie looking straight ahead. "You my eyes, my ears. Go."

Almost before Arden could close the door the Chrysler was moving out of the shadows onto the road. He watched it turn toward Toronto.

Inside the restaurant he ordered a grilled cheese sandwich and a beer, eating half the sandwich and making the beer last almost an hour while he kept remembering what had been said and what he had seen in Slip's car. What did the Russian mean when he said Slip had talked to people about Viktor, people he shouldn't be talking to. The police? Was Slip doing some deal with cops? Arden couldn't believe it.

Sitting there trying to look like he was enjoying his sandwich and beer, sometimes Arden's hand would start to shake and he found it hard to breathe. Instead of the beer he'd rather have a shot or two of rye, something to shock his nerves into steadiness. Finally, he walked to the front counter to pay the bill and ask the woman to call him a cab. She said sure, going where? When he told her Tuffy's on the beach strip she looked at him like he had two heads.

He was the patsy. He was the one the police would come to, knowing he'd been in Slip's car, riding with him, his fingerprints inside if they found them. They'll talk to him and he could tell them the truth, tell them he watched the Russian shoot Slip in the head, all he did was watch, the Russian made him watch, except the Russian would have an alibi, Arden knew. Viktor had an alibi and a patsy.

Or he could say what the Russian expected him to say. That he refused to be in the car with Slip after he showed Arden the gun, knowing that being in the same care with an ex-con and a gun would send both of them back to Millhaven. So whatever was going down, he'd say, he wanted nothing to do with it, and he got insistent enough about it that Slip let him off at the restaurant, saying he'd be back later. Arden had a sandwich and a beer while he sat waiting for Slip to come back, giving up after nearly an hour before calling a cab to take him to Tuffy's. It would work. That's how Viktor had planned it, always thinking a couple of moves ahead, like Slip had said.

He had no choice. If he told the truth, Arden knew, he could be charged as an accessory. And if he agreed to be a witness against Viktor, he'd soon be as dead as Slip. That wasn't a risk. It was a certainty.

He'd tell them the Russian's tale when asked.

And he knew he would be asked.

4

Harold Hayashida could see no benefit in rushing, nice day like this, the lake shining blue in the sun like the Caribbean. Hayashida had taken his wife to Jamaica the previous winter, leaving the kids with her parents. Two weeks of walking on the beach and drinking daiquiris every day, getting up every morning to see the sun rise over the ocean and feel it on their skins, the temperature back home not climbing above freezing all the time they were there.

The beach strip wasn't Jamaica and the lake was nothing like the Caribbean, but at this time of year the air temperature was almost the same. So he took his time on the way, stopping at a Hortons to pick up a large double-double, which he kept in the Chevy's cup holder, driving until he saw the cruisers on the shoulder of the road ahead with two cops leaning against one of the cars, telling stories. One of the cops looked his way as Hayashida slowed for the turn, bending to look in Hayashida's passenger side window as the detective lowered it.

The cop asked, "You alone today?"

"For now," Hayashida said. He knew the cop, one of those guys who never wanted to do anything more demanding than drive a cruiser, and never would. "Who answered?"

"I did." The other cop was a younger guy, blond hair and rimless glasses, looking like a high school math teacher. He reached for the notebook in his tunic pocket and started reading what he had written, doing it by the book. "Got the call at 11:23, arrived on site at 11:35, surveyed the car in the water, called the wrecker…"

"Who saw it first, the car?"

Flipping a page in the notebook. "Real estate agent, woman named Kormos, spelled K, O, R, M, O, S…"

Hayashida wanted to say the rookie didn't have to spell it, he could see the name on the real estate agent's sign at the end of the driveway, but he let the guy talk while he took his first sip of the coffee. Warm day like this, he still needed his hot shot of caffeine.

"She's the agent selling the place, came by to show it to somebody and there's the car under the water, you could see it easy with the sun at the angle it was earlier."

"Who's in it?"

The young cop blinked. "Forensics, they're…"

"How many? How old? That's all." Hayashida set the coffee back in the cup holder and swung the car into the lane, hearing the cop call after him, "I observed one male individual…"

The wrecker, a big oversized model, had been backed to the edge of the drop to the lake with a winch lowered to pull the Toyota out of the water. The car sat there at the end of the wire cable, halfway up the slope. The driver's door was open. A white-suited forensics team was taking photos. Two uniformed cops stood watching until they saw Hayashida's car approach and one of them said something to the other that made him laugh and nod. The driver of the wrecker sat behind the wheel smoking a cigarette and looking nowhere, waiting to do whatever he was told to do. A white Mercedes sat parked off the laneway, a woman behind the wheel talking into her phone, not looking pleased at all.

Hayashida carried his double-double to stand near the two uniformed cops staring down at the car and the body of Slip Winegarden slumped against the driver's door, the window up with a hole in the glass as round as Hayashida's pinkie. Hayashida was enjoying his coffee, which had cooled down to the perfect temperature.

"How you doin', sergeant?" one of the cops said, the one who made a comment that had made the other cop laugh.

"You check him out, the victim?" Hayashida said.

The cop said, "Opened the door when I saw him. Didn't touch him. Can't get more dead'n that guy."

"Know him?"

"Can't say I do. Car's registered to somebody named Winegarden, lists his address as Tuffy's, down the beach strip."

Hayashida turned to him. "He lives there?"

"What the car registry says. Gun's inside, looks like a thirty-eight. Phone too. Didn't touch a thing, left it for forensics."

"Who's the woman in the Benz?"

"Real estate agent. Came here this morning, saw the car in the water and called it in."

Hayashida drained the coffee, crumpled the cup and tossed it underhand into the open foundation of the house that once stood there, then walked to the Mercedes. The woman looked around as he approached, then spoke rapidly before putting her telephone in her purse and stepping out of the car. "Are you with the police?" she asked.

Hayashida introduced himself, handed the woman his card. He was impressed with her appearance: starched white blouse and black trousers, almost a masculine cut in them, playing against type because everything else about the woman, her makeup, her hair style, her jewellery were all feminine and expensive.

"I had no idea a body would be in that car," she said, reading Hayashida's card. "I came to look things over, I was going to show the property to a developer today, and I saw the car down there, thinking some kids maybe stole it and pushed it into the lake. I called you people and they said to stay here and wait for the tow truck and officers to arrive. They get here and there's a dead body behind the wheel and a bullet hole, I guess that's a bullet hole, as if I've ever seen one before, in the window." She looked around at a car approaching from the highway. "I cancelled my showing. Won't be able to sell the property for weeks now, I'll bet."

The car that had come down the lane stopped. A woman from the newspaper stepped out. Hayashida couldn't remember her name, didn't care. She showed her press card to the two uniformed officers, walked to look over the edge down at the car, and started talking into a small recorder.

"Hey." Hayashida watched as the uniformed cops and the woman looked back. It was the cops he wanted to talk to. "Close the damn lane to everybody including the press, and tell this woman to get her ass back in the car and out of here."

"I've got a press card," the woman said.

Hayashida said, "I've got hemorrhoids worth more than your press card to me," which made the real estate woman first gasp, then giggle.

"Know what I think?"

Hayashida was in Walter Freeman's office, Freeman reading Hayashida's notes while waiting for details from forensics. Hayashida was the senior homicide detective, a guy Freeman knew rarely made mistakes. His notes would tell them as much as they needed to know for now.

"What?" Freeman said, more of a grunt than a question.

"I think whoever did it, they didn't give a damn if we figured it was suicide or not."

Freeman said, "Looks like it, don't it?" He was reading about the wound to Slip Winegarden's bicep where the first shot struck him. That was a crock. Guy reaches around with his left hand to shoot himself on the outside of his right arm, then puts the gun in his right hand to shoot himself in the head? Or the other way around? The hell kind of Houdini trick is that? "We trace the weapon?"

"Charter Arms .38."

"Saturday night special."

"Pick them up downtown for two hundred bucks or a bag of crack, your choice. We'll never trace it. Funny thing is…"

"What?"

"Just two shells in it. Both fired. Why does a guy put just two bullets in a six-shot revolver?"

"Yeah, but if you're going to off yourself you only need one in the head."

"Still doesn't make sense, walk around with a gun, just two bullets in it."

"Maybe he couldn't afford any more. What else?"

"You notice the passenger window rolled down?"

"So the car'll sink for sure." Freeman tossed Hayashida's notes aside and wiped his eyes. Getting late, mid-afternoon. "Why not roll down the window on his side, the driver? You check his phone records?"

"Made a call from that location, or near it anyways, at 11:07, to a Toronto number. Call lasted thirty-eight seconds. Forensics figure he died between ten and midnight. Coroner might nail it down closer."

"Who'd he call?"

"You'll love this. He called Viktor Khrenov. Before you ask, yeah, we confirmed Khrenov was there, in Toronto. Or at least his phone was. It pinged off a tower two blocks from his home."

Freeman turned to Hayashida. "The Russian who owns the place on the beach strip."

"How well do you know him, the Russian? All I know is his name. Somebody referred to him as the crazy Cossack."

"Runs a construction company, a property management company, bunch of other stuff out of Toronto. Lot of charges laid, no convictions. Assault, theft, threatening. Pull his file, check him out. He's got a battery of sharp lawyers. Likes to hire ex-cons."

"Why's that?"

"Maybe they're grateful."

"Maybe they'll do stuff for him others won't," Hayashida said. "Like Winegarden." When Freeman looked over, Hayashida said, "He did two and a half out of three at Kingston and Millhaven, released on parole a year ago March."

"For what?"

"Theft over five thousand. Guess what he stole?" Freeman shrugged and Hayashida said, "Italian marble, rare stuff, from a construction site. It wound up in a building Khrenov was working on. They charged the Russian for possession, then dropped that and nailed Winegarden."

"Winegarden gets three for that?"

"Fourth charge. Judge had to slap it to him. He gets out and heads straight for a job running Tuffy's a week after Khrenov took it over. How's that for a good career move? Goes direct from picking his toes in Kingston to pouring beers on the beach strip."

Walter Freeman turned his chair to rest his elbows on his desk. "Winegarden gets time, the Russian gets off, Winegarden gets out and gets busy banging waitresses and slugging beer. What's a guy like that know about running a restaurant and a bar?"

"Bigger question: Why did somebody not give a damn if we knew it wasn't suicide when they could've made it look that way? Did I tell you forensics found glass fragments from the car's window on the ground, more than ten feet back from the edge? He shoots himself in the head, then drives into the lake. Now there's a trick."

"You say he was supposed to be managing that place on the beach strip for this Russian?" Freeman said. "What're they saying about him there, at the pub or whatever the hell it is?"

Hayashida was about to tell Freeman the strange part when Wes Delby leaned in Freeman's open door, saying he was sorry about being late and asking what he'd missed. Hayashida turned from Delby and frowned at Freeman. Delby'd started ten years ago, moving up fast from uniformed cop to full-fledged suit before getting himself over to Toronto and the so-called big-time. He started working undercover in narcotics until the dealers nailed him the first time he walked down Yonge Street, so he started looking into the construction business, running down bribes and union activities. He didn't do much better there, and when his marriage fell apart he decided to come back home and start over, get his life back on track. He continued doing undercover work on assignment from Toronto when they called and if Freeman gave his approval. Which Freeman usually did because it helped to build up points with the Toronto force but, frankly, he wasn't all that fond of Delby.

"He's a bit bent," Freeman said once to Hayashida, meaning Delby. "Nothing I can hang on him, and if I could tell which way he's bent and how far, I'd get him back directing traffic." There was more than that, of course. Everybody knew, you want to work undercover you need to be a little off-centre. Freeman's way of handling Delby was to keep him loose, choosing whatever Delby could handle if Toronto didn't need him or if he didn't have anything shaking back in the Big Smoke. Which was cool with Delby. Funny thing was, when Delby heard about Winegarden an hour ago he told Freeman he wanted to work on it. Almost insisted on it, saying he had a damn good reason.

"You know Wes grew up on the beach strip," Freeman said to Hayashida as Delby pulled a chair closer to Freeman's desk.

"I figured if you need another eye with this Winegarden thing, there's a good chance Khrenov's involved," Delby said to Hayashida. "Did some work on Khrenov last year, checking out building sites, subs and trades. Smooth bastard. Comes on like a dummy, can't speak the language very well, and you figure he should be schlepping bricks up a ladder or something, but I'll tell ya. The guy's not only the first guy across the finish line every time, all the other guys are dead on the track." He grinned and glanced back and forth between Freeman and Hayashida, looking for a reaction.

"So Wes is up to speed on Khrenov, if he's involved," Freeman said, "and he's got a feel for the beach strip." Turning to Delby he said, "You clear up everything on that woman in the east end?"

Delby sat back in his chair and nodded. He wore his thick hair too long, and his broad Slavic face was marred by a white scar on his upper lip. Hayashida wondered how he got the scar, but he was damned if he'd ask. "It's a suicide," Delby said. "He was leaving her, she found his rifle." Delby turned to Hayashida. "The woman who disappeared for two days, remember? Her husband doesn't know where she is and doesn't care, mostly because he's spending time in bed with a goddamn dental hygienist." He looked back and forth between Freeman and Hayashida. "Who the hell picks up a woman who spends an hour looking into your mouth, cleaning your teeth?"

"She went behind the furnace to do it, shoot herself," Freeman said to Hayashida. "Everybody thinks she's run off and she's down in the basement all this time, bullet in her head."

"We're thinking homicide, right?" Delby said to Hayashida. "Women sit in the car with the engine running or slice their wrists in the bathtub. Don't blow their goddamn heads off. But it's clear she did it. Used the husband's gun, which is a neat way of getting back at him for boinking the hygienist."

Hayashida nodded. He'd heard the woman's ten-year-old son found her. How's a kid grow up without scars after seeing that, scars that'll warp him for life? Sometimes he wished he didn't know as much about his work as he needed to know.

"Anyway, I'm done." Delby reached a hand to lightly punch Hayashida. "You want, I'm available."

Hayashida wasn't sure if he wanted the help. He didn't dislike Delby entirely. Just didn't like him enough to team up with him. In fact, Hayashida didn't like teaming up with anybody if it came down to it.

"I made a contact with somebody working for Viktor Khrenov," Delby said. "Nothing firm. Just planting seeds, that kind of stuff. Nothing we can use yet."

"What is it?" Hayashida said. "With who?"

Instead of answering, Delby looked at Freeman.

"It's all preliminary," Freeman said. "Hell, he hasn't told me who it is either."

"So tell us now," Hayashida said.

"I'd rather not." Delby avoided looking at Hayashida. "It's sensitive."

"Sensitive?" Hayashida said. "We've got a first-degree murder here, maybe connected with a serious operator in Toronto, somebody they've been trying to take down for years. Sensitive, hell. Does it have a bearing on this case, on Winegarden?"

Delby looked at Freeman, who shrugged. "It's Wes's call," Freeman said. "If he thinks he has anything, he'll tell you. Otherwise, he needs to keep his sources to himself, you know that. You come across anything connected with this guy Winegarden, you feed it to Harold," Freeman said to Delby.

Instead of agreeing, Delby said "Fill me in on what you've got for now," looking back and forth between Freeman and Hayashida.

"I'll get you a copy of the report," Hayashida said, standing up. At the door he looked back at Freeman. "We through here?"

Freeman said, "I guess we are," and shrugged.

Hayashida said nothing to Delby when he left, thinking he'd find something for the guy to do and keep him out of the way.

5

Here is how it went down at Tuffy's:

Arden arrived back around half-past midnight, shaking his head whenever anybody asked where Slip was. "Left me at the restaurant down near Walker Road," he said. "Nothing from him since. I had to take a cab back here." Play the game, he told himself. Just play the game until you can get out without losing.

At closing he collected the cash, put it in the strong box without counting it, and locked it in the room off the kitchen. Charm Darby had left for home, and the kitchen help who lived in the upstairs rooms had stayed downstairs until Arden arrived, leaving him to turn out the lights and lock things up.

Arden spent time staring out at the lake, thinking he should just walk away from everything he'd seen, everything he knew and suspected, get the hell away from this, leave it all behind.

And go where? The first time he didn't show up to meet his parole officer, the cops would run him down and send him back to Millhaven, automatic. So what's he do instead? Tell Renton he witnessed a murder, was right there in the car, watched the Russian put a bullet in Slip's head? Everybody saw him leave with Slip that night and come back alone. How's that going to go down? Who'd believe him? The Russian would get a herd of people to swear he was with them in Toronto or in Moscow if he wanted, anywhere far from the beach strip. None of Viktor's prints were in the car but there were plenty of Arden's, if they could still track them after the car spent a night in the lake. The police could come up with a dozen reasons for Arden killing Slip. Maybe to get Slip's job, or a fight over some woman, or getting even for something that happened in Millhaven. They'd have a hell of a good time explaining why he'd shoot Slip. The Russian could come up with a dozen more.

He went to bed, trying to calm down enough to sleep, trying to forget Slip's words just before the Russian shot him.

"*You owed me.*"

I'll never get to sleep, Arden thought, but he did anyway.

He woke to the sound of footsteps in the hall, and men's voices. It was past eight. He rolled off the bed and opened the door to see two men he recognized from Viktor's office, carrying a chest of drawers downstairs. The young one, a short muscular guy with hair to his shoulders, nodded at Arden as he passed. Arden recognized the chest of drawers. It had been in Slip's apartment.

"The hero's up."

Arden looked to see Goose carrying a large cardboard box.

"What's going on?" Arden said, already knowing the answer.

"Viktor wants his furniture back," Goose said. "I hear you're taking over. Let me know when you want to move up to his place. Give you a hand carrying your stuff there."

Arden said, "I think I'll stay here."

Goose walked past him. "Suit yourself." Then, over his shoulder he said, "By the way, I got Charm doin' the cash this morning since you didn't bother doin' it last night. She'll get it ready. And Viktor says 'Tell Arden hero hello for me.' That's what he calls you. 'Arden Hero'. How's it feel?"

Arden said, "How'd she get in?", knowing he had the key to the office and the strong box in his room. "How did Charm get into the office?"

"Viktor gave me his set of keys for her. Figured you'd be sleepin' in, have other things on your mind." At the landing he looked back at Arden. "You hear from Slip today, ask him where the hell he's been and tell him Viktor is really pissed at him." Just a hint of a smile when he said it.

Arden tried to keep himself busy all morning, washing glasses, telling Charm the menu looked good, as if he cared.

"You don't want to see the statement from last night?" Charm said, meaning the cash and credit card receipts. She was slim and attractive. Arden had seen her doing yoga on her break some mornings, out on the patio facing the sun over the lake. He wondered what had gone on with her and Slip. Maybe nothing sexually, but there might have been something else.

Arden said sure, he'd look at it in the office off the kitchen.

"Goose told me to get the cash and total up the charges, then he locked things when I finished and took the keys with him," Charm said. "I printed stuff out and left it in there, the office," meaning Arden would have to get his own key to enter. Then: "What happened to Slip?"

Arden said he didn't know.

Charm stared at him, waiting for more, then said, "He's not coming back, is he?"

Arden said he didn't know anything about that, and Charm bit her lip and stared at him again until he turned away and went to his room to get the keys.

Tuffy's took in just under three thousand dollars the day before, not great but not bad for a Wednesday. Most was in AmEx, Visa, Master-Card, plus debit cards. The rest was cash.

Arden stared at the printouts. Tuffy's didn't serve breakfast, didn't open until eleven for lunch. Based on last night, the place took in about fifty thousand a year in cash, he estimated.

He put copies of the deposit record and the credit card computer statement in the file drawer, telling Charm he'd be handling the cash, asking if she had any ideas how to make things smoother.

"Will you be running everything around here from now on?" Charm asked as if she knew the answer.

"It appears I am," Arden said.

He managed to eat some scrambled eggs and down a coffee. Then he walked the beach strip, all the way to the canal and back, looking at residents tending their gardens on one side of the lane and people in bathing suits spreading blankets on the other side, facing the lake. I watched a man get shot last night, he told them silently. I heard him plead for his life. Then I helped push his body into the lake.

He passed a woman his age, wearing a flowered print dress with blonde hair cut the way Marilyn Monroe wore her hair. She smiled tightly as they passed and he realized it was Josie short-for-Susan but it was too late to smile back or talk or even nod to her, as if he would have.

When he returned to Tuffy's he looked for things to do in the bar, washing glasses, straightening liquor bottles, making a couple of margaritas for somebody in the dining room, shaking the premix with tequila and ice, coating the rims with lime juice and coarse salt, then dumping the drink into a glass shaped like a cactus and handing it to the waitress.

The police arrived just after two o'clock, a Japanese detective and a younger guy who kept checking his reflection in every mirror he passed, and two uniformed cops. Charm came into the bar to tell him they were there to talk to whoever was in charge, and Arden said, "I guess that's me."

They came in, the Japanese detective leading the way, looking around the bar at two guys sitting at a back table and a couple of housewives sharing martinis in a far corner. Otherwise the place was empty. The uniformed cops separated, one standing at the entrance to the dining room, the other at the door leading to the patio. Arden was tempted to ask what took them so long to get there, but he played it the way he was expected to play it.

The Asian detective introduced himself and the younger guy named

Delby, and said, "Man named William Winegarden here?", knowing he wasn't. He looked around at the other people in the bar while reaching for his badge and flashing it at Arden, not long enough for him to read it, just to see it and maybe be impressed. Which he wasn't.

"Haven't seen him," Arden said, not moving from behind the bar, wrapping one hand in a bar towel.

"Since when?"

"Since last night when he dropped me off at the Esso station down near Walker Road and never came back."

Hayashida lifted a leg to settle himself on a bar stool, this time not taking his eyes from Arden. "Came back from where?" The guy called Delby began walking around the bar like he had lost something.

Arden told himself to be careful. "Beats the hell out of me. Said he wanted to talk to me about something, show me something down the road. Then I saw the gun."

"He showed you a gun?"

"Didn't show it. I saw it."

"Where?"

Christ. "On the dashboard. He put it there after we left here. That's when I told him to let me out, I didn't want to be anywhere near a damn gun."

"Why not?"

"Don't like them." Watching Hayashida, waiting for him to ask, knowing Hayashida might know by now. "Don't want to be around them." Then, tossing the bar towel into the receptacle, "I'm on parole."

Hayashida's eyebrows moved up his forehead. He asked, "What's your name?" Arden told him, and Hayashida said, "You in Millhaven?"

"Couple of years. You can look it up."

"For what?"

"Felonious assault. I broke a guy's neck. He'd raped my sister."

Hayashida nodded. "I remember that. Jesus, break a guy's neck with your bare hands? Where'd you learn to do that?"

Arden stared back at the detective, saying nothing, so Hayashida said, "Is that where you met Winegarden? In Millhaven?"

"We shared a cell for six months."

Hayashida looked around the bar again. The two men at the far table were watching, trying to hear what was being said. "You got a place we can talk?" he said. He told Delby to walk around, maybe go outside, just to get a feel of the place. Arden could tell by the expression on Delby's face that he didn't like the idea, but he went anyway.

Arden brought coffees into the small office off the kitchen, the one where Slip would count the cash before putting it in the small safe fastened to the floor. Arden sat at the beat-up desk, Hayashida in the only other chair there was room for. When Hayashida told him Slip's body had been found in his submerged car a few miles down the lake, Arden pursed his lips and looked away, shaking his head.

"You surprised?" Hayashida said.

Arden shrugged. "Nothing much surprises me anymore."

"He seem like the kind of guy might kill himself, all alone?"

"I don't know. I hardly knew him."

"Two years together in prison, six months in the same cell, a month working with him here, and you hardly *knew* him?"

"You're different guys in prison. You know that. Locked up you're one guy, out on the street you're another guy."

"You want to hear something weird? Your guy Winegarden had just two bullets in the gun. That's all. Two bullets in a six-shot."

"What's your point?"

"You pack a gun for whatever reason, protection, shooting tin cans off a fence, you fill up all the chambers, okay? So why'd he put two shells in the gun? He was going to shoot himself in the head, he'd need just one anyway. Of course, you're gonna shoot yourself in the head, you don't hold the gun in your left hand so you can put a bullet in your right bicep." He leaned closer to Arden. "Winegarden doing himself is the biggest crap story since Trump said he won in a landslide. You with me on that?"

Arden said, "Sounds like it," and looked away.

After watching Arden for a time, Hayashida said, "When's the last time you saw Viktor Khrenov?"

Ah, Jesus. Careful, careful… "Yesterday afternoon. He came by, walked around, checked things out."

"How long'd he stay?" Hayashida rose from his chair, began looking closely at things in the office, papers on the desk, the framed liquor licence, an old picture of Tuffy's when it was Tiffany's, a two-horse carriage parked in front with some women in long black gowns sitting in it.

"Half an hour. Maybe less."

"You see him go?"

Arden nodded.

"Not much time to visit. He go upstairs?"

Arden thought a minute, trying to remember. "No, he didn't."

"Winegarden has a room up there, doesn't he?" and Arden nodded. "Mind if I look at it, the room?"

Arden said, "You can if you want, but I don't think there's a damn thing there." When Hayashida blinked and started to frown, Arden said, "Two guys from Khrenov's company in Toronto were here this morning. Took out all the furniture. Far as I know, the place is empty."

"What time was *that*?"

"Quarter after eight maybe."

Hayashida wrote something in a small notebook he took out of his suit jacket. Nice suit, Arden thought, just to get his mind off what he had told the detective. One of those summer-weight outfits, light tan colour with a bit of a pattern, what they call a Glen check or something. He'd like to get a suit like that. Cost about a week's salary and you only get to wear it two, three months of the year, but still…

"So you're telling me," Hayashida was saying, "that before Winegarden's body was found, before anybody knows he's dead, your guy sends some other guys here to clear out his office?"

"Viktor's not my guy."

"Don't get smart. You know who I mean."

"Maybe he fired him last night, the Russian."

"He tell you that? The Russian tell you he'd fired Winegarden?"

"No…"

"Did Winegarden say anything to you about being fired, when you guys were driving last night?"

"No…"

"Why'd he drop you off at a gas station on the way? You didn't want to go with him in the first place, why didn't he bring you back here? And what's he doing looking at an empty lot on the Lakeshore around midnight?"

"I have no…"

"Okay, listen to me." Hayashida settled himself into the chair again, straightening his suit jacket, tucking his pale blue tartan tie into the waistband, wearing the tie with a pastel blue button-down shirt, the guy having a sense of style. "I make a call, one call, and your ass is back in Millhaven, understand? Never mind your parole officer, who I'm gonna talk to and get some things straight. You were in a vehicle used in a homicide, there was a firearm in the vehicle, you're consorting with known criminals, that's all I need. Ain't nobody going to save you, nobody to stand in front of a judge and say, 'Let the poor bastard go, he's not likely to offend again unless somebody else tries to boink his sister.' You're back in there and you know it, okay?"

Arden wanted to let the detective know he was pissed at Hayashida for making the remark about his sister, but he'd save it for some other time when he wouldn't have so much to lose or, for that matter, anything to lose. "I'm telling you what I know," Arden said. "I'm clean. I'm planning on staying clean."

Hayashida watched him, Arden knowing this was his style. Say as little as possible, make the other guy nervous, just sit there looking at him. Still watching him, the detective took a phone from inside his jacket, hit an autodial button and then hit another one and talked to somebody, giving them Arden's name and conviction, mentioning Millhaven, asking for a file report, a call-back.

"So how'd you do it?" Hayashida said, replacing the phone in his jacket. "The guy who raped your sister. Break his neck. How do you do that?"

Like a hundred other people wanting to know, all of them in Millhaven, as if he could demonstrate it for them. "There's a technique," he said.

"What's the technique?"

Arden shook his head.

"So you meant to do it. It was no accident, right? You did, what? Get him from behind, neck in the crook of your elbow, knee in the small of his back? That how it works? How'd you know how to do that?"

"Airborne regiment, special services."

"That's the army outfit that got disbanded," Hayashida said. "For torturing that poor kid in Somalia."

"I wasn't there."

"In Somalia?"

"When the kid was tortured. No part of it. Before my time."

"So you've been out of the army, what? Fifteen years?"

"Closer to twenty."

"Doing what since then?"

"Little bit of security. Worked as a trainer, helping old guys lose their beer gut. Tried some boxing, professional, out of a gym in Markham."

"How'd you do?"

"Had twelve fights. Won all but nine of them." He thought Hayashida might find this amusing. Most people did. The detective didn't. "Was a bouncer at a club in Whistler. Tried selling mutual funds. Got married once. No, twice."

This one Hayashida grinned at. "Trying to remember how many times you've been married?"

"Trying to forget."

More silence from Hayashida. Then: "How long did you wait at that restaurant, the one at the Esso station?"

"An hour. Maybe an hour and a half, I don't know."

"What'd you do? Have something to eat?"

"Ate a sandwich. Nursed a beer, waiting for Slip."

"How'd you pay for it?"

"Cash."

"Who brought you back here?"

"I had the woman, the cashier, call me a taxi." Knowing they would check everything, confirm it, look at the security camera recording, he started feeling a little better about things.

"When did Khrenov make you the boss here?"

"I'm just filling in."

Hayashida stood up. "You mind if we look around upstairs?"

"Not at all. You want to check my room, I'm in 203. Door's unlocked. Be my guest."

Back in the bar Arden poured himself a glass of soda water with a twist and sat alone, nobody wanting to approach him, not with police on the premises.

6

Goose sat behind the wheel of the Ryder truck the Russian had rented the day before, the one to carry all the junk from Slip's room back to Toronto. Took them nearly two hours to get from Tuffy's to where they were, normally an hour's drive, and they were still three miles from the office. Damn traffic, people driving an hour to work, sit on their ass in an office all day and take another hour to drive home. What kind of life is that?

The Russian had it down. For one thing, he knows how to plan ahead, Goose thought. Rents the truck to clear out Slip's room the day before the guy gets whacked. Got to hand it to him.

Which didn't warm him any toward Viktor. Okay, Goose was thinking, Viktor was smart and tough and sometimes funny, and now and then generous, but he screwed me over on this one, after telling me I'd be running Tuffy's. Screwed me over royally. What's he doing, handing the place over to some guy he's known for, how long? A month? Not much more than that. Does he really figure this guy, this ex-con, is going to be any better, any more trustworthy than Winegarden?

Goose had told Viktor he wanted that job at Tuffy's, wanted to get the hell out of the city and away from his ex-wife, get a place to work where he could spend time watching over things for Viktor, living by the water, meeting women who come in looking for a guy to buy them a drink. You take them upstairs, show them the view of the lake from the window, then the view from the bed. How you like the ceiling, sweetheart? You think about what colour I should paint it while I finish here, and you could move your hips a little if you don't mind. He laughed at that.

"What's so funny?" Heckle Dunne just wanted Goose to get them back to Viktor's office. There they'd unload all the crap in the back of the truck, tear it apart and tell the Russian what they found.

"Nothing," Goose said.

Goose went back to getting himself angry. What's with Viktor, he wanted to know, giving breaks to ex-cons? What, he thinks some guy who spent three, four years in prison, maybe they've got talent other guys don't have, just because they kept their mouths shut and did their time? How hard is that? And what's with this hardass Arden something, who breaks some guy's neck because the guy got it on with his sister and he gets time for it, for breaking the guy's neck? For that he's something special? He's a hero? That's what Viktor calls him. "Arden Hero." It's bullshit.

What this Arden character should have done, what Goose would've done to some guy who raped his sister, would be blow the guy away and duck the charge instead of letting the son of a bitch survive. Okay, he's in a wheelchair for life, but he's alive, isn't he? I mean, how dumb is that? You break the guy's neck when you should have offed him, then you call 911 to get him to a hospital. And when the cops want to know what happened, you tell them what you did, knowing you're facing time for that. That's what this Arden jerk did. What the hell's the world coming to when you can't give rapists a taste of their own medicine? No, Arden the hero beats 'em up and lets 'em get a good lawyer who tells the judge it was all consensual, there was no rape, the bitch was asking for it and besides, his client would never do it again.

Any guy who raped Goose's sister would've wound up eating his own balls before getting his head blown off. Goose didn't have a sister, but that wasn't the point. The point was, Goose knew how to deal with things better than that loser back on the beach strip. Get it done and get away with it. That's what's worth getting a reward for, worth getting a job like running that place on the beach strip. That's what Goose had been doing for, what? Five years now? Closer to six. Getting stuff done for Viktor, getting away with it and no hassles. All the shit Goose laid down for the Russian and never had a charge laid, neither he nor Viktor spent a night locked up. Wasn't that worth something? Should be.

Maybe Viktor thought ex-cons were tougher and maybe smarter in some way than guys like himself, guys who managed to stay on the street and out of prison, like Goose did. If they were so damn smart, they would've kept their asses out of jail in the first place.

The traffic began moving again but only for another hundred yards or so, and Goose got prepared to wait another ten minutes, sweating in this damn truck with Heckle Dunne, of all people. Meanwhile, Arden what's-his-name is there on the beach strip hustling women and throwing back all the cold beer he can pour. Goose pounded the steering wheel and yelled to nobody except the rest of the world, "Come on—move your goddamn asses!"

Heckle looked across at him and said, "Jesus, calm down a little," and Goose told Heckle not to tell him to calm down or else he might start calming down by throwing Heckle's ass into the traffic once it started moving again.

"This all?"

Viktor kicked the old wicker night table as if trying to wake it up, then turned it over to look underneath. Finding nothing, he dropped it to the floor and stood looking at the chest of drawers, upholstered chair, wooden desk, Windsor chair, bed headboard and other junk from Slip's room. Some of Slip's clothes spilled from a large cardboard box on the floor. Other smaller boxes were stacked behind it.

"His bathroom stuff's in that blue plastic box," Goose said, pointing to the side. "Nothing special there either. There's some junk in the bottom of his dresser, in a shoebox."

Viktor opened the drawer, put the shoebox on the dresser, pulled the top off and dumped out the contents. A pack of well-thumbed playing cards from the Flamingo in Las Vegas. Four photographs of a much younger Winegarden smiling at the camera, two of them with his arm around a dark-haired woman his age, both squinting into the sun. A set of car keys. A pair of reading glasses. A photo torn from a magazine of a young girl in a bikini stretched across the hood of a vintage Chevrolet Corvette. Pens, paper clips, a nail clipper, comb, a tube of lipstick, a cheque book with all the cheques removed, three condoms and an opened pocket pack of Kleenex.

Viktor held up the car keys. "His car?"

"Guess so," Goose said. "They're probably ten, fifteen years old. You can tell, nobody's used keys like that in years. Probably a spare set, tossed them in the box and forgot about them."

"The woman?", meaning the one in the pictures he was holding up.

"No idea. Some broad he knew, looks like years ago."

Viktor closed the shoebox and dropped it back into the bottom drawer. "His clothing?"

Goose said they had checked the clothes, all of them, and found nothing but old receipts and used Kleenex. "What'll we do with this crap when we're done?" Goose said. "Carry it to Goodwill?"

"Save it," Viktor said. "Save all. For police."

"They're comin' for it?"

"They will." Viktor turned and began climbing the steps out of the basement, then turned back to Goose. "Save box," he said, nodding at the old dresser.

Hayashida was downstairs at Tuffy's, sitting at the bar next to Arden, saying, "What a screw-up. You really screwed up, you know that?"

Arden looked at him, wondering what he was getting at.

"You tell me some guys show up here, first thing this morning, and take every damn stick of furniture out of Winegarden's room? I could make this whole rat trap a crime scene, you know that? Shut the place until the snow's piling up, if I wanted to." He turned from facing Arden to look across the bar into the dining room. "Everything about the victim's gone. It's like he's never been here. And you let 'em take it."

"You forget," Arden said. Staying calm. He had learned it as a child when his old man showed up drunk, went raving through the house, yelling and smashing things. The more violent he got, the more Arden stayed calm, became a rock, became invisible, became an invisible rock. He had a lot of practice doing that.

"Forget what?"

"I didn't know Slip was dead. So how'm I gonna tell them not to take any of Slip's crap in case you guys need it, seeing as Slip's dead and I don't know it? You ever think of that? And if I told Goose to leave everything there for whatever reason, first of all Goose would've kicked my ass halfway across the lake, and then Viktor would've fired me. What the hell could I do? Viktor tells them, 'Clean out the room,' I let those guys clean out the room. Not my place. Not my job."

Hayashida stared at Arden for a moment before looking at his watch. "Okay, you made your point," he said. "I had time, I'd go and see Khrenov myself, seize all that stuff on my own. Now I gotta count on the Toronto guys checking things out on my warrant." Looking at Arden now, talking like they're two old buddies sitting at a bar, talking the Yankees versus the Cubs. "What do you think they'll find?"

Arden said, "Damned if I know."

"Like, I know we were lookin' for money," Heckle Dunne said, sitting in the Ryder truck drinking Molsons from a can, stuck in traffic, the diesel engine rumbling, the windows down, hotter'n hell. Jesus, couldn't the Russian afford a truck with AC?

"No, we're not." Goose staring ahead like he could move all the traffic in front of him, push it the hell out of the way with a laser beam from his eyes. They were taking the truck back to the rental place. Get a cab back from there, maybe after they find a bar with cold beer and AC. How'd the world get through a summer without AC?

"You told me that," Heckle said, then took another mouthful of beer. "Said we'd be looking for cash, whatever. Don't you remember? Besides, everybody knows it."

"You think if we'd been looking for money, we'd've found it by now? You think it'd be so goddamn hard to find that much money lying around?"

"How much?"

Goose said nothing so Heckle asked again and Goose told him it was none of his goddamn business.

"I heard it was about maybe fifteen thousand." Heckle tilted his head back and drained the can. "That's all."

Goose said, "You don't think fifteen thousand dollars is a lot of money?"

Heckle crumpled the can with one hand and tossed it behind the seat. "Not to Viktor. You, me, somebody lifts that much from us, picks our pocket or whatever, yeah, we're gonna raise hell and break some bones maybe, I dunno. I just didn't think it was worth Viktor doin' what he did."

The traffic began moving. Goose dropped the truck into first gear and it lurched ahead. "What'd he do?" Goose asked, still staring ahead and frowning.

"Ah, hell, Goose." Heckle looked out the window. "Slip didn't run off with the fuckin' tooth fairy. Everybody knows that he's the guy in the car they fished outta the lake this morning. Cops're waitin' to contact his next a kin before they say who it is. All they're sayin' is that they're not convinced it was a suicide or an accident, probably because the Russian shot him about six times to make sure he was dead."

"Twice. Viktor shot him twice. But you say anything about it to anybody and you might wind up in the lake yourself, okay?"

"You were there?" Heckle looking at Goose with interest and maybe respect. "You seen him do it?"

"No, I wasn't there. Don't you start telling anybody I was there, okay?" He waited to calm down some. "Viktor told me. He tells me a lotta things. I know a lotta things you've got no clue about, okay?"

"He tell you why he killed Slip himself for fifteen grand?"

"Just drop that shit, okay?" Goose shot him a look.

"You miss him?"

"Who?"

"Slip. You guys were tight for a while. Saw you hanging with him when he came here, just out of the can."

Goose looked at him, then away. "We shot the shit a little, yeah.

We all do. So what?" Wondering if he sounded a little too defensive.

"So what did you think when Viktor did him?"

"What I thought, which is none of your business, is that Slip deserved it, okay? That's the way it works. You better remember that. It's the way it works with us. You play ball, keep your eyes open, your mouth shut and your hands in your own pockets, Viktor looks after you. Looks after you good. You try screwing around, get greedy, start thinking maybe you're smarter than he is, well, you see what it got Slip." He looked across, pointed at Heckle. "You remember that. You fuckin' remember that."

Heckle looked out the window at people on the sidewalk, walking faster than the traffic was moving. Damn traffic in the city these days. Shoot a guy yourself for fifteen grand? Why? Hell, there were a dozen guys Heckle could think of, they'd do it for a couple of thousand, do it for five hundred if things were tight, get it done right and clean. Why'd the Russian do Slip himself? And then, frowning a bit just as the truck moved forward another ten feet: Maybe he liked doing it. Maybe he enjoyed it.

He wondered if Natalka knew what Viktor did, what he could do if he wanted to. He also wondered if he would risk his own ass to get a piece of Natalka's. Maybe he would. She'd be out on the street herself in a couple of weeks like the other women Viktor had. Then she'd have to find something to do besides drive Viktor's big black Chrysler and get on her knees for him whenever he felt like it.

What if he didn't wait until Viktor found some other girl to hang on his arm? What if he said to Viktor, in so many words, hey, you're gonna be passing her along like you did the others. Why not pass her to me first? Would the Russian whack somebody for picking up his used goods? If Natalka flirted with him one more time, acting cutesy but letting Heckle know she wanted it from him, well, he'd see that she got it. "You want a beer?" Heckle said, trying to get thoughts of Natalka out of his head.

"Not one of yours," Goose said. "You find me a cold beer, I'll take it. Stuff you're drinking's probably like warm piss." Sometimes Heckle really got on Goose's nerves.

"Suit yourself." Heckle reached under the seat for another can. What, he wondered, would Goose say if he knew I was planning to bang Viktor's piece? Probably nothing to me. Bet he'd haul ass to tell Viktor all about it, though.

Arden worked it out standing at the window looking at the lake.

A guy shoots your buddy in front of you, inside a car, so close you can reach and tap him on the shoulder. Two shots, then he hands the gun to you, tells you to wipe the prints off it. Why's he do that? Hayashida told Arden the gun had just two bullets in it, a six-shot revolver, and wonders why Winegarden walks around with two bullets in his gun. But it wasn't Winegarden's gun. It was Viktor's. Viktor fired the two shots, then handed the gun to Arden, Slip's buddy. Why's he do that? Because Arden could've turned the gun on Viktor, one in the head and walk away. Or march Viktor up to the highway, call the cops, be a hero again. Viktor put two in the gun so he knew when he handed it to me I couldn't turn it on him.

He was testing me, Arden realized. He'd planned to put two in Slip's head, not even try to make it look like a suicide. This way, the people he wanted to know what happened would figure it out for themselves. He gives me the gun, and if I try turning the gun on him, I get nothing and he probably whacks me. He probably had another gun with him. He'd pop me with it, make it look like I did Slip. People would start speculating, thinking maybe it was a lover's quarrel, two guys sharing a prison cell all that time, who'd be surprised?

He tested me like he did with the money when I met him that first day, throwing it out the window, watching me pick it up like some beggar. I did what I was told. I wiped down the gun. I didn't try to be a hero. If I had, I'd be as dead as Slip now. Lesson learned. Slip was right. He's a chess guy like all those Russians, two moves ahead of you. Don't try to outthink him. Don't try to do anything except what he tells you to do.

"What, you want buy this stuff?" Viktor stood smiling at the Toronto detectives and two people from the forensics team, a man and a woman, inspecting all of Slip's stuff that Goose brought from Tuffy's.

The police could've used a warrant, would've got one if the Russian thought there was anything to hide and insisted on it, but there was nothing there, not in the furniture, not in Slip's clothing, nowhere. Viktor thought it was amusing, watching the officers do the same things Goose and Heckle had done a couple of hours ago down in the basement.

One of the cops threw him a look and went back to turning the furniture over, looking for hollow places where you could hide something, finding nothing.

Almost two hours later Goose and Heckle came back from dropping off the rented truck. Goose, having seen the police cars and forensics truck outside, stood looking at Viktor and spreading his hands, asking silently what this was all about.

"Looking for lottery ticket," the Russian said, grinning. "Make millions, give it all to widows and orphans, eh? Or maybe buy own doughnut shop. Cops never have to buy doughnut again."

One of the cops stood up, hands on his hips, and glared at Viktor.

"Have fun," Viktor said, and motioned Goose to follow him upstairs.

The police and forensics team left half an hour later, not saying anything to Viktor when they left, not even goodbye.

7

Everybody at Tuffy's knew it had been Slip in the car that was pulled from the water, knew it as soon as they heard about it. They didn't need the TV or radio to tell them, or customers coming in to pass along gossip.

What they didn't know, what no one knew, was Arden's role in Slip's death. So they avoided him all day and into the night, even after the TV stations showed a picture of Slip that must've been taken ten, fifteen years ago, before he got that hang-dog ex-con look.

Viktor called Arden near seven o'clock. Sarah, the front door hostess, leaned into the bar to tell him.

"You hear?" the Russian said when Arden picked up the phone in the bar and waited for Sarah to replace the extension in the dining room.

Arden said, "Yeah, I heard," thinking Victor's going to assume his line is being tapped because it probably is.

"What you think happened?"

"I don't know. I'm all confused."

"He seem fine, I talk to him yesterday. Fine to you too?"

"I guess. I could never tell with Slip."

"Police, they think maybe, what? They tell you?"

"They don't know what to think," playing the game along with the Russian. "They don't know whether he did himself or what."

A long pause from Viktor. Then: "Things good there. They good with you?", meaning Tuffy's.

"Not that busy." Arden was looking down the bar, not at the three guys watching the Jays play the Yankees on TV or the man and woman in the corner seeing who could pick up the other first, or the old guy in the booth reading a book and sipping his beer. He was looking at the blonde who had just come in through the beach entrance and was walking toward him, not looking around but watching Arden as though she expected him to bolt and, if he did, she would run after him.

Josie short-for-Susan sat on the stool nearest to Arden. She folded her hands and stared at him until he nodded, letting her know he was aware of her being there.

"I send Goose there every Monday starting now," Viktor was saying and Arden, who had been wondering about the blonde, turned away and lowered his voice. "What?"

"I tell you Goose comes, looks at what you put down, all the stuff from credit cards, other things, and cash. You give him what he wants, okay?"

"Why?" Arden looked behind him at the blonde staring out at the lake now, her chin on her hand.

"Why what?"

"Why send Goose? I can get everything to you, tell you on the telephone, send you an email."

A long pause. Is he thinking of what to say in case this wire's tapped, or is he pissed at me? Arden wondered. Then: "Show Goose. Every time, okay hero?"

"Sure." Arden waited to see what else the Russian had to say. It took him a few moments to realize he was listening to a dead line.

He hung up, took a cardboard coaster from beneath the counter, and walked to slide it in front of Josie, who shook her head at the sight of it. "What happened to Slip?" she said.

Arden said, "I don't know."

"Yes, you do."

"Look, if you don't want anything to…"

"Who killed him?"

"Why are you asking me?"

"Was it you?" Calm, like she was asking him what he had for dinner that night. Not accusing, just curious.

Arden closed his eyes, stretched his arms out, placed his hands on the edge of the bar, and leaned on them. "Look, lady…"

"My name is Josie. You know that. My last name is Marshall."

What the hell. He stared at her, dredging up as much anger and aiming it at her eyes as he could. "Okay, Josie Marshall. If you don't want anything to drink, don't loiter here, all right?"

She stared back at him. Green eyes, he noticed. He always liked green-eyed blondes. "Okay, I want a cup of hot tea with brandy on the side. On second thought, forget the tea."

Arden turned away to reach for the bottle of Hennessy and a glass. "Ice?" he said, and she nodded.

He set the drink in front of her and left, finding things to do at the far side of the bar, thinking about Viktor's decision to send Goose over to Tuffy's every Monday. Maybe he should pack it in, tell the Russian Goose could take over, he'd be on his way. Maybe head west and visit Donna Lee, see how she's doing, try to make things right…

"Can we talk a minute?"

It was Josie. Her brandy was untouched. She looked concerned, nervous.

"What about?" Arden said, turning to her and trying to forget about the Russian.

"Need two vodka martinis, dirty and straight up, three olives in each." It was Christine coming in from the dining room, talking to Arden but looking at Josie.

Arden took the batch of premixed vodka martinis out of the under-counter refrigerator, dumped crushed ice in a shaker, added the martini mix and shook it for sound effects so people in the dining room would think their drinks were freshly made for them. He squeezed in a bit of juice from three olives, pierced them with a toothpick, did the same with three other olives, added the olives to the martinis, and set both on a tray. He was enjoying his bartender chores. Even better, he was getting pretty good at it.

Christine had made a point of looking elsewhere, anywhere except at Josie or Arden. She took the tray of drinks and walked back to the dining room.

"You have time to talk?" Josie said, and Arden asked, what about? "You know what about. I want to know what happened to Slip. To Bill."

What the hell? Arden wondered. He walked closer, but not directly in front of her. "He your boyfriend?"

"No."

"Then why so interested?"

"Are you taking his job?"

"That's up to the owner."

"The Russian."

"You know him well? I see him talking to you sometimes."

"He comes in acting like he's Putin. Talks to me about the weather, asks if I like my drink."

"He ever try to pick you up?"

"Not me. He likes young women. Teenage girls."

Like the one with the pixie haircut driving the Chrysler, Arden thought. "If you're that interested then, yeah," he said. "I'm running things for a while, just to prove I can do what Slip did..." She looked up at that. "Watching over things for the Russian, that's all. Maybe spend the summer here. When it starts getting cold, I might go west, out to Vancouver where I don't slog through snow every day."

Josie said, "Why does the Russian trust you so much when he hardly knows you?"

Arden picked up a bar towel and leaned against the other side of the bar. "How do you know that, about him trusting me?" When she didn't reply, he said, "Slip tell you that? How much did he tell you about me?"

"He said you were a hero. Because of what you did to some guy who raped your sister."

"I'm getting tired of hearing about that."

"I hear that's what got you Slip's job."

"It's temporary, this job." He tossed the bar towel into the sink. "I'm here mostly as a figurehead." He started taking glasses out of the washer, getting ready for the rush later on.

"So are you saying the Russian's not letting you handle money?"

Which turned Arden around, literally. "Why would that be any concern of yours?"

She looked away, then down at her purse, withdrew ten dollars and put it on the counter, leaving her brandy untouched. "Good luck," she said, sliding off her stool and walking toward the door to the beach. "You're going to need it."

Christine came into the bar for some Cokes as the door closed behind Josie. "You know her?" Arden asked. "That blonde?"

"Lives up the strip, near the canal." Christine filled the Coke glasses from the fountain dispenser. She paused between glasses and looked down for a moment. Then: "You gonna tell us what happened to Slip?"

"Why does everybody think I know?"

She filled another glass. "You left with him. He was your buddy."

"I wouldn't say we were buddies…"

"He told everybody, long before you got here, he said 'This guy's somethin', my kinda guy, he does what needs to be done.' That's what he told everybody." Placing the Cokes on a tray she turned toward the dining room and paused to look back at him.

"He oversold me."

"So you're not going to say what happened last night?"

"I told the police."

"I meant tell us the truth."

"It *is* the truth."

"You're right." Christine headed for the dining room again. "He oversold you."

8

Toronto police tracked Slip's mother to a nursing home in Scarborough using his court records, saying they had something to tell her about her son, and she said she didn't know what the hell they were talking about because she didn't have any damn son. The Toronto cops couldn't tell if she didn't remember Slip, which was possible because the nursing home staff said she thought some of them were her own offspring, or if she'd disowned him. They gave up on her but found a sister driving a school bus in North Bay, the local cops saying they had news about her brother William, telling her they were sorry to say he was dead, possibly murdered.

"When?" she said, and when they told her it happened the previous evening, she said, "Hell, I thought he died years ago." She looked away and her eyes grew damp. "I guess I'm not surprised. A little sad, but not surprised."

The sister revealed that Slip had an ex-wife who moved back to Nova Scotia nearly ten years ago. She knew nothing else about her except that she had remarried, and she couldn't remember the husband's last name. They kept looking.

When Hayashida read all of this the next morning, he decided to release Slip's name to the media and ask for assistance from anyone who knew him, anyone with something to help with the investigation.

"You think it's a good idea?" Delby asked, "releasing it so early?"

"I think," Hayashida said, walking towards the copier, "it's a hell of a good idea. Draft something up for me to read and I'll pass it by Walter."

He had sent Delby to interview the staff at the restaurant next to the Esso station. All of them remembered a man in a tan windbreaker and khakis, maybe forty, forty-five years old, who had come in some-time after eleven and sat sipping a beer for an hour. They told the detective that the man, who matched Arden's description, had asked the woman at the cash register to call him a cab, then waited for it outside. The taxi company provided the records: Call received at 12:04 a.m., passenger entered cab at 12:17, requested journey to Tuffy's on the beach strip, arrived at 12:22, total fare eight dollars and forty cents, paid ten dollars leaving a dollar-sixty cent tip. It was all on the meter.

Which was a crock, Hayashida told himself. Why does Winegar-den drive to the edge of the lake at night with a gun, taking some guy he met in prison, a guy he admired and who people called a hero? Did Winegarden want a witness? To what? He didn't off himself, that's for sure.

Hayashida worked his way through things, holding on to what made sense, setting aside stuff he couldn't buy. He had talked to the restaurant staff, compared stories, memories, opinions, and they all matched. Then he'd driven down Beach Boulevard to talk to Josie Marshall, sitting in her kitchen drinking tea, enjoying her company. He always enjoyed Josie's company. He'd like to stay in Josie's living room the rest of the day and talk with her about anything except murder. Whatever she knew about Winegarden she wasn't ready to share.

When Delby brought him a draft of the press release asking the public for information about William Winegarden, a.k.a. Slip, Hayas-hida glanced at it and set it aside. Delby, in Hayashida's eyes, needed less ambition and more experience, but he was no dummy. He had a more open mind than Walter Freeman, who didn't care a hell of a lot about evidence and boring crap about citizens' rights. "Listen to what

I've got on this," Hayashida said, "and tell me what you're getting out of it."

He read his notes to Delby. About Arden agreeing to go with Winegarden to look at something down the road, practically at midnight. About Arden seeing the gun in Winegarden's car and insisting on being let out when Winegarden wouldn't turn back to Tuffy's. About Winegarden promising to come back in a few minutes and Arden waiting for an hour, cooling his heels, before taking a taxi back to Tuffy's.

"What sounds unreal to you?" Hayashida asked when he finished.

Delby pushed out his bottom lip to show he was in deep thought. "All of it," he said. "Except the sandwich and beer at the restaurant. And the gun."

"What about the gun?"

"This Arden guy, I don't know if he's clean or what. But he's cleaner than Winegarden. So I think if he sees a gun, he knows being around one gets him back in Millhaven or wherever. I think he'd say 'I'm outta here' and probably gets Winegarden to drop him off at the restaurant. That works for me."

"So why not take a cab back to Tuffy's right away?"

"Because he believed Winegarden would be coming back."

"With the gun?"

Delby blinked. "Okay, I got it. He wants out of the car when he sees Winegarden with the gun, how's he getting back in the car to return to Tuffy's if Winegarden's still got it?"

"Unless he thinks Winegarden's gonna get rid of the gun. Throw it into the lake."

"Except he didn't say that."

"Where does Winegarden get the gun, and for what?"

"His own protection. Maybe from the Russian."

"Or." Hayashida sat up. He hadn't thought about this before, what he was going to say. It had just occurred to him now. And he was convinced it was true. "Or this Arden character's lying and there wasn't a gun in the car when the two guys left Tuffy's."

"How'd it get there then?"

"Didn't walk, did it? Somebody else showed up with it."

"At the lakeshore, that vacant lot?"

"I don't know." Hayashida looked around. He hated admitting to Delby that he didn't know something he should know. "This fits somebody shooting him, Winegarden, inside the car."

"So we're back with this Arden guy. You think he brought the gun with him?"

"Don't know. Somehow I doubt it. But I'll tell you this. If Arden what's-his-name has the balls and the brains I think he has, okay, he wouldn't have stayed in the car with Winegarden when he saw the damn gun, but he wouldn't sit eating a sandwich and a beer waiting an hour for Slip to come back either, figuring he'd still have the gun with him. If there was a gun in the first place."

"So what was he doing there, at the restaurant? And, if you're right, who brought the weapon?"

"Arden'll know."

"So we put pressure on him?"

"We don't." Hayashida reached for the telephone. "Somebody else will."

Arden locked Tuffy's at one in the morning, counted the receipts and cash in the office off the kitchen, put the cash and strongbox in the safe with the total, and climbed the stairs to his room. In the darkened old frame building he could hear sounds from elsewhere—a radio playing in one of the staff rooms, the refrigeration and air conditioning systems humming and, from outside, freeway traffic on one side and the steady crash of waves hitting the lakeshore on the other.

The sounds made him feel safe. So did the heavy deadbolt he had purchased and installed on the door of his room that day.

In bed, waiting for sleep, he felt like a man walking a wire. He was safe if he kept his balance. Viktor had used him to calm down Winegarden on the way to the lakeshore and give Viktor a patsy, somebody Viktor could claim was the real killer in case the police tried to finger him. The homicide cop, Hayashida, seemed to buy as much of Arden's story as he could, with nothing to break his alibi about being at the restaurant when Slip was shot. But the police could never accept the suicide theory, not with the wound on Slip's arm. How, Arden wondered, had the Russian been so sloppy?

Because he didn't care. That's what Arden realized before sleep arrived. Viktor didn't care about little details like that, because he was totally confident that he would never be caught. And because he had Arden as a fallback.

He had to keep his balance. He fell asleep with that thought on his mind. Keep your balance. Walk the wire. Give the cop and the Russian what they want. Hold on to what you need.

"You got a phone message."

Charm Darby dropped a piece of paper on the table next to the scrambled eggs she had made for him.

The paper said he was to call Albert Renton immediately. The call had arrived at 9:15 that morning. It was almost 10:30 now. Arden had been up for half an hour.

"You took your time," Renton said when Arden called from the bar.

"I work late," Arden said. "Need my sleep."

"Get here by noon," Renton told him.

Renton's office was at the far end of the strip in a corner of the Corrections Canada training facility, the biggest employer on the beach strip. It had taken Arden ten minutes to walk there but he had insisted on finishing his eggs and swallowing another cup of coffee first. He said by noon, Arden told himself. So I'll make it by noon. No sooner. He knew that whatever Renton had to say wouldn't be good news.

It wasn't.

Renton made him wait in the outer office for fifteen minutes, which made it five minutes past noon when the parole officer held the door open for him. Arden sat in his usual place opposite Renton's battered metal desk, thinking if the parole board gave Renton a better office the guy might loosen up a little. You spend your day in a dump like this, you're always going to be pissed and look for somebody's ass to kick.

"I have been informed," Renton said, sitting opposite Arden with his hands folded on the desk, "that you are implicated in a murder investigation."

"Implicated?" Arden felt himself grinning before asking himself: the hell am I grinning about? "If you mean I'm accused, well, I'm not."

"I mean that you have an involvement, according to the investigators, in a suspected murder. That you were the last person to see the victim alive and that you may even have been present at his death."

"It's…" He was about to say bullshit but the word didn't seem adequate.

"Listen to me." Renton hadn't moved, hadn't changed the tone of his voice or the expression on his face. "You are two weeks away from having your parole revoked and being returned to prison to fill out the rest of your sentence, which, in case you have forgotten, is another year and three months. If this happens, you will not be eligible for another parole review under these circumstances. You either get yourself another job in two weeks or I'll declare you in violation of the terms of your parole."

Arden looked away and calmed his breathing. He would not react. He wanted to, but he wouldn't. He turned to stare back at Renton and said, "I had nothing to do with Winegarden's death. I had no reason to harm him at all. He got me the job at Tuffy's, and the guy was good to me, okay? If you want to send me away for working at that place, slinging beer and stuff, I can't stop you. But three, four weeks ago you said you weren't too happy about me being there but you wouldn't prevent me from working there. Well, I'm the same guy, and I did not harm Slip Winegarden. So why're you changing your mind now?" He had been careful not to say kill or murder.

Renton waited to make sure Arden was finished. Then he gathered the printouts from Arden's file and said, "Two weeks. You're still working there after that, you're back at Millhaven."

"You think that's fair?"

Renton, sliding the file into a drawer beside his desk, said, "You think I'm bluffing?"

9

Walking back to Tuffy's along the beach trail, Arden tried to decide where he would go, what he would do. Without a job he'd spend maybe a year in a halfway house. The parole board gave him a break because he'd had a firm job offer, because he'd had no previous criminal conviction, and because he'd been a model prisoner unlikely to reoffend.

But Renton didn't have to follow the parole board's decision. He could set his own rules, make his own decisions. He wants Arden to live in a halfway house like other parolees, he can do it. He wants Arden back in Millhaven, he can do that too. Arden couldn't stand the idea of living in a halfway house, being told where to go, when to come back, living with a bunch of guys filling in time until their next score.

Damn. He looked out at the lake, watched a steamer emerge from the canal, saw families playing on the sand and in the water. Standing there, he thought about his room back at Tuffy's. It was maybe the best job he'd had in years. Not a lot of money in his pocket, but enough. He was talking to people and feeling like he belonged somewhere, which was something he hadn't felt since the army. This would've been a good place to stay for the summer, build up experience, get a job doing the same thing at a straight operation, running a restaurant. Now it looked like it was going to fall apart. And what had he done to screw it up? Nothing. Except ride in a car with Slip.

He was damned if he'd go back to Millhaven. He would stay somewhere along the beach strip as long as he could, working at Tuffy's or somewhere else.

"Surprise him," Viktor told Goose that day. "Go talk to him, ask what he is doing, catch him offhand."

Viktor meant off guard, but Goose knew better than to correct Viktor. It took the crazy bastard twenty years to speak English like a three-year-old, and the Russian didn't appreciate somebody like Goose correcting him.

"What'm I looking for?" Goose said, wondering if he should take Heckle and deciding not to, the guy was a pain in the ass, always asking questions yet thinking he knew everything when he knew nothing.

"What, you want me draw pictures?"

Goose had been standing in front of Viktor, Viktor with his feet on the desk, heavy black boots and argyle socks, the guy was either a total loser when it came to knowing how to dress or ahead of his time, a fashion leader, who knew? He looked behind Goose. "Now see, time for my little *krolik*, eh?"

Goose didn't know what *krolik* meant, but he was sure it had something to do with sex. He turned to see Natalka, tiny little bitch, maybe five feet tall and twenty years old, wiggle past him in her short black dress, her feet crammed into little black shoes with high heels that made her ass stick out. She leaned across Viktor's desk directly in front of Goose, giving him a good view of her black panties with the lace trim, kissing Viktor's fat wet lips as he leaned toward her from the other side, it was enough to make a guy puke.

"Natalka and me, maybe we go to Vegas next week," Viktor said. Then, to Natalka, "Big surprise, eh?"

Natalka pranced around the end of Viktor's desk and made a show of jumping onto his lap and kissing him on the cheek, her arms around his neck like she's on a carnival ride. Her black hair was almost like a boy's, and her gold hoop earrings were large enough to slip an arm through. She was listed on Viktor's employee list as a chauffeur. "Drives like soldier, fucks like mink," Viktor told Goose after hiring her. "She learn to cook, maybe I marry her, eh?" Which Goose didn't believe for a minute. A month, maybe six weeks from now she'd be gone, and nobody'd be allowed to mention her name. He'd seen it before.

"Wait, wait, wait," Viktor said, standing and sliding the girl off his lap. "Goose needs to hear what I say," coming around the corner of the desk to Goose. Natalka jumped into his chair, her hands on its arms, and now she doesn't look like somebody's toy, now she's thinking about what she'd like for her own toy.

"Listen." Viktor has his arm around Goose's shoulder, his breath all onions and cigar smoke, and he's walking Goose out of the office. "This Arden, this hero, I like. I think he's good, got balls and smarts, you know?" He glanced back over his shoulder at Natalka while guiding Goose out the door. "He knows what's going to happen, he doesn't like my deal, well, too bad for hero, eh? He is lucky, he is back in prison. He is not so lucky, well, he is like Winegarden, okay? I need him there, Tuffy's, for time and need you here for time. Most, I need you make sure he is *there*, he does things I ask when I tell him, okay?"

They're in the outer office area now. Goose isn't sure what Viktor means, but he says, "You already told me that, Viktor. I said I'd do what you want and I will. But I could do what that guy's doin'. I could run that place on the beach strip, you know that. And I'd like the job. I don't need this big city shit no more. I'm gettin' too old for it. I've been with you, what? Five years at least. This other guy, this Arden jerk, what's he done for you, huh? What's he ever done for you that I haven't?"

Did he push Viktor too far?

Maybe not. Viktor nods and says, "I tell you what you get, then you get it. For now, do what I say, okay? You go, you surprise Arden the hero, he doesn't know you're coming. You watch him, tell me does he look nervous? Stuff like that. You let him know any day, any time, you or me, we are there, okay? He does not know we're coming. Is all big surprise, like I tell Natalka about Vegas. We know what he does that way, okay? Maybe we find what we look for, what Winegarden took."

"The money." Letting Viktor know he knew.

The Russian's face clouds. "More than money. He took more than money. One thing. You tell Mister Arden Hero he stays where he is until I say where to go, what to do, okay? You tell him where he goes, I can find. You tell him he goes back to jail, I find him there too and what needs to do, I can do. You tell him I want him there, Tuffy's. I need him there for police to think he and Winegarden is all connected, nothing with me, okay? I need you here. I find what Winegarden took, we make change. You want the job, you get the job." Then, pushing Goose lightly on the back, he smiles and says, "Go. Call me after dinner. We have steak and beer soon. Been too long since we have steak and beer, you and me."

Goose leaves, knowing some of what Viktor's referring to, guessing the rest. This guy, Arden, he saw what happened to Slip, but if he talks about it, he'll be back behind bars and he won't be safe there because Viktor'll get somebody to do him. Goose thinks he knows what Slip took and why, which is what got him killed.

Stealing fifteen large from the Russian's pocket would've done it easy, but that's not all that Viktor is concerned about. It's more than money. It's gotta be about what Viktor did, what he's done that could put him where Slip and Arden had been for a few years.

"I called Renton today," Hayashida said to Delby.

"Who?" Delby had just come in from somewhere, Hayashida didn't know where. He could've asked Delby where he'd been all day if he really gave a damn. Truth was, Hayashida didn't care, he preferred working alone.

"The parole officer for the guy who had to be with Winegarden when he was shot, Arden what's-his-name. Renton's up to date on what we're doing here. He'll pop the guy's ass back in Millhaven for working at Tuffy's, we say the word."

"Didn't the parole guy approve it, that job he's got?"

"Yeah, but he didn't like it. Didn't like Winegarden working there either. Tried to stop both but some lawyer specializing in rehabilitation for inmates or something objected, got Renton to give conditional approval. He argued that Khrenov doesn't have a record, Tuffy's is a legitimate business, he should let it go. You want to guess who hired the lawyer?"

"Viktor Khrenov, right? I figure he likes ex-cons 'cause they're tough, they're grateful, they do what the guy tells 'em to do. They come out after a few years in there, and they know more ways to avoid going back."

Hayashida didn't disagree but he wondered if that was always the case.

"Anyway, Renton tells Arden what's-his-name that he's got two weeks to get his ass out of Tuffy's, either as manager or as a guest, whatever, just get the hell out of the place. He doesn't and Renton recommends his parole be revoked and he'll be sent back to Millhaven for another year or so."

Hayashida stood up and slipped into his jacket. "The coroner still owes us the full autopsy report. Check it out and keep looking at anything new we can find on Khrenov. I'm heading out to Tuffy's to have a talk with old Arden."

"Gonna tell him to find a new line of work and keep Renton happy?"

"No, I'm going to tell him to stay where the hell he is so we can keep an eye on him. If he moves out of Tuffy's and makes it hard for us to find him, we'll pull him in for questioning. That's not going to make Khrenov happy. And we'll make sure Khrenov knows what we wanted to talk to him about." He dropped his Glock into his shoulder holster. "You want something to break, you put pressure on it, right?"

10

Arden had spent an hour walking the beach trail, trying to stay in the shade and out of the way of joggers, skateboarders, bicycle riders, people with enough time and energy to get out in the world, just for the fun of it. Now he was eating a late lunch in Tuffy's kitchen, a pasta dish that had been the dining room special the night before, penne with chicken in a cream and tomato sauce. Charm had warmed it up for him, adding a salad on the side, and he was enjoying it until one of the waitresses came in and said somebody at the bar wanted to talk to him.

Arden said, "Tell him I'm busy, he can leave a message." He hadn't eaten this well in years. Another reason to keep this job as long as he could.

The waitress said, "I think he's a police officer."

The hell. "He can wait."

"He said it's important."

"Is he a Japanese guy?"

"I guess." She looked at the card in her hand. "Hey-a-shy-da? Something like that."

Arden was half through the penne. He set it aside, wiped his mouth and told the waitress to put the rest in the refrigerator for him, he'd finish it later.

Hayashida wore a pale blue tartan blazer, summer weight, over blue linen slacks and a white short-sleeved polo shirt. He looked like a Tokyo golf pro. He was sitting at the bar. When he saw Arden emerge from the kitchen, he slid off the stool and headed for a booth in the far corner, away from the windows.

Arden stopped to pour himself a glass of soda water, then sat across from Hayashida. "I'd offer you something, but you'll just say you're on duty," he said.

"Maybe you could talk me into a Coke," Hayashida said. Arden stood to get one but the detective waved him down. "Sit for a minute." He looked around to make sure the bar was still empty. "So, how're you doing?"

Arden told himself to be careful. He'd rather get a hard question from a cop than this polite crap. That way he'd know what the cop was looking for. "I'm all right," Arden said. "How're you?"

"You settling in here, finding your way around, enjoying being a big-shot manager of a restaurant and bar?"

"I'm no big shot. Just a caretaker. Keep everybody working, count the take at the end of the day, lock things up at night."

Hayashida made a big deal of looking around. "Business isn't too good today. Might have to do something to pull in some customers."

"The hell do you want?"

Hayashida might have gotten mad at that and told Arden to show a little respect, but he didn't. You become angry enough, you're the dumbest person in the room, and Hayashida was anything but dumb. "First thing I want is to find whoever shot Slip Winegarden in the head and pushed him and his car into the lake. Second thing I want is for you to stop playing games and tell me what happened the other night, what you saw and what you did. I'm willing to wait for that, because the third thing I want is for you to stay here, working at this place, doing what you're doing as long as you can. I want you to watch what's going on and tell me about it when I ask you. I also want to know where I can get hold of you whenever I need to. How's that?"

Arden shook his head and looked out the window at the lake. A freighter was sailing east toward Montreal or maybe into the Welland canal on its way to Detroit and further north, all the way across Lake Superior to Thunder Bay. A different kind of freedom. Should've got a job on one of those, he thought.

"Are you listening to me?"

Arden turned to see Hayashida smiling at him. "Have you been talking to my parole officer?"

Hayashida sat back. "Now why would you think that?"

"Because he told me, just this morning, that if I'm still working here in two weeks he'll revoke my parole and send me back to Millhaven."

"I guess that's his right, isn't it?"

"And you're telling me I need to stay here where you can keep an eye on me, and you expect me to spill my guts whenever you rattle my chain."

"You'd be doing yourself a favour."

"And if I'm gone? If I just hit the road some morning and not look back?"

"Then you won't need Renton to get you out of circulation because I'll do it myself. I'll name you as a serious person of interest in a first-degree murder investigation. You may not go to Millhaven right away, but you won't be walking the beach strip, checking out the girls in their bathing suits like you did this morning," letting Arden know he was being watched.

"You like putting the screws to people?" Arden looked to his left and saw someone leaning into the bar, watching him and Hayashida together in the far corner. Seeing Arden look at him, the guy leaned back into the restaurant. Arden caught his breath.

Hayashida was talking to him. "If you're asking if I get my kicks doing this... What's the matter with you?"

Arden was breathing quickly, almost hyperventilating. They were going to put him back behind bars to serve out his term and maybe more time, a hell of a lot more time, if they could put him in the car out on the lakeshore that night, watching Slip get shot.

"You okay?" Hayashida looked at him like he was afraid Arden was going to be sick.

Arden said, "Why don't you just put the cuffs on me now? You're telling me one thing, Renton's telling me the opposite. I do what you want, Renton sends me back to Millhaven. I do what Renton wants, you try nailing me for Slip's murder. Whatever I do, I'm screwed."

Hayashida started sliding out of the booth. "Don't have the grounds to put the cuffs on," he said. "When I do, I'll let you know." He stood up, buttoned his jacket. "I'm telling you again. You stay here, tell me what I need to know, and I'm fine. I want to know who's running things out of Toronto and what they've got to do with Slip Winegarden, the only suicide in medical history who shoots himself first in the head and then in his arm, or vice-versa. Hell, even Houdini never tried that. You leave this job without my permission and I'll see that you get a lot of time to think about what happened to Winegarden the other night. You think that's not fair? Too damn bad."

The detective left Arden wondering if he should wait for Goose to come in or go out and try to explain what he was doing spending his time talking with a cop.

He went out to meet him.

Goose was sitting at a table in the restaurant, picking his teeth with a business card. "You need to see me?" Arden said.

Goose pocketed the card, stood up and sidestepped Arden, heading toward the bar. "Let's go," he said, "you can pour me a beer," walking to the same table where Arden and Hayashida had been two minutes ago.

Arden poured a draft beer in a glass tankard and set it in front of Goose, who was wearing a muscle shirt with TEQUILA & TACOS stamped on the front, his biceps and triceps looking like partly inflated balloons but hard like rocks. Goose watched Arden, saying nothing, even after Arden sat across from him. When Goose still didn't speak, just sat staring at Arden, Arden said, "What?"

"How're things?" Goose said.

"They're fine," Arden said. "We're doing okay."

"Not havin' no trouble?"

"None at all. What's your point?"

"You not havin' any trouble, why've you gotta talk to a cop alone in here, practically whisperin' together?"

"He's a homicide detective, Goose. Hell, you know that. He's trying to figure out what happened to Slip."

"So what'd you tell him?"

"Told him the same damn thing I've been telling him for three days. Slip dropped me off at the restaurant. I waited an hour for him, had a beer and a sandwich, then gave up and came back here. End of story."

"You sure about that?" Sipping the beer.

"Come on, Goose."

"What'd he mean about you quitting here, he gives you a helluva lot of time to think about what happened to Slip? What's he mean by that?"

"It means he wants to know more."

"About what?"

Arden about to lose it. He raised his voice. "About Slip, that's…"

Arden thought Goose was about to strike him with the tankard, the way he lifted it off the table and pulled his arm back. Instead, he flung it across the bar to the opposite wall. It shattered and fell to the floor, leaving a trail of beer across the tables between them and the wall, and bringing two waitresses in from the dining room, one of them covering her mouth with her hand, the other wiping her hands on her apron.

"Don't worry, ladies," Goose said to them. "I'll get my man Arden here to clean things up when I leave."

Arden became a rock, not reacting at all, not even moving his eyes, while Goose kept smiling at the waitresses, showing his gold tooth, until they withdrew to the dining room. Then he turned to Arden, the smile gone. "That cop, the Jap," he said, "he wants to keep your ass here so he can squeeze you to tell him what's goin' on with Viktor, right? Am I right?"

"He wants to know about Slip. That's all."

"So why's he want you here? He can drag you in, keep you for two days with no charge, you know that, put pressure on you downtown, wherever. I heard him, okay? I heard him say he wants you to stay here so you can tell him what he needs to know, and that's got nothin' to do with Winegarden. It's got everything to do with Viktor. The cops here, they've got a deal with the Toronto cops, lookin' for ways to nail Viktor. Been trying for years to figure out what he does, all the action he's into. And you know what? *You know what?* They ain't never gonna do it. Not unless some asswipe like you gives them stuff nobody should be talkin' about. That's why he wants you to stay here, squeezin' you to tell him what you know about Viktor. And guess what? Viktor wants you here too. He doesn't want you skippin' town, go some place where he can't talk to you easy. So if you start thinkin' about movin' on, you better start thinkin' about somethin' else. That's my advice to you. If I was you, I'd take it."

Arden hadn't moved, hadn't even blinked through Goose's lecture. Now he said, "I stay here, my parole officer will send me back to Mill-haven."

"For what?"

"For hanging around people like you."

Which Goose thought was funny as hell. "People like *me?*" He threw his head back and laughed. "Man, you *need* people like me around you right now. We're your friends, you know that." He kept giggling as he spoke. "Come on. They're always bluffin', them parole people. They bluff like a guy facing four aces who goes all in with nothin' but a coupla deuces. Smart guy like you should know that. They're squeezin' you, you jerk. Cops and parole guys, they work together like two hookers in the same bed. You don't gotta do nothin' except what you're supposed to be doin', which is runnin' things for Viktor, keepin' an eye on the place, tellin' him or me what's goin' on. That's what you gotta do. Think you can do that, hero?"

Goose stood and stretched, looking around, out at the lake and the sunbathers, most of them women in their bathing suits, lots of bikinis. "It kills me, Viktor calls you a hero. Hero, my ass." He looked down at Arden, who was watching him, still unmoving. "You're a snivelling piece of shit to me. By the way, you'll be seein' more of me and Heckle around here. We'll be droppin' by any time, no notice, no phone call." He walked away, heading for the beach exit of the bar, gesturing with his hands as he spoke. "Might let you pour us a beer again, Heckle and me, just to see how it goes. Heckle, he used to play ball as a kid, second base he tells me. Got a hell of an arm. Probably toss a beer from here all the way to the lake."

He went out the door without looking back.

Arden sat with his head in his hands for maybe a minute. Then he walked toward the kitchen, looking for a mop and a broom, telling himself it was time for him to quit letting others push him around, and wondering what Goose meant about the Toronto cops and local cops getting together to bring down Viktor.

"I could ask to what I owe the honour of this visit, second in two days," Josie said, pouring iced tea from the plastic jug in her refrigerator, "but I'm not sure it's an honour."

"Of course it is." Hayashida took the glass and sat back in the kitchen chair next to the window overlooking Josie Marshall's garden. It had once been well tended. Now the grass was uncut, the shrubs were overgrown, and Josie's old Honda Civic sat in a far corner, its front-end smashed, two tires flat, weeds and a maple sapling growing around it, the paint fading in the sun. On the trail beyond the garden people jogged, skated or walked, most looking toward the wide stretch of sand leading down to the lake. Hayashida slipped his jacket over the back of the chair and loosened his tie. "I am here," he said as Josie sat across from him with her own glass of iced tea, a slice of lemon on the rim, "because I don't know anyone better qualified to tell me what's going on."

"And I don't know anybody," Josie said, "who spreads the BS thicker than you."

"Come on, I'm serious." Hayashida had been a sometime partner of Josie's detective husband Gabe Marshall. After Gabe was found naked on a blanket, shot through the head apparently with his own weapon, Hayashida was about the only person, on or off the police force, who refused to buy the official opinion that it was suicide. It wasn't. With a little assistance from Hayashida, Josie proved it was murder, cementing a bond between them.

"If you're talking about Slip Winegarden's murder," Josie said, "I don't know anything more than you do. Probably a hell of a lot less."

"But you know more about Slip, I'll bet. Good tea, by the way."

"Then drink it quick."

"You don't like me being here."

"Don't sound hurt. I don't like a lot of people being here, all of them men."

"But he was here, wasn't he?"

"Who?" Taking a long swallow from her glass.

"Slip. We know he was. Don't ask how, okay? And obviously we don't care why. He knew your telephone number, he came to see you. The two of you got together some times, not together at other times, including times he was here when you weren't home. So he had a key, right?"

"No, he did not have a key, wrong. He just knew where to find one. And don't go looking for it because it's not there anymore. After a while, when he asked if he could leave some papers here, stuff about Khrenov, I told him absolutely not. I didn't even want him in my house after that. If he wanted to hide whatever he had on the Russian, he'd have to find some other place. That was the deal."

"What did you two talk about when he was here?"

"Who said we talked?" Leering and teasing. "Okay, we talked. That's about all we did, especially over the past three, four months."

"Did he talk about Viktor Khrenov?"

"A little."

Hayashida watched her, saying nothing.

Josie spoke first. "Is he the guy who shot Bill?"

"Bill?"

"That's what I called him. I didn't call him Slip when I was with him. I still think of him as Bill."

"So you were that close."

She stood up and carried her empty glass to the sink. "We went to bed together exactly three times. Older women on their own are choosy about who they get naked with. Makes it easy to count. Three times. You want pictures, drawings, positions, forget it, Harold. You get statistics, nothing more. The other times he was here, we discussed movies, music, and assholes in government. Sometimes even assholes in the police department." She began rinsing the glass, talking over the sound of the running water. "If he was here when I wasn't, guess what? We didn't talk about anything. That's all I've got to say."

"How did he scare you?"

"How did who scare me about what?"

"Winegarden. About Viktor Khrenov."

"How was your iced tea?"

He finished his drink and set the glass on the table. "Good."

"Come back anytime. For tea."

Hayashida stood up and slipped on his jacket. "You probably don't need me to remind you about the risk of withholding evidence."

"No, I don't."

"Incidentally, I like that you changed your hair. You make a good blonde."

"Thanks. I make a good meatloaf too, in case anyone cares."

"You miss him?" Pausing at the door. "Slip?"

She shrugged. "Sure. I also miss Sinatra and slow dance music. And Gabe. I'll always miss Gabe. So don't ask me about missing Slip."

Opening the door and looking out at the garden, Hayashida said, "When are you getting that old car hauled away?"

"It's not an old car. It's a garden fixture."

She closed the door and leaned her back against it, her eyes closed, waiting for the tears to stop.

11

"So what kind of name is Heckle?"

Natalka guided the Chrysler down Yonge Street, sitting on a black leather cushion to help her see over the steering wheel, driving the big car smoothly through traffic with no sudden stops, no horn honking. She was taking Heckle to a construction site near the docks. A truck was waiting there for him to drive east and load it with stuff he didn't know about, didn't need to know about, then take it back to the site in Toronto.

"I got no ride," he had told Viktor when Viktor told him to do it. "Goose is gone to Tuffy's, remember?"

Viktor had opened a door and hollered upstairs for Natalka to take Heckle downtown and there he was now, sitting alongside her, watching her skirt ride above her knees, asking himself how much he'd risk to spend half an hour between them.

"My middle name is Hecla," he said, "which was my mother's middle name. It's a place in Scotland. My mother was Scottish. My grade six teacher told me in class one day that I should be named Heckle instead of Hecla and everybody heard her so it stuck."

"You didn't mind people calling you that?" Looking sideways at him, big dark eyes.

"Better than the first name they gave me."

"What was that?"

"Cormac."

She laughed. He knew she would. "Cormac? Where did they get a name like that?"

"Irish. My father's Irish. It's an Irish name."

"Cormac?" She said it again, laughed again. "Cormac Hecla? They gave you strange names."

"That's why I liked Heckle." Getting defensive. He didn't want this woman laughing at him, even if it was just his name she was laughing at. "Hey, Natalka's kind of strange, right?"

"It's Ukrainian. Like Natalie. Natalie's a nice name. Natalka's just as nice, only different." She looked across at him again. "Anyway, I don't care about names."

"What do you care about?" Heckle wanting to keep her talking, wanting to stay with her in this car and not drive some rusty truck thirty miles each way alone.

"I care about me."

"You selfish?"

"Maybe. Doesn't matter. My mother told me to look after myself first and that's what I'm doing. Take your hand off my knee."

"If I don't, will you tell Viktor?"

"Maybe." She swung the big Chrysler around a parked taxi, then back into her lane, smooth as silk. "Maybe not."

"You gonna marry him, Viktor?" Not moving his hand.

"Viktor doesn't want to marry anybody unless she's got more money than him."

"So you're just hanging around, having fun."

"Kind of. I know the guy as well as you do. In a couple of months he'll give me a one-way plane ticket to somewhere like he did the others. I heard about that."

"What'll you do then?" Moving his hand up, slowly.

"I'm sure not going to spend another winter around here. Maybe go to the islands, Miami, I don't know. I'm just having fun. Why not have some fun, right?"

"You have fun rolling under the sheets with Viktor, him smelling like a sauerkraut fart?"

She said nothing, keeping her eyes on the road.

"Don't you think about doing it with somebody close to your own age, got muscles instead of hair in his ears?"

"Okay, that's far enough." Pushing his hand away.

Heckle sat staring ahead, knowing she was looking across at him now and then, while she drove. He made a fist with his left hand and raised his arm, flexing the bicep like he's doing some kind of exercise, giving her a little show.

She looked away. "What would Viktor do if he saw you doing that just now, what you were doing with your hand on my knee?"

"Don't know," Heckle said, "I'd do whatever I needed to do so's he wouldn't find out." Then, as serious as he could get, "You'd be worth it, you know. You'd be worth the risk. I'd take my chances with you," and she looked across at him again, this time with a different look on her face, and he smirked. He couldn't help himself. He felt good seeing her with that look on her face.

"This cop, this Japanese cop, he is homicide?"

"Handlin' the case." Goose sat in Viktor's office with his legs stretched in front of him, wishing he had a cold beer, after spending nearly two hours in traffic getting back from the beach strip. "Slip's case."

"That is all he wants from hero, what he knows about Slip?"

"I'm pretty sure."

"You think he knows, Arden hero, about what we know, what we get from inside them, the police there?"

"Don't think so. I mentioned how we know what they're doin' down there and how the Toronto squad is supposed to be gettin' together with them on some kind of what they call a joint operation, and he didn't react."

"You think he stays there, at the bar?"

"He runs, the cops nail him. He stays and parole sends him back to Millhaven, someplace like that. The cops, the Jap guy, they set it up that way."

Viktor thought about it, then grinned. "That guy, he has got nowhere to go, huh? He is rat in trap."

"Are you worried about him talkin' to keep his ass out of prison?"

"You tell him he is not safe there, not from me? You tell him that?"

"Couple times."

"So what is he going talk about, eh? Not about me. Not about us. Only him was in car with Winegarden. You and me and Natalka, we are all here that night, right? Here in my place making popcorn." Viktor laughed at that. He thought popcorn was funny.

Goose nodded, then looked around. "Where's Heckle?"

"Coming back with hardware for Front Street."

"He pick it up from those guys, that gang in Oshawa?" Goose and Heckle were assigned to transport goods to building sites where the tradesmen could install it and claim not to know its origins, stuff that fell off some truck, what do they know? It was the Russian's strategy of keeping different parts of his business separate, nobody knowing what was really going on, only Viktor having the whole picture. Brilliant guy, Goose thought more than once. If he'd been straight, if he'd fitted himself in with connected people downtown, he'd have done well and not have cops and inspectors nosing around him all the time. But he wouldn't have as much fun maybe.

Viktor nodded, looked at his watch, the gold Rolex with diamonds where the numbers should be. "Should be unloading now."

"You want me to go pick him up?" Goose rising out of his chair.

"Stay, stay. Natalka took him there, she bring him back." Viktor beckoned to Goose with his hand. "Show me money we take in, tell me what we are doing, how much we are making. Then how much we say we are making."

"Don't be silly."

Heckle slipping his hand around her breast, nuzzling her neck. "Nothin' silly about this. I'm fuckin' serious. And vice-versa."

Boats floated in the marina off Ward's Island ahead of them, the sun low in the sky while some woman on the radio talked about what a mess the rush-hour traffic was today, everything backed up all across the city.

Natalka closed her eyes and Heckle lifted his head to kiss her, forcing her lips open with his tongue, which didn't take much effort, he could tell she wanted him to do it, she wanted him to do everything.

"We'd better get going," she said when he pulled away, sitting back and looking at her, imagining what was under that black dress.

"Wait a minute, wait a minute." When she looked at him, her hand on the key getting ready to start the car, he said, "You're talking about going south, maybe Jamaica, some place like that, right? You'll go when you figure Viktor's going to give you a slap on the ass and say bye-bye, right?" When she said nothing, he said, "So why wait for Viktor? We can go together, you and me, to Florida. Lauderdale to start with, and then maybe out to the Bahamas."

"You're crazy." But she was smiling at him, still not turning the key.

"Why? Why are you saying I'm crazy?"

"Because if I go to Florida, some place like that, I'm not going there with some guy who's scuffling for work, leaving me to wait on tables just to pay the rent. I'm not skipping off with a loser. Not me."

"So you're telling me you need a guy who's got money to throw around like Viktor does?"

"Something like that." This time she turned the key, starting the car.

"I've been planning to get that kind of money. See, I got a buddy down there, he's actually my cousin. I stayed on his boat a year, year and a half ago, a fifty-four-foot Sea Ray. Jesus, it's nice. Bigger and nicer than any of this stuff," pointing toward the marina. "You should see this boat. If you were a boat you'd be it, because you're both that beautiful," and she rolled her eyes and looked away. "Really, I stayed on it with him for a week at Harbour West Marina, we had a blast, him and me. He's a good guy, makes three, four million a year bringing in blow from Peru, selling it to the Angels, the Hells Angels. They bring it north. He doesn't do retail, strictly wholesale. It's safer that way. Been doing it nearly ten years now. He knows who to pay off and how, he's safe as a church, you hear me? Anyway, he offered to cut me in, handle the inside stuff..."

"What's the inside stuff?"

"You know. Details. Schedules. Help move it north, be his

go-between with the bikers, all that shit. I'd make a million a year easy the first year. He told me I could. He's a good guy, we were tight together, him and me. He grew up in Jersey. My parents used to take me there to visit my aunt and uncle, and we'd hang out, him and me. Name's Roman. He trusts me because we're family. I give him the word and we're down there hanging with him, and I start tapping into what he's up to. You can make so much money down there so fast, it'll make your head spin, really."

"So why didn't you go when he asked you?"

"I had to come back. My mom was dying. Jesus, it was terrible. I stayed with her, me and my old man, except he was drunk most of the time so it was mostly just me. I got busted, never mind for what. Did a year, then came out and got a job on one of Viktor's sites, hanging drywall and stuff. One day he saw my build, saw me with my shirt off, heard I'd handled myself in a couple of situations with some rough guys. He said he'd hook me up with Goose, doing whatever needed doing, Goose and me. I jumped at the chance. Hated doing drywall. Viktor wants me to be his muscle, I'm his muscle. Why not?" Lowering his voice, touching her arm. "You haven't seen me with my shirt off yet. I mean, I work out a lot, you know? Watch what I eat, live right, don't do no hard drugs."

She put the car into gear and swung it onto Front Street. "How big did you say your cousin's boat is?" she said.

12

Arden told Charm he was going for a walk. It was three days later, three days Arden spent trying not to think about what Renton and Hayashida and Goose had told him, the three of them using his ass like a soccer ball whenever they wanted.

When Charm said she would call him on his cell if anything came up, he told her not to bother, he wasn't taking his phone with him. Truth is, he never carried it with him because the only person who called him on it was Viktor, who had called twice so far that day, once to make sure he had Arden's number and another time to tell Arden he should add lobster to the menu because it was cheap these days, that's what Viktor had heard.

He left Tuffy's through the bar door to the beach, heading north toward the canal. Everybody has fun on a beach, he was thinking. Kids, men, women on rollerblades, and bicycles passing him in both directions. Others lay sprawled on blankets or laughed and splashed in the water. He remembered his aunt and uncle taking him to a Lake Erie beach on Sunday afternoons in the summer when he was a kid. He knew what it was like to love the water, the first chilling pleasure when you dive in, the thunder sound of waves when under the surface, the sense of deliverance when leaping out of the water into sunshine. After watching Slip Winegarden and his Toyota roll into the lake, he had no interest in the water. But it would be good to watch other people enjoy it, take his mind off things for an hour or so.

Halfway to the canal he saw a metal bench facing the lake, fixed onto a concrete pad so it couldn't be moved, a tall tree shading it. He walked to it and saw, on the back of the bench, a metal plaque that said the bench was dedicated to the memory of Evelyn Bodden 1945 – 2017. Below it were words set among musical notes. *Thou swell. Thou witty. Thou sweet. Thou grand.* He stood reading the lyrics, hearing the melody in his mind and imagining the kind of woman who would inspire those words as a way of remembering her, thinking it must be her husband, wondering what it said of their life together, and what words he would choose if he loved someone that much.

A woman spoke to him from behind, saying "You going to sing or sit?"

He turned to see Josie Marshall watching him, her head tilted, her face a mask.

"I was wondering what kind of woman would inspire somebody to describe her this way," Arden said.

"A wonderful woman who loved old Broadway tunes by Cole Porter, Gershwin. People like that. People nobody knows anymore. Music nobody knows."

"And Rogers and Hart." He nodded at the plaque.

She arched her eyebrows. "I'm impressed. You study Broadway musicals in prison?"

Which annoyed Arden. "Who the hell are you anyway? And how'd you know where I was?"

She sat at the far end of the bench, crossing her legs, looking out at the lake. "I'm Evelyn Bodden's daughter and I paid for this bench. I chose the words on the plaque."

"So you get to say who can sit here?"

"Not a bit." Still looking away. "You want to sit, then sit. There's room."

Arden looked around. This was the only bench in the shade, and he was tired of walking. He sat.

"How long did you know Slip?"

She paused as though waiting to decide to answer or not. "Not long. Just after he started working there. He told me about meeting you in jail or whatever. I called him William. Bill, actually. And you know who killed him."

He took his time to look directly at her. Red blouse, white pants, sandals with rhinestones. Blonde hair a little brassy. Full mouth. And those green eyes. "What do you know about it?"

"I know you were there when he died."

"Who told you that?"

"A friend." She looked away. "A cop."

"I had nothing to do with it."

"But you were there."

"The cop is wrong."

"Sure he is."

"I liked Slip. He gave me a break."

"Nice. What'd you give him in return?"

"There wasn't a hell of a lot I could do at the time."

Looking back at him. "So what could you do for him now?"

"Nothing."

"You could tell the police what you know."

"And I'd be charged as an accessory. That'd be bad enough. I talk to them and Viktor puts me in cement and drops me in the lake. One way or another I'd soon be dead, either here or back in jail."

She actually smiled. "Gee, I thought I had problems."

The hell am I doing here? Arden wondered. He began to stand, thinking he'd walk further along the beach strip. Walking helped him think.

She extended an arm to stop him. "I know you didn't kill him. But some people want to believe it. Or get other people to think you did."

Arden sat down. "How come you know so much?"

She shook her head. "I'm staying out of this if I can."

"But you want the police to find who killed Slip. So how're you going to stay out of it?"

She breathed deeply, which did attractive things to the front of her blouse. "I don't know. All I know is…"

"What?"

"Why he was killed."

"Because he was caught skimming money out of the place."

Her looking quickly at him, then away.

"That's it, right? I mean, I could figure it out…" Not all of it, he realized. Remembering when he was sitting in the back of the car listening to Viktor tell Arden why he was going to kill Slip. *He talk to people about me.* That's what Viktor said, that was the reason Viktor gave Arden for shooting Slip. *People he should not be talking to about me.*

Josie rose from the bench. "It's all yours," she said. Smoothing the front of her pants and starting to walk away.

"Wait a minute." Arden was at her side. "Listen, maybe you can help me."

"With what?"

"I'm being set up. The police really think I was involved in Slip's murder…"

"You were."

"Okay, I was there." Looking around and lowering his voice. "I was there, and I was as surprised as Slip. He was executed, pure and simple. I had no idea it was going to happen but I was there and the guy…" He closed his eyes, willed himself to calm down. "The guy who shot Slip has an alibi and I don't."

"So the murderer has an alibi, and you don't. Nice trick."

"Because he planned it that way. He planned everything, including having me there so that, if things get too hot for him, he can, I don't know, find some way of proving I was with Slip and I had a reason for killing him."

Josie stood staring at Arden, both of them in the shade of the tree, other people in bathing suits either lying in silence in the sun or squealing in excitement in the water. "You know what I think?" she said finally.

"What?"

"I think you're basically a sweet guy who's in over his head. And I also think I should stay far away from you."

"I'd like to talk to you more," not wanting her to go.

Turning, she said over her shoulder, leaving him there, "Maybe in some other life."

"What are you looking so smug about?"

Goose was driving Heckle to Heckle's apartment, which was a dump on Sherbourne Street. Heckle had no car and he paid maybe five hundred a month in rent. Where's he spend all his money?

"Smug?" Heckle kept looking out the window at people on the sidewalk, sometimes twisting in his seat to get a longer look at a woman he figured was worth the effort. "I'm not smug."

"Well, you're something different. Last couple of days you look like you won a fuckin' lottery or something."

"Yeah, well." Heckle still not looking at Goose, figuring Goose might read too much from his face. "That'd be luck, wouldn't it?"

"Winning a lottery? It's all about luck."

"I don't believe in it, in luck. You make your own luck, right? My old man told me that a long time ago. You count on luck getting you through life, you're a fool. That's what he told me."

Goose grinned. "He ever tell you that being an arrogant prick can piss people off?"

Heckle said nothing, figuring maybe he'd said too much already.

Goose said, "You want to take a run to the beach strip tomorrow?"

"What for?"

"Viktor wants me to keep surprising the hero. Wants him to think one of us could be there any time, showing up to check things out. I told him tomorrow should be your turn." Goose rubbed one side of his jaw. "Gotta go to the dentist tomorrow. Probably have a fuckin' tooth pulled."

"How do I get there?"

"Can't use my car. The goddam dentist is up in Kingsville."

"So I rent something? I'm not driving that three ton truck there and back, no air conditioning in it."

Goose shrugged. "Check with Viktor. Maybe he'll get Natalka to drive you, if she's not out shopping or something."

Heckle kept staring out the window, not wanting Goose to see him grin.

13

Arden woke to rain, and thunder somewhere far off. He liked the sounds. They were comforting. Lousy for business as long as the rain lasted, but he didn't care.

"Might rain all day," Charm said when he came into the kitchen for breakfast. "That's what they say. You should check for leaks upstairs. Slip had been looking into it, said there's a leak in the roof on the lake side. Never got around to fixing it. You want more coffee?"

Arden shook his head. Then he said, "Charm?"

She was walking away. She turned and said, "What?"

"Thanks."

"For what?" No smile. Charm laughed and smiled with other people, never with him.

"For telling me stuff like that, stuff I should know about. You run this place better than I do. Everybody knows that."

"Uh huh."

"So I'm just letting you know that I know. That's all."

"What's your point?"

He shook his head. This wasn't going the way he wanted it to go. He just wanted to talk to someone. He realized it yesterday, sitting with

Josie Marshall on the bench in the shade, facing the lake. He could have sat there all day talking, or maybe just watching the people in the water, and the birds. He remembered some politician saying that when he retired all he, the politician, wanted to do was sit under a tree, drink wine, and watch people dance. He would like to sit under a tree with somebody like Josie Marshall and drink wine and talk. They wouldn't need the dancing but that would be all right, they could talk about dancing. It seemed like a reasonable ambition, sit under a tree with somebody like Josie Marshall and watch people dance but, hell, he couldn't even talk to Charm.

"I'm not sure I have a point," he said to her. "Just letting you know how I feel, that's all."

She turned to look at him. "Guilty? You're feeling guilty?"

He smiled and nodded. "Yeah, I guess. I mix drinks, clean glasses and tell Viktor how much he makes every day while you and Christine and Carter and the others, you keep the place going."

"Well, don't." She walked toward him and bent to speak in a lower voice. "Don't feel a bit guilty about that. You know why? I'll tell you why. 'Cause you're the man who has to deal with Viktor. You're our…" She looked away, trying to find the word. "You're our shield from Viktor. He deals with you, he don't deal with us, and that's how we like it. All of us." She straightened up and began walking away. "All you gotta do is deal with Viktor and those fools he sends over here and leave us to do our thing, and we're happy to have you around."

Arden thought about her words the rest of the morning, through the thunderstorms that rolled in from the west and out onto the lake. He thought about it when he went up to the top floor and saw water stains in one corner, following them to the storage room below the attic. Then he got a ladder and climbed into the attic with a flashlight, finding the leak coming through some old flashing at the edge. He'd have to get it fixed, maybe get Viktor to approve it first.

He was still thinking about it when the sky cleared after lunchtime and the air became cooler and fresher, not nearly as humid, him standing at the window in the bar, watching people return to the beach.

"How about a goddamn beer?"

He turned to see Heckle Dunne grinning at him and lifting a leg over a bar stool.

"Hell of a job you got," Heckle said when Arden walked past him. "Spend time staring at bitches in bathing suits, pour yourself a cold beer when you feel like it. Viktor really pay you for doing that? Make it a draft, in one of them big glasses."

Arden poured a beer for Heckle and set it in front of him. "That'll be five bucks," he said.

Heckle watched him over the rim of the glass, taking a long swallow before setting the glass down and drying his mouth with the back of his hand. "You're fucking kidding me," he said.

Arden turned away and began wiping down the bar. "Where's Goose?"

"That any of your business?"

Arden looked back to Heckle. He would be easy to take down, Arden told himself. The arrogant ones always are. "No," he said. "You're right. It's none of my business."

"I'm doing his job today. Came here to look around, see what needs to be done, watch you work your ass off, which is a joke…"

"The roof leaks."

Heckle said, "The what?"

"The roof. It leaks when there's rain. I went up and checked it myself. We'll need somebody here to find it, replace some flashing. Place could probably use a whole new roof."

"Hey." Heckle gestured with the hand holding the beer glass. "Something needs fixing, it's up to you to look after it. You got a leak in the roof, you haul ass up there and fix it."

"With what?"

"I dunno. Tar, glue. Find it and fix it."

"Viktor tell you that? Did Viktor order you to come here and tell me how to run this place? I doubt it. I seriously doubt it."

"You don't think I've got Viktor's ear? You don't know shit if you think that. 'Cause we have, Goose and me. Nobody's closer. You'd have a crap if you knew how close I am to Viktor." And he seemed to find this funny because he giggled before taking another long swallow of beer. Then: "Give me the numbers on the place, the stuff Viktor wants."

"You mean yesterday's? This week's? This month's? This year?"

"Whatever."

You sap, Arden thought. You thick idiot. Charm had shown him the figures that morning, a printout from Excel. He recited them from memory. "Beverage sales up 13.4 per cent YTD, food sales up 28.3 per cent YTD. Those are gross. Nets are up about 10 per cent for beverages, less than 5 per cent for food. Food costs are up 12 per cent gross, which explains the lower net."

Heckle blinked. "What's this net, gross, YTD?"

"Goose knows."

"Yeah, well, Goose ain't here," Heckle raising his voice, trying to sound like a threat.

"Viktor wants nothing written down. Not by me, not by anybody." Which wasn't quite true, but Heckle bought it.

"Okay, tell me again, slow."

Arden repeated the figures to Heckle, who nodded his head, trying to remember them. "Wait here," he said, and slipped off the bar stool to walk through the restaurant and out the door, nearly running.

Arden watched him trot to the black Chrysler with darkened windows sitting in the lot. He opened the passenger door, giving Arden a view of a woman's bare legs, her sitting behind the wheel, and leaned into the car talking to her. Arden had seen that car before. He knew who the legs belonged to.

"Okay, now show me the stuff," Heckle said when he came back from the car. He drained his beer, looking at Arden.

"What stuff?"

Heckle stood holding the glass, using it to gesture toward the kitchen. If he throws the glass, Arden told himself, I'll break his arm. "In the office you got. Goose told me to check it out, make sure everything's tickety-boo."

Arden raised his eyebrows and smiled. "Tickety-boo?"

"You know what I mean." Heckle set the glass on the bar. "Where you keep the cash and stuff. Make sure you're not, you know, setting some aside for yourself."

"It stays in the register drawers until closing. Then it's locked in the room until Goose or somebody comes to pick it up, take it to Toronto. Viktor knows that. Obviously Goose knows it too. How come you don't?"

"I know, I know," Heckle said in a voice that confirmed he didn't know. "Just need to look around." He started walking toward the kitchen.

"You can't get in," Arden said, following him. "It's locked." Meeting Heckle at the door and taking the key out of his pocket, he said, "Don't touch anything." He stepped around Heckle and opened the door.

Heckle walked in, looked around. "This your office?" he said. "What a shit hole. No wonder you spend all your time in the bar." He sat in the chair facing the computer screen, his back to the window looking onto the beach, the view hidden behind cheap plastic Venetian blinds. He was swivelling around in the chair, looking at books on the shelves, the open filing cabinet, the worn carpet. "What's that?" Pointing to the small safe in the far corner.

"What's it look like?"

"You got the combination, right? And the black broad, Charm something? I hear she knows it too. What's she need it for?"

Arden began waving him out of the office. "Let's go or I call Viktor, tell him you're screwing things up here, costing us money."

Heckle said, "Hey, I'm here for him, you know, for Viktor," but getting out of the chair anyway.

"So am I," Arden said, closing the door behind them and locking it again.

Back in the car, Heckle said, "The guy's a total doofus."

Natalka put the car in drive. "So he's a doofus." She looked at her watch, the Cartier that Viktor had given her. "We've got an hour to kill. You going to spend it telling me about him?"

"I got a better way to spend it," reaching to rub her stomach, the fabric of her dress stretched taut across it, then moving his hand down, watching her begin to smile, not heading for the highway but staying on Lakeshore Road where the motels were.

Arden was more amused than upset by Heckle Dunne. Viktor and Goose were pros. What Viktor did to Slip had been done with reason and planning. It didn't make Viktor any less of a murderous bastard, but he was different from Heckle who acted on impulse, a guy who believed everything he told himself about being smart because he was younger and maybe more ambitious. It would lead to disaster for him, Arden believed. Worse, it could lead to disaster for people around him.

"You scared?"

Heckle was lying naked on the bed, watching her reach to unfasten her bra. Jesus, she was beautiful.

"About what?"

"About this."

Now her panties. "Scared of what? Being in a motel with a guy?"

"You know what I mean."

Walking toward him, swinging her hips and her shoulders, then bending from the waist to reach him. "It's exciting, I guess."

"You guess?" Grabbing her waist and pulling her to him, then rolling her onto her back, hearing the sound of traffic on Lakeshore Road, catching a look at the clock radio to see the time, remembering that they'd have to leave in an hour, get back on the highway and to Viktor.

14

For two days, Arden made a point of walking to the bench that Josie Marshall had purchased and dedicated to her mother. On the first day he went twice, finding no one there at noon and returning later to see three teenage boys sitting on the back of the bench, their feet on the seating area, pointing at people in the water and laughing at others walking on the sand, finding it all amusing.

The next day he went three times. Once the bench was unoccupied and he sat alone, asking himself what the hell he was doing there and knowing the answer. He waited almost an hour before returning to Tuffy's where Charm told him Viktor had called twice, the first time wanting to speak to Arden, the second time saying that he had called Arden's cellphone, asking why the hell he hadn't answered it either.

"I need talk to you," Viktor said when Arden called him back, "it is now, not later."

"I'm here," Arden said. "What's up?"

"Where were you, no cellphone?"

"On the roof," Arden lied. "Looking at the leak. Didn't Heckle tell you?"

"Tell me what?"

"We've got a leak in the northeast corner. Not bad now, but it'll get worse unless we fix it. Could use a whole new roof as a matter of fact."

Viktor appeared amused. "You know buildings now? You know building roofs? You contractor and hero too? I know building roofs. I decide what is to be done."

"I'm just reporting," Arden said. "Looking after things. It's what you pay me to do. And it's not a build, it's a repair. The leak's at the corner joist. Some bad flashing there. Looks like the soffit needs replacing too."

Viktor grunted. "No fool you, eh?"

"I did some roofing, some framings when I needed the work."

"I send Goose, couple guys from site, do roofs. Send them this week, maybe next week. Good what you do, watching over place. Okay for roof. Now. You got problem with Heckle? That is why I call."

"He doesn't know what he's doing. He comes here, throwing his weight around like he's somebody important, and he's not. Not to me anyway. He wanted to see inside the office. What for? I let him in but I watched him. The only thing he seemed interested in was the safe where we keep the cash."

A long pause. "Why does he need to know? About safe?"

"You'd better ask him. Look, Viktor, you can send anybody you want here to check things out, okay? It's your place, I get that. But when it comes to watching the money it's either my job or somebody else's. If it's mine, I'll watch it for you because…" Because that's what got Slip killed, he was thinking. "Well, it's my job. You want somebody else to do it, that's fine with me. You get them and I'm gone."

Which Viktor didn't like. "No, no, no, hero. You stay. I speak to Heckle, tell him leave things to you. Doing good job, you are. Is okay." And he hung up.

Arden was shaking when he replaced the receiver and walked out the door to the beach, telling himself he needed to relax, wanting to find the bench empty or with Josie on it, but it was neither. Two white-haired women were there, one knitting and the other leaning toward her, talking nonstop in her ear. An hour later he came back and found a man his age seated on the bench reading a newspaper in the dying light of the day. He walked back and forth along the lane a few times, waiting for the man to finish his paper and leave. The man remained, so Arden walked back to Tuffy's to find the bar was crowded with baseball players and their wives and girlfriends celebrating a victory, some breaking into a chorus of "We Are The Champions." "We could've really used you," Christine said when he returned. She was annoyed, angry. "We've been run off our asses since you left."

The next morning he left Tuffy's before breakfast, enjoying the chill in the air as he walked north along the beach trail, and there she was. He recognized her from the back, sitting upright in the middle of the bench, looking at the water, no one else around. He stepped in front of her and said, "You got room on that bench for me?"

She wore her hair up, held in place with a tortoise-shell comb and leaving a few tendrils hanging to catch the onshore breeze. She had a book in her hand but it was unopened and Arden suspected it was a prop, something to bury herself in when she wanted to avoid company and conversation.

"You plan to do a lot of talking?" she said.

"No."

"Good." She slid to one end of the bench, saying nothing. She was wearing blue pants that ended mid-calf and a white cotton sweater, and she opened her book and crossed her legs.

Arden sat at the other end, leaving space between them. He stared out at the lake. Some mornings, if the light was right and the air was clear, he could make out the skyline of Toronto on the far horizon. But a morning haze hung over the lake, and he settled for watching cormorants fly east in small flocks, black against the pale sky.

He grew conscious of her glancing at him from time to time, sometimes at his face, sometimes at his jeans and the deck shoes he had purchased the previous weekend, the brown leather still rich and shiny, worn without socks.

"You don't wear socks," she said.

Still looking out at the lake. "Try not to."

"You get athlete's foot that way."

"Good. Always wanted to be athletic."

She closed the book. "I saw you the other day. Sitting here alone."

He shifted, turning to face her. "I was looking for you. Thought you might like the company."

"I come here in the early morning. Sometimes during the day I come back, and if nobody's here I'll sit and talk to my mother." She looked at him for a reaction. When there was none, she said, "I imagine her giving me advice like she always did, especially after my husband was murdered."

"What does she say when she talks to you?"

She stared at him, then looked away. "Forget it. Forget I mentioned it."

"Whoa." Afraid she would stand up and walk away. "I'm sorry. I meant, whenever you talk to somebody like that, we all do, you imagine them speaking back to you, having a conversation. I wasn't making fun of you."

"Mother couldn't speak for the last eight years of her life. She'd had a stroke. Destroyed her ability to talk. But she was as wise as ever. Maybe more. She would write…" Josie looked away, blinked. "She would write with chalk on a little blackboard. That's how we talked back and forth, me speaking and her answering me on a blackboard. Then she had a second stroke, and that one killed her."

Arden could have said he understood, he was sorry for her loss, all that fluff. Instead he waited until she dried her eyes, then said, "Why didn't you come and sit beside me when you saw me here? Or just walk past, wave hello?"

"Tell me who shot Slip."

"I thought you called him Bill."

"When he was alive. When we knew each other. Now he's gone, he's just Slip Winegarden. So who shot him?"

"It wasn't me."

"Never thought it was. So who was it? Viktor? Was it the Russian?" When Arden said nothing, she said, "Don't you have enough courage to tell me?"

"I think you know."

"If he killed Slip that easily, he'll kill you as well."

"If he needs to. But he won't. I'm his patsy. If he has to save his skin, if the police start coming on to him about his alibi, he'll point at me, find a way to put me there, not him."

"So that makes you safe?"

He tried to think of an answer to that. When he couldn't, he said, "How'd you get mixed up in this?", sliding along the bench closer to her. "Okay, I understand you'd be upset about Slip's murder if you two were, you know, an item or something…"

"Item?" Like she found it funny.

"Whatever. Although I don't recall you two looking like you were hot for each other whenever you came into the bar. Hell, I hardly remember you speaking to each other."

"We weren't an item, whatever that is, and we weren't hot for each other, as you put it. Okay, we fooled around a little at the beginning, that was months ago. We all make mistakes. I made mine, we got over it."

"No, you didn't." Saying it like he knew it was true. "You're not shocked that some guy you had a fling with is dead. You're a bit saddened and a lot scared. So how come?"

She shook her head, looking away. "What happened the day after Slip was shot? What happened at Tuffy's?"

"The police came around. Talked to me, talked to Charm and the rest of the staff. Viktor called, to make sure our stories were straight, his and mine."

"Before that."

"Goose and a couple of guys showed up for the stuff out of Slip's room, take it all back to Viktor."

"Why?"

"They were looking for something."

"Like what?"

"Money, I assume."

"Had to be a lot of money, right?"

"What's your point?"

"How's he going to hide a lot of money, say thousands of dollars, and not have them find it easily?"

"Maybe he put it in a bank."

"Maybe."

Arden looking away, frowning. "Maybe it's not money they were looking for. Is that what you're telling me?"

"I'm not sure I'm telling you anything."

"So tell me why you don't come into Tuffy's anymore."

"Does anybody there want to know? Do they ask about me, wondering where I am?"

"No," running the question through his mind even as he answered it. "Who'd you have in mind? Viktor?"

"Do me a favour," she said, standing up, this time getting ready to walk away. "Let me know if the Russian or that big bald-headed guy he keeps around…"

"Goose."

"Let me know if they start asking about me, okay?"

"How do I do that? Call you on the phone?"

"I'm here every morning." Over her shoulder, walking back toward the canal and home.

15

"I'm not going back to your place. It's a dump."

Natalka leaned against the wall in Viktor's office, her arms folded, wearing a flowered print dress that made her look like a schoolgirl. Viktor had warned her never to wear jeans, pants or shorts. He insisted she wear only dresses or skirts, clothes she could buy herself at good stores on Bloor Street. She'd bring them back, model them for Viktor, a dozen expensive dresses and skirts, coming and going from the bedroom to the living room and strutting like she's in Paris. He would send half of them back, keeping the ones he liked, the ones that turned him on. That was fun for a while but she missed wearing T-shirts and tight jeans with heels to show off her ass.

"I'm not saying…" Heckle took another look out the window and down at the parking lot, making sure Viktor wasn't back from the construction site downtown. "I'm not saying we're going back there. And I'm moving, anyway. Soon's I get my condo downtown, along the lake."

"What condo?" She seemed amused by the idea.

"I'm negotiating, all right? You gotta deal with these bastards. You never pay the asking price, you deal with them," making a fist and showing it to her, "squeeze them until you get the price you want."

"I thought we were going to live on your friend's yacht in Lauderdale."

"That's where we go to make the contacts, okay? Anyway, so we won't go back to my place. I'll get us a room downtown. The Royal York, maybe the Four Seasons…"

She smirked. "You can't afford the Four Seasons."

"I sure as hell can. Get us a king-sized bed, order room service."

"For an hour?"

Heckle said, "Whatever." This wasn't going well. He wasn't thinking on his feet like he should.

She pushed herself away from the wall. "This is crazy. You know that, don't you? You know what Viktor would do if he caught us?"

"He's not gonna catch us, we're down in Lauderdale."

"I don't think we should do this anymore."

"This? What's this? What're we talking about?"

"You know." She began walking out of Viktor's office. "It's crazy, what we're doing."

He grabbed her arm, said, "Come on, you like it, you know you do."

Pushing his arm away. "I'm not staying around here forever, I told you that. If you want to come along when I go, you better have a lot more to offer than an hour in some hotel or a story about some guy you know on a yacht in Florida."

She headed for the door and Heckle called after her, "It's not a story, it's the truth. The guy's waiting for me to show, waiting for *us* to show…"

She was out the door and heading upstairs to Viktor's apartment. He would have to wait for her to return, no way was he going up to the penthouse with her now, not with Viktor in town.

Goose arrived at the open door, looking at Heckle, back to where Natalka had gone, then back at Heckle again. "The hell's going on?" Goose said.

Heckle tried to walk around Goose, get out of Viktor's office, until Goose put a hand on Heckle's chest, stopping him.

"I asked you what's going on," Goose said. "What's this about some guy waiting for you to show?"

"Nothing." Heckle stepped back, away from Goose's hands. "I was telling her about a buddy I got in Florida, wants me to come down for a vacation some day, chill out on his boat, that's all."

"Vacation? You talk to Viktor about that?"

"Not yet. I will. Just a week off maybe. See what he says."

"You said 'us'. You said somebody's waiting for 'us' to show. Who's us?"

"A friend of mine, might come down with me. What the hell is this? You're listening in on what I'm saying now?"

Goose stared at him, trying to read the truth in his eyes. "Look, you're a smart guy, good-looking, women go for you, you got big plans, fine. But you're not that smart, okay? You're not as smart as you think you are. Not yet."

Heckle started to speak.

"Shut up and listen to me. Natalka's smarter'n you in some ways. Women like her always are. You start falling for whatever she's layin' on you, you're gonna find your nuts under a hammer, understand? I'm your friend, your buddy, but no way am I going to put myself on the line for you if Viktor thinks you're interested in playing pinch and giggle with her, with Natalka, you hear me?"

Which made Heckle laugh. "Pinch and giggle? Is that what you think? Jesus, you sound like my grandmother. Pinch and giggle," walking away, shaking his head and talking to himself.

Two hours later Goose was in his pickup, ready to go home, when somebody called from across the parking lot.

It was Heckle trotting toward him, his face twisted in anger, his fists clenched. Goose knew what was coming. He'd been preparing for it.

"What the fuck'd you say to Viktor?" Heckle said, opening the passenger door and climbing in.

"You want a ride home?" Goose staying cool, knowing how to handle this.

"I want to know what you said to Viktor, got him to fire me."

"He didn't fire you. He's just sending you back to the work site, get your hands dirty, learn how to take orders, do what you're told."

"*I don't need to know how to take fucking orders.*" Screaming it loud enough that Goose wanted to push him out of the truck and give his ass a good kicking. "I'm not hanging any more drywall. He thinks I'm hanging drywall, he's nuts. I'm out of here. I'm gone." Looking around, shaking with anger.

"There's no drywall to hang. They're just starting to pour footings down there. Look." He tapped Heckle on the shoulder, the younger man not looking at him. "I'm doing this for your own good. You may not know it, but getting you away from that little bitch…"

"Who?" Looking at him now, still angry.

"Natalka. I see her coming on to you. She wants to play that game, don't let her. Best thing to do is tell Viktor. He'll deal with her when he wants to. You just don't want to be around when it happens, okay? You work downtown for a while and you're away from her. She wants to piss off Viktor, she can do it without you, okay? Like I say, I'm doing you a favour…"

"A favour? You think you're doing me a *favour*?" He opened the door and got out of the truck. "You don't know jackshit, man." When Goose called his name, Heckle told him to piss off and slammed the door, walking away without looking back.

Viktor watched it all from his office, the window open so he could hear some of the words Heckle called back over his shoulder at Goose. Give him a week, a month maybe, of dumping concrete in the sun, Viktor thought. That'll change him, hotheaded little bastard. Smart guy in some ways, dumb in others. Might even be dumb enough to think he can do to Natalka with his hands what other men do with their eyes. How *bezumnyy*, how crazy, does somebody have to be, think they can do that almost under his nose? And what is this, asking questions about the safe at Tuffy's, going where he shouldn't be?

Viktor did not want to think about it again. Goose was right, telling him about Heckle, telling him how Natalka had been teasing the boy, how Heckle was trying to be a *bol'shaya shishka*, a big shot. He thinks Natalka wants him to *yebat* her? He can't tell when a woman's teasing him, thinks she's serious. Stupid punk, needs his balls broke. Would have got it too, if Goose had not talked him out of it, saying the kid was okay, he would learn his lesson. Viktor knew who Goose was loyal to, how far Goose would go. He'd send Heckle downtown, out of the way and far from Natalka, leaving him to deal with other things. He'd send Goose back to the beach strip and find out what Slip Winegarden had taken, and what he'd hidden besides the money. Viktor knew there was more. He just didn't know what it was for sure. Or where.

16

Hayashida always knew there was something about Wes Delby he didn't like, aside from the fact that the guy was nearly twenty years younger and cocky as hell. Most undercover cops were like that, hoodlums with badges. But this was something else. What he'd found out was enough to get Delby suspended. Or should be. He dealt with it when Delby showed up after lunch, confronting him near Delby's desk.

"You waited a week to tell us that the victim of a homicide case we're investigating was a source for you?" he said to Delby. "What the hell were you thinking?"

They were in Hayashida's cubicle at the far end of the office, as far from Walter Freeman as Hayashida could arrange. Hayashida wanted to shout, yell, maybe throw things, but he kept his voice low.

"Okay," Delby said, slouched in a chair in the corner, his hands behind his head. "I can understand why you're a little angry…"

"A little angry? I don't know whether to chew gum or kick ass. And I'm all out of gum."

Delby said, "That's good. That's from some movie, isn't it?"

Hayashida, still sitting, rolled his wheeled chair toward Delby. "Look, you smarmy prick…"

"Hey," Delby said, but he sat up and leaned away.

"…I'm going to see that you're suspended and face charges on this…"

"*He was a confidential fucking source, all right?*" Delby stood up, breathing like he'd just come up three flights of stairs. "What, you don't understand that?"

Somebody a few cubicles down called out, "You need a hand there, Harold?"

Hayashida ignored the voice. "As soon as he became a *dead* fucking source you owed it to us, to *me*, to say you'd been working him. Don't you think that's a goddamn factor in a homicide case?"

"Could be." Delby was still standing, nodding at the guy across the room who had stood up in his cubicle to ask Hayashida if he needed help.

"*Could be?* A guy talking to you, he works with Viktor Khrenov, he's talking to you about who knows what, it doesn't matter, and you're a cop? That's a goddamn motive to have somebody put a bullet in his ear, wouldn't you say so?"

Delby shrugged. "Possibly."

Hayashida tilted his head and almost smiled. "A tree stump. I start out thinking I'm talking to a police officer, a de*tec*tive, and instead it's a fucking tree stump in a cheap suit."

"Hey, I said…"

Hayashida turned his chair around and wheeled back to his desk. "Fuck off, Delby. I'm taking this up with Freeman…"

"He knows."

Hayashida turned back to stare at him.

Delby was grinning, he couldn't help himself. "I told Walter just now, and he sent me over here to tell you. He said these things happen, but it doesn't change a hell of a lot and it might help get this case done. He said he would review things later, but for now I should feed you everything I know about Winegarden. Then it's up to you whether you want me working with you or not. So that's what I've been doing. Filling you in on Winegarden and me. So. You want me still working with you?"

"Oh, yeah," Hayashida said. "Like I want a Drano enema. Look, you better put every goddamn thing down about this on paper for me."

"It's supposed to be verbal…"

"Yeah, and it was supposed to be in my hands the minute you heard about Winegarden being shot too. Put it on paper and sign it. I don't care how many copies you make. I want it in your words so neither you nor anybody else can start saying, somewhere down the road, that I got it wrong, that I didn't hear you correctly, that you were misquoted. I don't want bullshit like that. Put it in my hands by the end of the day."

"Okay, he screwed up a little." Walter Freeman sat cleaning his fingernails with a toothpick, avoiding Hayashida's eyes. "He'll get a letter from me in his file, mess up his chances for a promotion for a while."

"He shouldn't be on the force, Walter." Hayashida was standing, hands in his pockets. He wanted Freeman to look at him, not at the crap he was pushing out from under his fingernails. "He sure as hell shouldn't be in homicide. Not after this."

"He won't be working with you if you don't want him." A quick glance up. "I assume you don't." Freeman set the toothpick aside and talked to his fingernails. "You're going to need help with this and I've got nobody available right now. Who else you thinking of using?"

"Start with my own source."

"Who? Don't keep this one secret."

"Guy named Arden."

Freeman looked at him, confused.

Hayashida said, "He's the guy, took Winegarden's place. I think he might've been there when Winegarden got shot." He stood and headed for the door. "He's on parole and he wants to stay that way. He sure as hell is not interested in going back to Millhaven." Hayashida turned to walk away. He'd had it with Freeman.

MEMO
CONFIDENTIAL – EYES ONLY
TO: Detective Sargent Harold A. Hayashida
COPY: Superintendent Walter Freeman
FROM: Detective Weston Michael Delby
SUBJECT: William Winegarden, a.k.a. Slip (deceased)

I first contacted this individual on April 18 of this year through his Parole Department case manager, Robert Scanlan. The subject had indicated to Scanlan that he wished to end his association with the prime subject of an on-going investigation with Toronto Police Services (File #10-2141), one Viktor Petro Khrenov and his firm Odachni. Khrenov is a naturalized Canadian having arrived from Smolensk, Russia in June 2002. Khrenov's activities are associated with various offences including fraud, theft, bribery, extortion, assault and possible narcotics distribution as well as suspicion of murder.

Winegarden served two years in prison as a result of a conviction for theft over $5000 involving building materials destined for a Front Street construction project. At trial, Winegarden claimed the theft was conducted by him without Khrenov's knowledge. This was an obvious falsehood but no proof was submitted substantiating Khrenov's involvement, and despite various offers Winegarden refused to confirm Khrenov's role in the theft. For his reward, upon his release Winegarden was appointed manager of Tuffy's, a restaurant and bar on the beach strip.

I recorded eight encounters with Winegarden (coded in my files as "Merlot") between March 8 and July 11, all at various locations on the beach strip. Winegarden refused to implicate Khrenov specifically in any illegal activity, indicating only that he wished no longer to be associated with Khrenov or Odachni. He proposed that he provide documents enabling us to proceed with serious charges against Khrenov personally and Odachni on a corporate level. He feared Khrenov or individuals associated with Khrenov would prevent him by force from dissolving his association with them.

At no time was he specific about his activities or about his personal plans. During our last encounter he indicated that he was "close" to providing material we could use to lay charges leading to a conviction of Khrenov. He claimed to have documents identifying the activities and those involved. The timing, in his opinion, was not yet right.

Our last meeting was at approximately 10:15 a.m. on July 11. We met at a bench located approximately 100 metres south of Fourth Avenue and ten metres east of the beach trail. The meeting was brief—less than three minutes. Winegarden appeared positive about developments and assured me that he would provide the documents before Labour Day.

I made two efforts to contact him via my intermediary between that date and his death, the last one on July 24.

I have neither copies of the documents promised nor any indication of specific offences that could be linked to Khrenov or his business.

"What the hell?" Hayashida said aloud. Delby had left something out. He carried the one-page memo toward Delby's cubicle, which was empty. "Anybody know where Delby is?" he called out when he got there.

"Said he's gone back to Toronto for something," a detective named Castor said.

"How about Freeman?" Walter Freeman's door was open, his office empty as well. "Where's he gone?"

"Damned if I know," Castor said.

Hayashida stood outside Freeman's office looking this way and that, as though somebody could tell him just how Delby managed to contact Winegarden for all of those meetings. He had used an intermediary, somebody who'd know times, dates, locations when they got together. So who the hell was it?

17

He met her the next morning, sitting on the bench dedicated to the memory of her mother. He brought two coffees in foam cups from the kitchen, one black for him, one with cream and sugar for her.

"Too early for margaritas?" she said when he handed her the coffee. She was wearing a knit cotton top, shorts and sandals. He tried to keep his eyes off her legs, for now anyway.

"That might be pushing things. Coffee's safer, makes a better impression."

"A better impression? How nice. I'm not used to meeting gentlemen in the morning." She paused, the cup near her mouth. "That didn't come out the way I meant it."

"Doesn't matter." He sat next to her looking out at the lake, the water like glass. He could sit there all day. He *might* sit there all day.

"Thanks for the coffee." She sipped it and frowned. "Next time leave out the sugar. Cream only."

"I'll remember that."

"I saw you jogging by my house a few times."

"On the way to the canal. Just to watch the boats pass. It's a nice house."

"Who told you where I live?"

"Can't remember. Anyway, I won't show up at your door unless I'm invited."

"You work hard, keeping yourself in shape."

"A hangover from the army. Becomes a habit."

"Was that a problem when you were in prison, getting exercise?"

"Not really. Nothing much else to do. Besides, you gotta do it. Keep in shape, get the right attitude, and you're able to protect yourself."

"From what?"

"You don't want to know."

"Slip told me you'd gone to prison because you broke a man's neck."

"Something like that." Everybody wanted to talk about it. Arden didn't.

"For raping your sister."

Arden sat back, spread his arms across the back of the bench and looked away.

"Does this bother you?" Josie asked. "To talk about it?"

"I'd rather not."

"You don't think he deserved it? The guy whose neck you broke?"

"It's complicated."

"Was he paralyzed? After you broke his neck?"

"More a dislocation than a break. But pretty bad. Bad enough to screw up his spinal cord. He's got partial paralysis below the waist. Sits in a wheelchair, can walk with crutches."

"You feel guilty about it?"

"I feel more guilty about cheating on my first wife than about what I did to his neck."

"So you won't talk about it."

"Not easily."

"I have a problem picturing you in prison, hanging out with people like Slip. I mean, Slip was no boy scout, but he was no hoodlum either. He wouldn't beat people within an inch of their life."

"Or break their necks?"

"I seem to be saying all the wrong things today." She turned toward him, crossing her legs. "Anyway, you seem out of place among people like that. Criminals, I mean."

"You start talking about criminals, about people who break the law, and most people picture somebody making a conscious decision, like deciding to rob a bank. Sometimes it's not like that. Sometimes you get nailed by the law and you don't deserve it."

"You mean people who are wrongly convicted? I see their cases on TV shows."

"Yeah, but it can be more subtle, more..." He couldn't find the word. He turned a little, facing her, liking the idea of looking at her while he spoke and having her watch him, except she wasn't, she was looking out at the lake. "Can I tell you a story?"

"I'm listening." A quick glance at him and back to the lake again.

"That was a saccade."

"A what?" Looking at him and beginning to smile.

"Saccade. What you did just then. Looking at me, then away so fast."

"It was a glance."

"No, a glance takes longer. See, with a glance you want to absorb things, really fast. A saccade is like... it's like you're just checking to see if something is still there."

"I was looking to see if you were still there? I could hear you. Why'd I have to look?" Before he could answer she looked away. "You're making this stuff up."

"No," he said, softening his voice. "No, I'm not. Really. See, believe it or not, I wanted to be a teacher. Couldn't afford to go to college. That's why I joined the army."

"So instead of learning how to teach people to read, you learned to shoot them?"

"Something like that." Arden looked away, then back at her. "You know what book I enjoy reading most? A dictionary. It's the only book I had when I was jailed. I borrowed others, but I kept that one. Anyway, look it up sometime," and he spelled *saccade* for her, letter by letter. Then he looked away again, thinking he had said too much, he'd been trying too hard.

"What's the story," she said finally. "The one you were going to tell me before I got the grammar lesson."

He smiled and twisted his body to face her again. "I had a friend from the army, a good buddy I stayed in touch with after we left, after they broke up our parachute regiment and discharged most of us, no severance, no pension. He was from Sainte-Adèle up in the Laurentians, a great guy, good skier. Couldn't handle things when he left the army. Wandered a bit, then married a French-Canadian girl. He's English. They had a couple of kids, living up in the mountains, him sometimes working as a waiter, a real misfit. Anyway, he made a connection, some tourist he met from the States who had a buddy handling weed in North Carolina. He went down there and hit it off with them, the rednecks and all. They called him Frenchie down there, although he's no more French-Canadian, Québécois, than you or me. He just taught them a few French sayings, swear words mostly. He was a good driver, a cool guy, and they got him trucking the stuff up and down the coast, a lot of it into Washington D.C. if you can believe it, practically right on Pennsylvania Avenue. He'd go down there a couple of times a month, spend two, three days on the road, come back to Sainte-Adèle with eight, ten thousand dollars, relax with his kids, drink beer and play cards for a week or two, and head south again."

Arden grew aware of Josie leaning her head against his arm, the one still stretched across the back of the bench, watching him and smiling with that mouth of hers, the bottom lip full like she's always pouting a little, he'd love to bite that lip.

"This went on six, seven months, and everything's cool. Eventually they get busted, four of them, the three guys growing the weed and making the contacts, and my buddy Frenchie, their mule. They all get fast-tracked to court, and after their first appearance their lawyer tells them if they fight the charges they're sure to lose, and if they lose they're facing ten to twenty years. The state was pretty upset at all the weed going through it. They thought it was giving the state a bad name. Which was pretty funny because a lot of the stuff they were peddling was being smoked on Capitol Hill and all across Georgetown. On the other hand, the lawyer says, if they plead guilty and save the court the cost of a trial, since they were first offenders the judge was prepared to hit them with two years in a Club Fed, minimum security place. They'd live in cabins, cook their own meals, play tennis, and relax. They behave themselves and they're out in a year. Naturally, they fall all over themselves taking the deal."

She was listening, hanging on every word.

"So they show up in court and the lawyer and the DA tells the judge everything's settled. The judge gives them all two years, just like they were promised, and they all relax a little. Then the lawyer says three of the guys've got families and asks if they can have a week to settle their affairs before going to prison. One of them, of course, is my buddy Frenchie. The judge agrees, they get the date to report to a place outside Raleigh, and off they go."

"Didn't the judge know your friend was coming back to Canada?" She was watching him, sipping her coffee.

"Either he didn't know or didn't care. Anyway, my buddy comes back to Sainte-Adèle. They've saved enough money for his wife and kids to get by for a year without him, and he feels good about that. Not good about spending a year in jail, but that his family can pay the rent and not starve."

Arden shifted in the bench a little, getting closer to her.

"The day before he's supposed to report for prison, he buys a one-way air ticket to New York City and on to Raleigh, catches a bus to the airport in Montreal, and checks in. At the preclearance gate a U.S. immigration guy asks him the purpose of his visit, and my buddy gives it to him straight. 'I gotta report to prison in North Carolina tomorrow,' he says. The customs officer asks for details, and my buddy tells him. So the immigration guy says, 'I can't let you into the country.' My buddy asks why and the immigration guy says, 'Because you're a convicted felon. You're barred from entering the U.S. ever again. Sorry. Those are the rules,' and essentially tells him to get lost."

"That's crazy," Josie said.

"It's bureaucracy. If my buddy'd said, 'I'm going to lie on a beach for a week' he'd've been waved through. But he tells the truth and the immigration officer tells him no exceptions, says get the hell out, you're a convicted felon and there's no way you're getting into the States."

"So what did he do?"

"What *could* he do? He went home and relaxed for a couple of days, figured he'd wait a week and see what his options were. Three days later a couple of Mounties show up with a warrant, clamp him cuffs and deliver him to the border. Two sour-faced FBI agents escort him to North Carolina as a fugitive from justice—how about *that?*—and he gets six months added on to his sentence, which disqualifies him for the Club Fed place where his buddies are. They're cooking barbecue and hanging out together, laughin' and scratchin', and Frenchie's sharing a medium-security joint with a thousand tough guys off the street. The only good part was, he got a refund for the airline ticket he had bought to get there. Rode down on Washington's dime."

"Didn't he explain what happened?"

"Sure he did. Over and over. You think it mattered? The guy's a convicted felon, he's not an American citizen, never paid taxes in the States, he's what they call down there an alien. All they said was, 'Gee, that's tough' when he told them about the immigration guy not letting him in."

"What's your point?"

"Point?" Arden shrugged. "Not sure there is one, except maybe you can get your ass in a wringer just for telling the truth. It makes a good story. Anyway, I heard he's back in Montreal, living on the street. Wife left him when he was in prison, took the kids with her and never came to see him, like she'd promised. Guess I should look him up sometime." He snapped his fingers. "Wait a minute. Maybe the point is, even when you try to do what's right you can still get screwed."

"My husband used to tell me stories like that. I like having a man tell me stories. Reminds me of my father."

"I've got lots of stories. Some are funny, some aren't. I'll tell you the funny ones some day."

She seemed to think about that, then stood up a little too quickly. "I have to go," she said. "Thanks for the coffee," handing him the empty cup.

"I've got another point," he said as she began walking away. "About the story."

She paused and looked back at him.

"My point is." He stopped, thinking what he had been about to say. "My point is, I'm kind of in the same position as my buddy. Whatever I do, I lose. Big time. I've got a parole officer who wants to put me back in prison."

"For doing what?"

"For having a steady job. How about that? And I've got a cop who says if I quit my job he'll do the same thing. Ask for my parole to be revoked."

"Why?"

"He wants me to stay and tell him about things."

"What things?"

"You want to guess?"

She looked at him for an extra beat or two. Then she said she hoped he worked it out, turned, and walked away.

Arden sat on the bench looking at the lake, which wasn't smooth and glassy anymore. He remained there for an hour, willing her to return.

18

Goose got a call that morning from the foreman on one of Viktor's projects down on Front Street, a twelve-storey office building, lots of glass and concrete. As he did with all of his projects, Viktor set up the tender and got the deal, then hired outside project managers to manage it, guys who knew the score, knew how to get the building up. They did it while tolerating surprise visits from Goose, who Viktor sent to look things over, Goose having spent ten years in heavy construction himself, knowing what works and what doesn't, what can be done over-night and what takes a week.

Viktor didn't cut the project managers much slack when it came to hiring trades to pour the foundation, work the high steel, handle the cladding. He wanted companies that could do the job and know how to work with him, cutting corners to buy themselves more work down the road. "You scratch my balls, I scratch yours, eh?" Viktor said once. Goose told him the phrase was, "Scratch my back, I scratch yours," and Viktor said he knew, he knew, but he liked his version better.

"Your guy didn't show up this morning," the foreman said to Goose, calling him from Front Street. He meant Heckle. "Leastwise, he's not here yet and it's after nine o'clock, so I figure he's not gonna show. Not that I need him. Got enough broom pushers as it is. I'm just letting you know, right?"

Son of a bitch took a flyer, Goose thought. Which was probably a wise move on his part.

Goose usually got along with Heckle. The guy could be funny now and then. Heckle had started out promising the world to Goose and Viktor, happy to have caught their eye, walking up and introducing himself when they were going through one of Viktor's condo projects. "I'm not gonna hang drywall all my life," Heckle had said to them. "See, I got plans. Maybe I could work out something with you, Mister Khrenov," ignoring Goose.

Viktor had been amused. He said nothing, just looked at Goose and grinned, later telling Goose to look the kid up, see how bad he wanted to work, what he'd do and what he wouldn't. He liked the kid's attitude.

"What can you do?" Goose asked, and Heckle had said, "Whaddaya got?" When Goose started complaining to Viktor about his workload, how he was run off his feet checking with the project managers, keeping things in line with the trades and their unions, threatening a little muscle when some didn't fall into line, Viktor suggested getting Heckle, giving him a chance to learn the ropes. Goose did, and a week or so later he was complaining to Viktor about it.

"Kid's got an attitude," Goose told Viktor after a couple of weeks. "You know what he said to me the other day? He said he wants to be you in a couple of years, doin' all the things you do, have all the money you got. Got an ego the size of a Mack truck."

"Maybe we let him, eh?" Viktor said. "See how high he climbs before he falls." Which might have been one of Viktor's least smart decisions. Heckle was ambitious, he was smart, he was cool when the pressure was on, making runs for Viktor, never asking why or for what. Trouble was, he wanted to go too far too fast, pissing off everybody he dealt with, telling them they'd soon be taking orders from him, so they'd damn well better move their ass when they were told to. "Slow down," Goose said to him when he heard about it.

Heckle laughed and said, "I'll slow down when I'm dead," and Goose said he knew some guys that could arrange it, Heckle being dead.

Goose wasn't sure he should tell Viktor about Heckle not being at work, not doing what Viktor told him to do. This would really make Viktor pissed, and nobody enjoyed being around Viktor when he was pissed. Besides, the kid might show up later, he might just be sick, who knew? Goose thanked the project manager, and suggested he cross Heckle's name off the employee list if the kid didn't show by noon.

So where is he? Goose wondered when he hung up. Probably picked up some girl last night and is in bed with her. Or stoned from whatever drug he favoured these days. That'd be the worst thing he could do. He did that, he'd better be gone for good.

It had taken Heckle five minutes to get into the Silverado and two minutes to pry out the ignition switch with a hammer and screwdriver, slip the blade under and go to work. He'd chosen an older Silverado, made before they started using chips, transponders they call them, to open the door and start the engine. Made it damn near impossible to heist one. Heckle had learned about heisting cars as a kid. He'd driven a BMW for three days when he was in high school, driving it away when the owner left it running with the keys in it and the AC going, just so he could come out of Tim Horton's with a hot coffee and get into a cool car.

Heckle didn't want a BMW. They were cop magnets with a young guy like him behind the wheel. Pickup trucks were better, hardly ever stolen and sometimes not driven every day either.

The Silverado cruised nicely along the highway toward the beach strip, already filled with gas by the owner, thank you very much, loser. Heckle had pulled all the cash he had from the bottom drawer of his dresser, just over five hundred. Now he wouldn't have to spend any of it on gas.

Take it easy, he told himself, keeping the Silverado in the slow lane. Nice day like this, find some good rap on the radio, you can do what you need to do. Show Natalka a few tricks maybe. Or maybe just hit the road, head somewhere out west. Anywhere but under Viktor's thumb. No more of that shit.

He entered through the kitchen door, nodding to everybody, letting them think he was there as Viktor's man, subbing for Goose.

It was just after noon and everybody was busy, the dining room nearly full, people digging into meals, some with wine bottles on the table. How much does Viktor make from this place anyway?

He watched Charm Darby working with the cooks, moving burgers, pasta and sandwiches out of the kitchen on their way to the dining room, good-looking woman for her age, if you like dark meat. When he nodded to her, she gave him a look and turned away. He walked to the office and tried the door. He considered forcing the lock, he could probably do that in a flash. Instead, he went back to the kitchen and looked into the bar. Arden Hero was pouring drinks, mostly draft beers, putting them on trays for Christine and the other waitresses to carry to the dining room. What the hell kind of work was that for somebody, supposed to be a tough guy, after spending a couple of years in the slammer?

Back in the kitchen, he called Charm over from where she was dropping sliced tomatoes on plates. "I need to talk to you," he said.

"What about?" Charm said. "I'm real busy here."

"Take two minutes. It's for Viktor, he sent me in. Finish what you're doing, then come back to the office. Bring your key. Make it quick. Viktor's waiting outside. And don't tell asshole in the bar, okay?"

"Arden?" Charm said.

"It's about him," Heckle rubbing his thumb and forefinger together, giving her a hint it's about money. "What he's doing. Viktor's pissed."

Charm looked worried. "The key's in my purse."

"Then get it, get it. Viktor's out there, the engine running. I don't want him coming in here, do you?"

He went back to the office, around the corner from the kitchen. She showed up a minute later, the key attached to a steel ring with a rabbit's foot on it. He angled his head toward the door and she put the key in the lock, turned it, and just like that they were inside. "Now the safe," he said, and that stopped her.

She looked at him with a different expression. She'd bought the story about Viktor waiting outside, but this was slowing her down. It was Thursday, almost a whole week's cash in there. "What about it?"

"Open it," Heckle telling her like it was the most obvious thing in the world. "See, Viktor figures Arden's been skimming from him every day, every week at least. That's what Slip was doing, right? And you know where that got the stupid bastard. So what we need to do is, we need to count what's in there, put it back, and compare it with what he says we've got on Monday."

Charm blinked, frowned, tilted her head. "They won't match."

"What won't match?"

"Whatever's in there now and whatever gets picked up on Monday. There'll be all the cash from the weekend added, so what good's it going to be to know how much is in there now?"

Holding himself in, keeping his patience, Heckle said, "I know that. You don't think I know that? You don't think I told that to Viktor? But you know him, you can't tell that dumb Russian anything. Besides," feeling good now with a different story, back to thinking on his feet, "this way he'll know just how much he might take in on a weekend. See, the big deal is, you can't let what's-his-name in the bar know we counted the cash, else he'll be on to Viktor. So just open it, get me a pencil and paper, I'll count it, put it back, and you can go finish slicing tomatoes."

"This is…"

"What?" Still keeping himself calm, ready to tell the bitch to hurry up, do what you're told.

"I have to get it."

"Get what?"

"The combination."

"What for? You open it every fucking day."

"We changed it."

"Who changed it?"

"Arden. He said it's a good idea to change it every now and then, otherwise the combination gets passed around."

Heckle breathed deeply and nodded. "So you're telling me, what? You haven't memorized it?"

"It's written down on a piece of paper. In my wallet. I'll have to get it. Just take a minute."

Heckle was ready to ask if she really thought it was smart to carry the combination for the damn safe around in her wallet with her, or maybe tell her that she had better move her black ass because if Viktor got all worked up out there in the car there'd be hell to pay, but she was already gone. He crouched down, staring at the safe, built into the wall, be a hell of a job getting it out. Maybe he should've blown it, find somebody who can work with whatever it takes to blow this piece of crap open. Then he'd have to share it, have another damn hand in there, wanting part of the action. This was better. She bought the story, Charm did. That's the beauty of having a guy like Viktor around. You drop his name and everybody craps their pants afraid to…

"What're you up to?"

It wasn't Charm's voice.

He turned to see Arden standing over him, one of his hands wrapped in a bar towel. Heckle got to his feet. "I need the combination," he said, sticking to his story. "Viktor needs to know how much is in there."

"Then tell Viktor to get over here and check it himself." Arden was rocking on his toes, flexing his fist inside the towel.

"He's out in the car waiting," Heckle said. His voice cracked on "waiting," making him sound like a little boy.

"Good," Arden said. "Let's go bring him in here."

"No, you don't want him in here." Heckle was on his feet, his eyes like ping pong balls, jumping from the desk to the bookcase to the windowsill, looking for something to use against Arden, who outweighed him and stood half a head taller. He was looking for a glass, a hammer, a club, something to swing, something to knock Arden out of the way.

"Get out of here," Arden said quietly. "Now."

Behind Arden, Heckle could see Charm and Christine and one of the chefs taking it all in, watching Arden the fucking hero play the big man.

"You want me out of here," Heckle said, "you fucking come and get me," which he hoped gave him time for some kind of advantage. Heckle had his own strength, he reminded himself, pressing two-fifty, three hundred pounds…

He felt Arden's hand on his arm without having seen it move, it . was that fast. Heckle twisted and tried pulling away but Arden pulled the arm up behind him, using Heckle's momentum to shove him face-first against the wall with so much force he broke Heckle's nose. Arden raised the arm even further until Heckle screamed in pain, and Arden's free hand seized Heckle's hair, pulling his head back, every step return-ing from his parachute regiment training, the special unit that had taught Arden hand to hand combat, and how to break or dislocate a man's neck.

Arden wasn't interested in breaking anyone's neck. He turned Heckle around, Heckle's head back now so he couldn't see where he was going, blood streaming past his mouth and down his chin, Arden's hand feeling like it was going to snap his arm, with his other arm waving in the air ahead of him.

Arden frogmarched Heckle past Charm and Christine, who stood back with hands over their mouths, and past Carter, whose eyebrows were raised in approval and admiration, heading for the kitchen door leading to the beach. "Somebody open it," Arden said, Heckle neither screaming nor struggling anymore, and when one of the kitchen boys opened the door Arden marched Heckle to it. Releasing Heckle's hair and arm, Arden lifted his right foot to Heckle's ass and booted him toward the beach. Trying to twist away, Heckle struck a steel pole hold-ing an overhead light fixture just beyond the door, leading with his face, his mouth open in a prepared string of threats and swearing. The collision with the pole broke one of his front teeth off almost at the gum, producing a new torrent of blood, and Heckle fell to his knees, his head down, the sand beneath him turning crimson.

"Jesus Christ," he said, and Arden could see he was crying from pain and humiliation.

Using the pole for support, Heckle managed to stand, holding his head and spitting blood. Arden stood watching him for a moment, feeling a low swell of regret at what he had done before tossing the bar towel at Heckle, then closing the door and locking it.

"He's leaving," Christine said a couple of minutes later. Arden had poured himself a finger of Crown Royal, drank it, and was about to pour another measure and drink it too. Instead, he carried the drink to a window where Charm and two waitresses stood staring out at the parking lot. At tables seated along the windows facing Beach Boulevard, diners nudged each other and looked out as well.

Heckle was holding the bar towel to his mouth and stumbling toward a rusty pickup truck at the far end of the lot, near the curb. Blood was staining the towel, and a cut above one eye had opened, launching another stream of red onto his cheek. He climbed into the truck and drove away slowly.

"Should we call the police?" Charm asked. "Or Viktor at least?"

Arden shook his head. Somebody would have to be told. He just wasn't sure who. Or in what order.

19

Hayashida had a name for anyone he was angry with. He called them Charlie, no matter what their names were. "Shape up, Charlie," he would say, or, "Charlie, you're so full of shit your eyes are brown." He never called Walter Freeman that, but he had called his wife Charlie a few times in the middle of an argument. "Don't tell me how to live my life, all right, Charlie?" and his wife would either break up laughing and the argument would end there, or she would become even more angry and what might have been a civil disagreement would erupt into domestic war.

Wes Delby had never heard Hayashida call him Charlie before, so when Hayashida poked him in the chest with a forefinger and said, "Who the hell do you think you are, Charlie?" Delby blinked and said, "Charlie? Who's Charlie?"

Hayashida ignored him. "You're not running your own show on this one, damn it. This is first-degree murder, with some organized crime charges involved. So get serious. You wanna play games, go back to hustling crack dealers or whatever you do when you're dressed like a bum. But not now, and not if you're working with me."

They were in the coffee lounge at Central, in a far corner near the men's john, Delby having come out still zipping up his fly when Hayashida pounced on him.

"Let me guess," Delby said. "You're upset because I didn't tell you who my contact was, between me and Winegarden."

"For a start. Who the hell is he?"

"I'm not sure I have to tell you." Hayashida began to boil over again, and Delby said, "You know what's wrong with you, with this whole department? You all play your games, waiting for stuff to happen. It's small town thinking, two-bit stuff. You say, 'I'll push a button here, push another button there, and see who jumps,' and it's all crapola, Harold. The people I deal with in Toronto, the Russian and the guys working for him, they've all got PhDs in working around the law, they're not a bunch of guys breaking streetlights and stealing bikes. They play different over in Toronto. You want to find out what's happening there, you don't sit on your ass, you get out on the street with them, okay? That's what I do. That's the way it gets done."

"Being on the street didn't save your contact's ass, did it?"

"But it's how we'll find out what happened with him. Bet on it."

"Who were you using to get to Winegarden? I want their name."

"Forget it."

"You want me to get Walter Freeman on this?"

"That's your answer, Harold? Run to Walter? I don't have to reveal any of my sources until we lay a charge, you know that." Delby looked across at four cops sitting at a table, watching and listening to Delby going up against a senior cop, a guy popular with the rest of the force, twenty years on homicide, everybody owed him favours. He turned away from them and lowered his voice. "Okay, you want to talk to them? You want to know how I set things up with Slip?"

Hayashida played along. If Delby wants to save face, not look like such a jerk in front of the other guys, Hayashida would help him for now. "Yeah," he said. "I do."

"I'll go see them, get them to talk to you if I can."

"*If* you can? They've got something to tell us, they damn well better say it."

"It's complicated, okay?"

"When?"

"Today. Tonight, if I have to."

"Do it now."

"I can't do it now. I'll try tonight, maybe tomorrow morning."

"That's the best you can do?"

"It's the way it works. I don't choose how it happens. They do. If Slip had something he wanted to tell me, he got them to contact me. If I needed to talk to him … hell, you figure it out."

"Jesus Christ, Wes." Hayashida shaking his head.

"What?"

"Just set it up as soon as you can, all right?"

Delby might have gone to the beach strip right away. He wanted to. But he didn't want to change the way he had set things up, and he sure as hell didn't want to ask "how high?" whenever Hayashida told him to jump. Besides, he had a right to hold onto his sources until a charge was laid or somebody higher up ordered him to. He was damned if he'd cave in to some hotshot who was five years away from cashing in his pension.

So he found other things to do for the rest of the day. He'd let the four guys watching from the table, all of them thinking Hayashida was getting tough on him, let them know he was nobody's tin can to kick around. He'd play things the way he always did, and hoped they would pay off.

Heckle pounded the steering wheel in between wiping blood from his eyes and mouth, heading for the North End of the city where he had spent some time on the street, couple of years ago, knew guys in the bars along Sherman Avenue and Barton Street.

The son of a bitch.

He tried not to breathe through his mouth. Cold air on his broken tooth was like having an ice pick shoved into his gums. Breathing through his nose was just as bad. Both nostrils were plugged with blood and he could feel it running down the back of his throat, making him want to pull over and throw up, which he did once, just outside of one of the old steel company factory gates, leaving a red puddle the size of a saucer on the ground.

He hit three bars, two on Barton and finally one on Sherman, guys sitting at the tables elbowing each other at the sight of him, the bloody towel still held against his cheek. At Argonne's on Sherman, he recognized a guy named Lowell. Everybody called him Wingy, thin guy with long stringy hair, worked for a while as a glazier until a sheet of double-diamond shattered and nearly took off his left arm, slicing the muscle and tendons and leaving a scar across his forearm from elbow to wrist, leaving him barely able to raise a glass of beer in his left hand. Wingy got hooked on morphine to kill whatever pain he was feeling, the story went, and did some dealing to pay the bills and feed his habit. Somewhere along the line he made a contact in Buffalo. Cheap revolvers were coming in from various places, even Russia, landing in the States for as little as fifty bucks, worth three hundred by the time they crossed the border. Heckle had met a couple of bangers out of North York who talked about their man Wingy in Hamilton, saying he could come up with just about anything they needed. Wouldn't come into Toronto, didn't like the place. Stayed where he was, hanging at a couple of bars around people he could trust. One of the bangers said, "You ever need a popper, you see Wingy," not meaning something to make popcorn with, that was obvious.

"Hey," Heckle said, sitting next to him, the guy having watched Heckle come into the place, unsteady on his feet.

"I know you?" Wingy said, his hair to his shoulders and about enough hair in his moustache to fill a thimble, you shave it off. He had a Molson in front of him.

"Heckle. We worked together a while. Place in Scarborough, big condos."

Wingy looked away. "You say so." Then looked back. "The hell happened to you?"

"I need a gun."

"You need a fuckin' doctor."

"Seriously. I need something right away. What can you get me?"

Wingy twisted this way, that way, checking the door, looking at the bar. Everybody else in the room had turned back to their drinks or to the two hookers sitting together across the room. "What're you talking about?"

"You know. Come on, damn it."

Wingy looking directly at him again. "How much've you got?"

Heckle calculating in his head. "Three hundred."

"Three-fifty."

"Okay, three-fifty. And loaded, right?"

"Get it for you tonight."

"Not tonight, goddamn it. Now."

Wingy took a long drink from the Molson.

"Look at me," Heckle said, wincing at the pain. "Some asshole did this to me and I need to…"

"Shut up."

Heckle sat back in his chair.

Wingy still didn't look at him. "I don't want to hear what you want the fuckin' gun for."

They sat like that for a minute or more, Wingy staring somewhere beyond the bar, Heckle wiping his nose on the towel now and then, trying to sit still, trying to stay in control. Then, still not looking at him, Wingy said, "If you've got the cash, go into the men's crapper, leave it inside the thing where you get paper towels. Open it up, put the money inside and fuck off. The money's there, what time is it?" He twisted in his chair to look at the clock on the far wall, did some calculation. "You get back here at seven, go around the back, open the dumpster lid, look for a cereal box."

Heckle said, "Cereal box? What, like corn flakes?"

"Don't you got some other place to be?" Wingy said, and Heckle got to his feet and walked to the men's room.

He drove the Silverado to a mall on Barton Street, a sad place with a store promising that nothing it sold cost more than two dollars, another place selling used furniture, a tattoo parlour, a pizza joint, and three empty storefronts. The cut on his lip had dried, and he could breathe more easily through his nose. He parked the truck and stretched out on the seat, feeling tired, feeling wiped, thinking of Natalka walking out of the bathroom, removing her bra as she approached him, and the feeling was so good, felt so warm, that he fell asleep.

He woke to the sound of rain falling on the truck, and he had to remind himself where he was and what he needed to do. He drove the Silverado back toward Sherman Avenue, stopping at a Tim Hortons and leaving the towel in the truck. He drank coffee and managed to swallow a yeast donut, watching the clock behind the counter move toward seven.

He drove to the bar, parking the truck a block away and walking around to the back. There were two metal dump bins behind the bar, one so high he'd need some kind of ladder to reach the lid, the other smaller and grey, off to the side. It had to be in the grey one, and it was. Shredded Wheat, the box sitting on top of a stack of old papers, flattened cardboard boxes. He almost smiled at the sight. His father used to eat that shit. Every morning, Shredded Wheat.

It looked like a new box. Wingy must have bought it today. He took it out, the lid was cut off. Layers of them, the biscuits his old man ate every morning, one layer on top and another under it and a small black revolver on the bottom. An Armscor .38, cheap and ugly piece of junk, what Goose called a card table gun. "Don't need to pick off mice at a hundred feet with a gun like that," Goose had said. "Just needs to work good across a card table and over a stack of chips." Heckle opened the chamber, six rounds inside. He'd like to have gone in the bar and thank Wingy personally, knowing that getting what you wanted out of life was all about making contacts, knowing the right people, counting on them when you needed them and having them come through. The guy had come through for Heckle. He wouldn't forget that.

Steady rain, the light growing weak with the heavy overcast sky. He'd thank Wingy some other time, not that the bastard needed to hear it, and headed the pickup down to the beach strip, feeling the gun against his thigh growing warm like a lover.

20

It was almost seven-thirty when Wes Delby pulled up at Tuffy's. Damn rain sounded like it would never stop, not a summer rain either but cold like the rain you get a month before it turns to snow. The air felt more like November than July, and he wondered what the hell was happening with the weather, wasn't it supposed to be getting warmer?

He went into the bar, as crowded as he had ever seen it, maybe twenty, twenty-four people in there sipping beers and fancy drinks with plastic swords in them, most of them women too old to have spent the day in a bathing suit on the beach. Some of them, the ones sitting with other women, looked over when he walked in, sizing him up, a good-looking guy out on his own. He sat as far from them as he could, down near the end of the bar.

Arden was drawing draft beers for Christine to take into the dining room, paying attention to the pour, taking pride in producing an even head on each glass. Christine saw Delby come in and spoke to Arden, who looked quickly toward Delby without moving his head, then back to the beer. When Christine took off with her tray of drinks Arden approached the detective, picking up a towel and looking all around on the way, making sure everyone had the drinks they needed.

"What can I get you?", he said, wiping the bar in front of Delby.

"I'm waiting for a friend." Delby smiled, made a show of looking around, searching for a familiar face.

"You here as a customer or a cop?"

Delby still smiling, keeping things light. "You have a preference?"

"Could've used one of you guys here this afternoon."

"Something happen?"

"You know a guy named Heckle Dunne?" Arden keeping his voice low.

"What about him?"

"Came in here today throwing his weight around..."

"Works for Khrenov, doesn't he? Shows up here with the guy they call Goose to check up on you, the same guys who used to check up on Winegarden?"

"Not this time. He was screwing around, wanted to know the combination to the cash safe in the back office. He said Khrenov sent him, which was obvious bullshit."

"You call Khrenov about it?"

Arden looked away. This might have been a mistake. "Handled it myself."

"What do you mean, you handled it yourself?"

"I told him to get his ass out of the office."

"And?"

"He didn't."

"You want to draw me a picture?"

Arden spread his hands. "Tried to pull him out, he wouldn't come, turned him around, marched him to the door to the beach, threw him outside."

"Easy as that."

"Not really. Along the way I think I broke his nose and he lost a tooth."

"You hit him?"

"Not me. A utility pole out back. He bounced off it."

Delby stared at him, smiled, looked away, turned back. "You're telling me you roughed up one of Viktor Khrenov's men, the guy who owns this place? How's he going to take that?"

"Not badly when I tell him Heckle had been trying to get his hands on the cash in the safe."

"Dunne could lay an assault charge on you."

"Not likely. He prefers to stay away from you people." Arden looked down the bar. A guy in a Blue Jays T-shirt was standing with his hand raised like he was in school and wanted to leave the room. Arden looked away, saying nothing to Delby who watched Arden pour two beers for the Blue Jays fan to carry back to his buddy at a table against the window, and ring up the sale.

"What'd Heckle want with the combination to the safe?" Delby said when Arden came back.

"You think he was picking numbers for a lottery ticket?"

"I don't believe the guy was stupid enough to try and rob Viktor Khrenov."

"I hear the two most common elements in the universe are hydrogen and stupidity."

"You want to be a fucking comic or you want to be straight with me?"

"The only thing I want to be is left alone. By you, by your buddy Hayashida, by Viktor Khrenov, the lot of you."

Someone called Arden's name and he saw Christine at the other end of the bar holding a tray, waiting for him to do some drinks.

When he came back, Delby said, "So you beat him up in the office."

Arden leaning on the bar, keeping his voice down. "I didn't say I beat him up. I tried to get him the hell out of there, that's all."

"Show it to me, the office where the safe is."

"Why? You saw it when you were here with Hayashida."

"I should take another look. In case Khrenov's guy decides to press charges."

"You think a guy like that, he's going to run to the police and say, 'Somebody kicked my ass, I want you to pick him up and put him away'? Not bloody likely."

"I don't need him to press charges, you know. I can do it myself or get one of the duty cops to do it, if I see enough evidence. Look, I'm trying to keep you out of trouble here. The place is a cubbyhole, that office, right? Tiny little space. Get two guys in there, maybe somebody gets sideways, whatever, it can happen. Then maybe it's not assault, not worth prosecuting anyway. Just show me, give me an idea what went down."

Arden stood staring at Delby like he was something Arden should be wiping off the counter with.

"Hey," Delby said, starting to lose it in front of the ex-con, "you know, I can count at least three things here that, if I pass them on to your parole officer, they'll put your ass back in Millhaven, okay?"

The rain, Heckle told himself, would keep people off the beach, away from the back of Tuffy's. Which is where he wanted to go, not in the front, it'd be nuts to walk in the front door with or without the Arms-cor in his hand. He'd slide in the back, he knew his way around. Pop the son of a bitch and go.

He'd need to get rid of the pickup, find another way to get home, probably with Goose. He parked the Silverado on the street, two blocks to walk through the rain to Tuffy's but that was all right, the rain, the dark sky, it was what he needed.

Tuffy's was lit up like a birthday cake, people going in the front entrance off Beach Boulevard, some of them running through the rain. Maybe now should be the time to hit it for cash, they'd be stuffing the safe tonight, but Heckle was smarter than that. He had one thing to do. He remembered his old man telling him: *You learn to do one thing and you do it good. You do one thing at a time, that's all you need. Do one thing at a time and do it good.*

He walked around back, staying in the shadows without needing to because there was nobody on the beach trail to see him, not in this cold rain. Lights from the kitchen lit the ground next to the door where Arden had thrown him up against the steel pole. Jesus, he had to have done it on purpose. He'd lined him up like a bowling ball and threw him at the pole. That's when Heckle didn't have a .38 in his hand and didn't have a reason to whack him, but he sure as hell had both now.

He went to the back door and tried the knob. It was locked. Okay, people come and go, the kitchen help, they're in and out of this door all the time, coming out for a smoke or dumping crap in the garbage cans, he knew that, he had seen them. Next prick who comes out gets pushed aside, Heckle's on his way to the bar, puts a couple shots in the hero's head and how do you like it, asshole? Then he's gone, people too scared to think about doing anything but run, get the hell away from him. He calls Goose, gets home, stays warm and dry and tomorrow he's on his way to somewhere, which made him think of Natalka, but just for a moment. A light had come on, shining through the window on the other side of the door from the kitchen, the window of the shithole office where the safe was.

He couldn't see anything for sure, just a shadow against the closed plastic Venetian blinds, but he knew what he was looking at. The shadow was standing long enough for Heckle to pull the Armscor out of his pocket and aim. Then the shadow was gone, dropping below the windowsill to floor level, where the safe was. Just as he figured. There was so much cash from tonight, they had to dump some in the safe. He's opening it now, slipping in more cash. I should be inside, Heckle thought, be in there and clean it out, get on my way now. Kill two birds with one stone. Well, one bird anyway... And just like that the guy was standing again, the shadow straight up like he was daring Heckle to do it. Heckle Dunne never needed two green lights to cross the street, and he took a step forward and fired.

Like catching a baseball in a mitt, that's how firing the .38 felt, like the ball coming straight down the line to you from third base and into your glove, he'd played some baseball, wasn't bad either, handling shortstop or second...

The shadow froze in place with the shot, no sound of glass breaking, just the shadow stiffening and giving Heckle the next shot, this one where it needed to be. He took another step forward, raising the Armscor to align it with the shadow's head and this shot seemed louder. The shadow dropped right out of sight, and Heckle was gone.

The kid was maybe fourteen and living in one of those glitzy million-dollar joints near the canal. Where the hell did a kid that age get enough money for a new iPhone except from rich parents? He was jogging along, the phone to his ear, talking and laughing into it. "They're gonna kill me, I show up soaked like I am. Did you know it was gonna rain?" Coming down the paved beach trail wearing striped shorts, Nikes and a Roots hoodie keeping his head dry.

"I nearly forgot. Did you see what Danielle was wearing? That yellow top? I thought she was going to fall out of…"

Heckle grabbed the kid's hand, the one holding the iPhone, and jerked it away from him. He thought about showing the kid the Arms-cor, scare the shit out of him, some kids thinking their phones grow out of their heads, but not this punk. The kid stopped long enough to look at Heckle, who gave him a brief stare before turning and walking away, not changing his pace a step. The kid made a noise that might have been a whimper, then started running again.

21

Goose had met her a couple of weeks ago, teasing her about her looks when she brought him the egg salad sandwich he'd ordered, telling her she was one good-looking chef, and her teasing him back for eating such nothing-tasting food, a macho-looking dude like him. He read her name tag, Arlene, and said he didn't think he'd ever met a woman with that name, and she said back to him that he'd never meet another Arlene like her, sticking out her tongue a little after saying it, and he was hooked. They had drinks a couple of times, him downing a beer, her asking for a mai tai of all things, saying she'd have dinner with him some night but not right away, she couldn't, maybe being careful, maybe being busy, he didn't know.

Finishing his lunch he offered to take her out for a steak dinner when she was off work that night. This time she told him okay, but if he picked up a couple of good steaks from the Sicilian butcher over on Dupont and brought them to her place, she'd cook him a better steak than he'd get in any restaurant downtown, and it'd be good if he brought a bottle of decent red wine as well, a Merlot would be nice.

And he did. Two T-bones, some Merlot from Chile—the French stuff was too expensive—and a bunch of flowers from a grocery store on the corner. Her apartment was in the back of a house on Bathurst Street, not a bad place, what you get when you're somewhere around forty and gone through two marriages, three kids, and who knew how many guys. She'd fixed herself up by the time he arrived around six, looking not bad for her age. You could do better, Goose told himself when he came in, but that would mean hitting bars and clubs or getting on the internet. He never felt good at the places downtown where you didn't know if you were talking to a princess or a hooker, and the internet was a crapshoot. He was old-fashioned, he guessed, figuring the best way to meet women was face to face, knowing who they were and them knowing who he was. Or as much as he'd let them.

She gave him her life story. Her two oldest kids had moved out and her youngest, a son, was working a pizza joint on Yonge Street until eleven, sometimes he didn't get back until after midnight or later, what're you gonna do?

She cooked the steaks okay, not that great but she didn't ruin them, with a baked potato on the side, and some pie she'd picked up on the way home. After they ate, they sat together in the living room, the old sofa almost collapsing under Goose, the size and weight of him, her waiting for him to make a move, him waiting for the right time and the right mood, thinking he could've gone to a poker game that night, one of Viktor's guys was throwing it, when his cellphone rang. He excused himself, being polite, pulled it out of his pocket, looked at the screen and asked himself who the hell was Bobby Dickson? He pressed the kill button on the phone, put it back in his pocket and remembered they had been talking about movies.

"Now, you want me to get all hot and bothered," Arlene was saying, "you put me watching a movie with Al Pacino in it." She giggled. "Better still, you can put me anywhere near him."

"You kidding?" Goose said. "Pacino? He's a little guy, an *old* little guy, all wrinkled up. The hell you want to go to bed with a prune for?"

"I'm not talking about the way he looks now, I'm talking the way he looked in those Godfather movies."

"You weren't even born then. When they were made."

"Doesn't matter. And now, okay, he doesn't look as good as he did then, but… You gonna answer that?"

His phone showed the same damn name, Bobby Dickson, whoever he was. Somebody at a job site downtown? He pressed the green button, brought the phone to his ear and said, "What?"

"You gotta come and get me, okay?"

Whoever it was, he sounded like Heckle. "Who is this?"

"Listen, don't give me that shit, like you don't know me. You said, *we* said, any time one of us is in trouble the other guy moves his ass, right? I'm on the beach strip…"

Goose stood up, turned his back to Arlene and started walking away, lowering his voice, knowing this wasn't going to be good. "The hell are you doing down there?"

"Trying to fix things…"

"Fix what? And who's Bobby Dickson?"

"It's his phone. Listen…"

"What're you doing with his phone?"

"*Goddamn it, will you listen to me*?" Even Arlene heard that from where she was sitting, looking out the window like she wasn't listening. "I'm on…" Heckle swallowed, Goose could hear him swallow over the phone. "I'm on the beach strip, you know where that war monument is near the canal, a big circle with a flagpole in the middle, on the lake side? Okay, I'm sitting on one of the benches. There's a driveway next to it, just pull in there, I'll get in. I did something, I got something done that I had to do, okay? I had to do it. How long'll you be?"

Goose looked over at Arlene, thinking it's a cold rainy night, he could be in her bed in ten minutes, maybe less, then telling himself that she'll still be around later tonight and if not, she'd probably be just as available tomorrow night.

"Give me an hour."

He could see the light show down the road about half a mile away, on the lake side where Tuffy's was. Had to be six, seven or more cruisers there and a bunch of other cars, all but one lane of Beach Boulevard closed off with a long line of cars waiting to get through. He wondered: This have anything to do with Heckle?

Goose pulled into the lane alongside the war monument, in the space between Beach Boulevard and the berm that marked the paved beach trail and the beach itself. The rain had let up on the way and the clouds had gone east, leaving a strange red glow in the sky to the west, beyond the bay. Goose sat in his car staring at the memorial, an open space lined with stone plaques and framed maps of some battle from World War II, a bunch of local guys died in it. There was no one at the memorial, nobody on the benches where Heckle said he would be. Goose turned to look at the berm and beyond it, where the sand went all the way down to the water, nobody there for sure in this rain. If the crazy bastard is over there on wet sand, Goose was thinking, he can stay there.

He turned at a sound from the passenger door. Heckle was trying the handle. Goose leaned across the seat to unlock the door and Heckle was inside, his hands in his pockets, wet and shivering.

"What the hell happened to you?" Goose said, and Heckle said, "Just get the hell out of here," sliding down below the level of the window glass. Backing out, Goose took another look at him. "You look like shit," he said. "Somebody beat up on you?"

A police cruiser flew past, coming from Tuffy's, its lights flashing but no siren. Goose pulled onto Beach Boulevard, watching the cruiser shrink in size ahead of him and glancing across at Heckle. Even in the weak light Goose could see that his nose was broken, one eye was turning black, his bottom lip was swollen and the front of his shirt was stained with blood.

Heckle caught Goose looking at him. "You wanna take a picture?" he said.

Goose told him to mind his fucking manners and tell him what was going on, reminding him that he could dump Heckle's ass into the canal and leave him there or just take him back to Tuffy's, because whatever the hell was going on back there, Goose knew Heckle had been in on it.

"I taught a guy not to fuck with me," Heckle said, and Goose was about to ask if this was the same guy who tried to rearrange Heckle's face, when Goose's phone rang. This time when he looked at it the caller's name wasn't displayed as Bobby Dickson. This time it read Viktor Khrenov.

When they closed Tuffy's, the police sent the customers home after taking their names and phone numbers, and checking ID. Staff members were herded into the dining room to be questioned individually. They were told not to talk about anything they saw, or thought they might have seen, with each other or with anybody else.

Harold Hayashida left all of this up to the ID guys, which wasn't quite right because two of them were women. He stayed in the short corridor outside the office, watching and listening to the forensics team, two in the office itself, two outside on the beach, big arc lights making it look like noon where they shone down on the sand. From his angle he could see the victim's shoes and the blood pattern against the wall above the safe.

He'd been halfway home when the call arrived, and his first thought was: There goes the damn weekend. Well, it was probably going to rain every day anyway.

"No casings," one of the forensics men said, coming in through the door to the beach. Which meant the shooter probably hadn't used an automatic weapon.

"Sergeant?"

A uniformed cop holding a clipboard had come in through the front door.

"We have a fourteen-year-old male, lives with his family in one of those new condos down the lake. Says about an hour ago he was talking on his cell, walking down the beach trail out there, and some guy ripped it out of his hand, took it."

Hayashida said nothing, just kept looking at the cop, waiting for him to get to the point.

"Kid's name," looking at the clipboard, "is Bobby Dickson. He told his parents, and they called it in. Then they heard what happened here and brought the kid in, he's outside with them, because they thought it might have something to do with," the cop nodded toward the office, "this."

"He get a description?"

The cop nodded, handed the clipboard to Hayashida to read for himself.

Goose shut the phone off, tossed it on top of the dashboard and looked across at Heckle. "Tell me now," he said. "Tell me right now, no bullshit, not a goddamn whiff of bullshit. What happened at Tuffy's?"

"What'd Viktor say?"

"Never mind Viktor. What happened?"

Heckle was sitting up straight. They were on the highway now, no chance of a cop looking in. "That asshole Arden. I stop off to have a beer and he starts coming on like King Shit, telling me what to do, pushing me around and then sucker-punching me, he and a couple other guys, pushing me out the back door. I lost a tooth. Jesus Christ, I need a dentist, something. Lookit this," and he pulled his upper lip aside, showing the broken tooth up front. "You think I'm going to take that crap? Would Viktor take that crap? Would *you* take it?"

Goose said, "Never mind me. Just get to what you did."

"I got a buddy in the city, the North End. Owed me a favour, so he got me a thirty-eight and I went back and blew that prick away."

"Where?"

"Where what? At Tuffy's."

"Where were you when you shot?"

"I was going to go inside, face to face, let him see who was doing him."

"So did you?"

"Didn't have to." Heckle looking through the windshield reliving things and starting to feel good about it. "He walked by the window right in front of me, the jerk. So I got him that way, two shots, one to the fuckin' head, end of story."

He waited for Goose to say something, maybe even congratulate him, tell him he was one stand-up guy or something like that. But all he heard was Goose breathing deeply. Then Goose said, "Where's the gun? You still got it?"

"Yeah, I…"

"Give it to me," Goose reaching under the seat for a rag he sometimes used to wipe down the car now and then, check the oil level.

"The hell you want it for?"

"Just give me the goddamn gun." Goose had the towel in one hand and held it toward Heckle, who reached into his pocket and withdrew the Armscor. "What're you going to do with it?" he said, and Goose said, "Put it in my hand," glancing at it when Heckle gave it to him.

Heckle sat back, his arms folded, trying to ignore the pain in his mouth. "You think I'm going to let some guy jump me, kick the shit out of me and forget about it? Or come crying to you or Viktor? Like hell I would. I did what any of you guys would've done, right? Wouldn't you and Viktor done the same thing?"

"Shut up a minute," Goose said. There was a bridge past the next interchange, a creek below it, a deep ravine. He didn't want Heckle talking until they got there, and he didn't want Viktor calling again either.

With the bridge in sight he slowed down, pulled over to the right, ignored the horn blast from the trucker who had to swerve to get around him, and said to Heckle, "Roll down the window," the Armscor still in his hand, the oil rag keeping his prints off it.

Letting up on the gas he brought his right hand holding the gun across his chest, then flung the gun out the window and over the railing.

"The hell you do that for?" Heckle said. "I could use that…"

"What'd I do it for? *What'd I do it for?* To save your dumb ass, that's what. You're telling me you shot Arden back there, standing out in the rain like some goddamn bum? Well, you didn't…"

"I sure as hell did," Heckle said.

"*No, you didn't.* You shot a cop, you stupid shit. *A cop.*"

22

Walter Freeman called from his home, asking Hayashida if he wanted to take the lead on this. Hayashida said "goddamn right," watching Wes Delby being rolled out of Tuffy's in a body bag. Walter told him to get a team together, choose whoever the hell he wanted, pull in Toronto and the Mounties if he thought it would help, and Hayashida said he'd put something together. When Walter asked what else he could do, Hayashida gave it some thought, picturing Walter at home in his big condo with his feet up and a glass of port in his hand.

Finally, Hayashida said, "You might start by having somebody check the phone records of a kid named Dickson, Bobby Dickson. Lives down here on Beach Boulevard. He had his iPhone stolen tonight by somebody who matches the description of Heckle Dunne, out of Toronto. Dunne's a punk. Works for Viktor Khrenov, who he probably wanted to call."

"You think Khrenov ordered this guy to get Delby?"

"Khrenov's smarter than that. Delby wasn't the target."

"What was Delby doing there anyway?"

"Probably trying to dig into something he didn't know about."

"Or maybe he did and *we* didn't know about it. Wasn't he supposed to get you the name of whoever he used to reach Winegarden? Wouldn't it make sense for him to be down there for that?"

"Doesn't explain why he's in the office, checking out the safe where they keep the cash."

Walter thought about that, then said, "Okay, this is your show. Who else do you want with you? You head things up, take charge and keep me up to date on what's happening. Jesus, I'm getting calls already from reporters. I'll start referring them to you and you can pass 'em on to whoever you want. Got anybody you like to get started, get hustling for you?"

Hayashida named three detectives, the first three who came to mind, he didn't care who they were, he preferred working on his own. The only cop in a suit he'd enjoyed working with had been Gabe Marshall, and look what happened to him.

"I'll let them know, pull them off whatever they're up to, have them call you right away," Walter said. "Right now I need to contact Delby's family, get a release done, put this Heckle guy's description out—the hell kind of name is that anyway?—go through all that stuff," reminding Hayashida to keep him informed, as if Hayashida needed reminding.

When Hayashida hung up, another cop was standing in the doorway, holding a white iPhone in a plastic bag. "This is the kid's phone," he said. "Found it at the side of the trail, down near the war memorial. Forensic'll check for prints. And there's a pickup truck over on Beach Boulevard, reported stolen out of Toronto. Couple of people, waitresses, said they saw Dunne get into it or one like it when he left here earlier. We're dusting it."

Hayashida nodded and brushed past him on his way to the bar where Arden sat in the far booth, his arms on the table, looking down at his hands.

"You want a drink, it's okay with me," Hayashida said. "I'd have one myself, but…" He shrugged.

Arden looked at him, then away.

"What was Delby doing here?" Hayashida said.

"I'd told him about Heckle and me. I taught him a lesson, roughed him up a little. Delby said he'd check and maybe make sure there'd be no assault charge against me. He wanted to see the office, get an idea of what happened. Two guys in there, it gets crowded, so I hung back and stood in the doorway. Delby wanted to know where the safe was, what Heckle had been doing, and I told him. Delby kneels down to look at the safe, stands up, I turn around, heading back to the bar, and I hear the shot. I look around and he's staring at me, like 'What just happened?' and the next one, Jesus, the next one…"

"What I meant was, what's Delby doing *here*? At Tuffy's?"

"Said he was waiting for a friend."

"That's all? Waiting for a friend?"

Another uniform cop approached and Hayashida thought: Jeez, we got anybody left on the street tonight? Must be three dozen here, maybe more. This one talked to Hayashida, but looked at Arden as he spoke. "Got a guy on the phone, wants to know what's going on here. I tried putting him off but he won't hang up, he's getting a little pissed. Actually he's getting *really* pissed and wants to speak to this guy," indicating Arden. "Says he owns the place. Got some kind of heavy accent, Russian or something. I keep telling him there's a murder investigation going on and he says he knows about it, he wants answers from the guy running the place, not from a bunch of cops."

"You tell him he's unavailable?" Hayashida said.

"A bunch of times. You want to tell him yourself?"

Hayashida looked at Arden, pointed to the phone. "You got an extension to that line?"

Arden said, "Hello, Viktor," and waited for something, anything. When he heard only breathing he said, "You still there?"

"Hero," Viktor said. "You okay? Not shot?"

"I'm fine." Saying as little as possible.

"What am I hearing? Somebody shoots police officer there, kills him? Is that right?"

"That's what happened."

"Who?"

"The police don't want his name released."

"Not him. Who does it? Who shoots policeman?"

Arden leaned to look into the bar where Hayashida was holding the receiver against his ear. Hayashida nodded. "I think it was Heckle. So do the police."

"Why?"

"Probably because he thought it was me. He was outside. Shot through the window. He came back here after I threw him out a couple of hours ago. He wanted the combination to the safe. I told him to forget it, I wasn't giving it to him, and he wouldn't take no for an answer." Arden looked back at Hayashida who was frowning at him, shaking his head. "I've probably said too much already. I think you should speak to the police about details, all right?"

"Where is he now, where is Heckle?"

"I have no idea. The police are looking for him. Look, everybody here saw him earlier when I got a bit rough with him, just to get the little bastard out of here. It looks like he came back with a gun, went around back and thought it was me in the office. The blinds were pulled down, all he must've seen was shadows." More breathing sounds from Viktor, and Arden said, "Viktor?"

"They listening?"

"Who?"

"Police. They listening to us, you and me, now?"

"Hell, I don't know…"

Another pause, this time without any breathing sounds, and Hayashida called from the bar, "He hung up."

Heckle still couldn't believe it. "You're shittin' me."

Goose said, "Nobody's shittin' you. They called Viktor, the police. Told him there'd been a shooting at Tuffy's, a cop'd been shot. It's his place, so he'd better get on it. Viktor doesn't want to come anywhere near the place now."

"How…" Heckle started. Then, "What the hell's a cop doing in the office there, bending down like he's opening the safe?"

"What's it matter? The guy's dead and you're the shooter, right?"

"I didn't mean to shoot a cop."

"Yeah, that'll go over well in court."

"I'm not sticking around. I wasn't gonna stick around. That's why I was there, at Tuffy's."

Goose looked at him, waiting for him to start talking again.

"No way was I going to hang drywall for Viktor or nobody. No fuckin' way."

"So you shoot a cop instead."

"It was an accident."

"Well, you're gonna get twenty-five years to life for your accident. And you still didn't tell me why you were at Tuffy's."

"I needed money to get the hell out of here and go down to Florida or somewhere, me and a friend."

"Where were you going to get it?"

"Borrow it. Out of the safe. Maybe just five thousand. Take it out, send it back to Viktor later."

"You're so fuckin' crazy, you know that? You do that, you might as well have sent your balls back with the money because Viktor would've got them somehow."

"What's he care? He pisses that much away every day."

"You poor dumb son of a bitch."

Hackle said, "Hey. If they'd come through, given me the combination, let me check how much money was there, we'd be on our way by now."

"We? Who's we? You and your friend? What friends've you got? Hell, I'm your only friend, or I was until you got too stupid for me to know you. You were gonna pay the freight for both of you, you and your friend? Why couldn't your friend get the scratch to go? Why should you pay his way on your own?"

Heckle said nothing. He was thinking of his father eating Shredded Wheat. Working as a welder every goddamn day, worked his ass off just so's he could eat Shredded Wheat every morning. Dropped dead, forty-five years old, walking across the floor of the Legion Hall carrying a beer. Who the hell wanted a life like that?

"You listening to me?" Goose slapped the back of his hand against Heckle's shoulder. "Why couldn't this other guy…"

"It's not a guy." Heckle swept his hand away. "It's a girl."

"Some broad?" Goose almost laughed. "You were gonna do this for some broad? Some cheap piece you picked up downtown, maybe does BJs in the alley for twenty bucks a throw? Are you kiddin' me?"

Heckle said, "Shut up."

"You are such a goddamn loser."

"You don't know what the fuck you're talking about."

The traffic was getting heavier as they got closer to Toronto. Goose looked over his shoulder, checking for an open lane. "Blows away a cop, a *cop*, so he can bang some cheap piece down in Florida."

"She's no cheap piece. So just shut up about it, okay?"

"So who is it? Lady-fucking-Gaga?"

"Natalka."

Goose actually slowed the car, taking his foot off the gas to stare at Heckle.

Heckle looked at him. "See? You think you know everything about me, and you don't really know shit. She's in love with me. What, you thought those times we were late getting back to the office, the times she goes shopping, you think we were stuck in traffic? Like hell we were. She's gorgeous, man, and she thinks Viktor is a stinking asshole, which he is, and you know it. She can hardly wait to get away from him."

Somebody behind him was hitting the horn, telling Goose to move his ass, he was driving below the limit.

"I had her back to my place, in my bed, just last week." Heckle couldn't shut himself off, couldn't let the logic of keeping his mouth shut overcome the pleasure of surprising Goose, the guy who called him a loser, treated Heckle like a bum. "Hour and a half, two hours without stopping, know what I mean? When's the last time you had anything that nice?" He leaned over to look Goose in the eye. "Anything *nearly* that nice? Only piece you've talked about is that waitress you've been trying to bang the last couple of weeks. Looks like a witch and is old enough to be my grandmother."

Goose told him to shut up, and took the next exit, Mississauga Road, saying nothing until he pulled into the first residential street he saw and stopped at the curb. Heckle had been staring out the window silently, feeling good that he had put Goose in his place.

"Okay, listen to me," Goose said. "You better do what I say or you have no idea what's gonna happen to you, no idea at all, okay?"

Heckle had his hand to his mouth, trying to soften the pain of the broken tooth, staring at the houses on the street. Big houses with swimming pools in the back, maybe maids to cook your breakfast, take care of the kids, wipe their asses, you're the guy who hires her so she gives you a quickie now and then. That's who lived there. People like that, didn't have a worry in the world. Not Heckle Dunne. Nobody ever wanted Heckle Dunne to live like that, live that kind of life.

"You want me to help you, you do every damn thing I say." Goose reached to nudge him, get his attention. "You don't want to do that, you can get the hell out of the car right here and I don't know you, I never met you, anybody asks me. You getting the picture?"

Heckle lowered his head into his hands, not wanting Goose to see him cry.

23

Arden was drinking the coffee Charm Darby had brought him. She stood with her hand on his shoulder, saying nothing for a while. Then, "They told me I can go home now, but I'm not. Going home, I mean. I can't. I'm going somewhere else."

"Where?" Arden said.

"My sister's. She's already picked up the kids. They told me, the police, that they'd come around and check my place all night, if I wanted them to."

"He's not coming back for you or me or nobody. Heckle's long gone."

"He might be back. I don't want to be around if he is. Besides, I need to talk about it, you know? I can sit up, talk to my sister and get it out. What I saw, I mean. We won't be opening tomorrow, will we?"

Arden said, "Not a chance. Maybe not ever."

"I need a job."

"So do I."

"Where're you going to be? You're not staying here, are you?"

Arden didn't have an answer.

Hayashida nodded to Charm, coming into the bar as she was leaving.

"You're lucky," he said, sitting across from Arden, and when Arden looked at him, eyebrows raised, he pointed at the coffee mug and said, "Somebody finished off the last cup in the kitchen." Arden offered the rest of his but Hayashida said if he wanted one he'd get it at the Tim Hortons down the beach strip, he didn't need caffeine, he was running on adrenaline.

"You know a guy named Joe Googins?" Hayashida said.

It took Arden a moment. "Goose," he said. "Works for Khrenov."

"That's who Heckle called on the kid's cellphone. Called him twice within maybe five minutes of shooting Delby. We're looking for Googins now, whatever he's driving."

"Heckle maybe called for Goose to come pick him up."

"We're pretty sure he's the guy who left the beat-up Silverado down the strip. Probably match the prints in the truck and on the phone, both places, for sure."

"Where was Goose when Heckle called him? You know yet?"

"Phone company'll pin it down for us. All we know is that it wasn't around here, it bounced out of Toronto." Hayashida said, "Tell me what you think. About Googins."

"I don't think Goose was in on this. He's too smart for that. Heckle probably called him, asked for a lift home."

"We don't think he was involved either, but we're pretty sure he is now. We've got a trace on his number. He talked to Viktor Khrenov from somewhere between here and Victor's place about an hour ago."

"Filling Viktor in on what happened."

"Probably. Probably has Dunne with him too." Hayashida looked back along the bar toward the restaurant where one of the women from forensics, fingerprint specialist, was gesturing to him. He slid off the stool and said without looking back, "Last guy in the world I'd want to be right now is Heckle Dunne."

Goose had sent Heckle in to register his own name, seventy bucks for a small room at the back of the motel, three miles from the airport. The place got most of its business from hookers and people catching an early morning flight. The motel offered shuttle service to the airport, the shuttle being a ten-year-old minivan. "Get some sleep," he'd told Heckle in the room, "you're gonna be busy tomorrow."

"Doing what?" Heckle said. He was on the bed, still dressed.

"Hauling your ass out of here." Goose left, taking the room key with him.

Natalka was propped on pillows reading a magazine with the picture of some famous person on the cover, someone Viktor had never heard of. She was wearing an oversized T-shirt that barely covered her pretty little ass, her *popka*, sitting with her legs stretched in front of her.

Viktor watched her through the open bedroom door, remembering the first time he saw her. Goose had been driving him down Bloor Street, Viktor thinking of business or something, not about sexy young girls, which he thought about at other times. There she was standing at the window of Birks, one hand on the glass staring at the jewellery, all the diamonds, biting her lip like she was trying not to cry, her *popka* nearly bursting her jeans, and Viktor told Goose to pull over, let him out.

He walked to stand behind her and said, "What happen, I buy you bracelet?" he said, pointing to the one nearest her in the display window.

She turned to look at him and stayed cool. No smile, no "Who the hell are you?" Instead, she had told him she preferred the Cartier watch.

"So what happen, I buy you Cartier watch?"

She had looked him up and down this time. He'd been at a meeting that day, wore a sports jacket, trousers, white linen shirt, good Italian loafers. When she finally smiled and said, "Maybe lots of things," he waved Goose away from the curb, telling him to go to the office on his own, and flagged a cab. He took her for a drink at the Four Seasons, impressed that she didn't make a big deal out of it, as though she practically lived at the place.

He bought her the Cartier two days later, and she was wearing it now. How long ago was that? he wondered, and believed it might have been too long ago.

The headlights of the car turning into the parking lot four stories below caught his eye. He watched it stop and walked away from the door, waiting for his phone to ring. "I'm downstairs," Goose said when he answered.

"Come up," Viktor said, "bring that piece of crap with you," meaning Heckle.

"I think you better come down," Goose said. "Heckle's not with me."

"What, you throw his ass out on road?"

"He's in a room near the airport. I gotta tell you some stuff you need to hear, Viktor."

When he told Natalka he was going out for an hour, maybe more, she said, "That's nice," not taking her eyes from the magazine.

"Okay," Goose said, driving out of the parking lot, "I'm tellin' you this because you need to know it. It could be a pile of bullshit, Heckle bragging about nothing, if he's that stupid, but if it's true…" He glanced over at Viktor, who was staring straight ahead, like he was at a movie and was waiting for the picture to start. "Well, I hope it's not true. Okay?"

"We sent everybody home," Hayashida said. It was almost midnight, he and Arden sitting in the bar. "Still looking for the weapon, in case he tossed it before he left. May not find it until the morning, if at all. Could have thrown it in the lake."

Arden said, "Why'd he wait?"

"For what?"

"Why'd he wait so long to come here and shoot through the window, thinking it was me? I'd beat the crap out of him. He was lying in the sand, bleeding like a stuck pig, everybody watching him. Guy like that, if he'd had a gun on him he would've used it on me, maybe on everybody who stood there looking at him."

"He went somewhere to get it."

"Back to Toronto?"

"Maybe. What's it matter?"

"I don't know. Did he get it from Viktor? Or from Goose? I figured they're too smart to give a hothead like him a gun. Unless they expected him to use it the way they told him to."

"I'm still confused about what Delby was doing in the office," Hayashida said, not wanting to let Arden know about Delby's claim to doing undercover work there. "Did he say he wanted to look into the file drawers or something?"

Arden shook his head. "Wanted to see the safe. He looked around the office, saw where I'd pushed Heckle, bent down to look at the safe and stood up. Then bang. Through the window twice."

"What's so special about the safe?"

"Damned if I know."

Hayashida watched him, waited for Arden to get uncomfortable, then said, "Time for you to let us know."

Arden, not sure what he meant, said, "Let you know what?"

"What happened to Slip Winegarden."

"I already told you."

"Not everything you didn't."

"Why should I now?"

"What've you got to lose?"

Arden leaned forward, getting closer to Hayashida. "Did you ever think that maybe, just maybe, we're seeing this from the wrong angle?"

"I don't know what you're talking about," Hayashida said, shaking his head.

"Did you ever think that maybe Heckle didn't get this dumb idea to come back here with a gun and blow my head off, that he didn't get it all on his own? That maybe Goose or Viktor, it would have to be Viktor, figured they could use Heckle to get rid of me?" He leaned back in the chair. "You know one of the first things Slip told me about the Russian? That he's always thinking ahead, he always figures out what you're going to do before you do it and he never, ever gets himself in a place where he can be nailed for anything."

"So what?"

"So instead of Heckle showing up, looking for a gun to come here with and blow my goddamn head off, why wouldn't he go back to

Toronto and tell Viktor, who maybe said, 'Here, take this,' give him a weapon and figure he's rid of both of us, Heckle and me? Wouldn't that be Viktor's style?"

Hayashida sat sucking on a back tooth. Then: "Two questions. You think Viktor's gonna greet Heckle with open arms and a loaded thirty-eight after Heckle tried to get into his safe, take his cash? That's what this was all about, wasn't it? You don't really buy that crap about Heckle being here because Viktor sent him over, did you?"

"How would Viktor know? About Heckle being here, trying to get into the safe? Nobody here told him. Heckle could've just said he and I got into it over a beer, a woman, anything."

"Okay, bigger question. Why would Viktor want Heckle to kill you in the first place?"

Arden sat staring at Hayashida, saying nothing.

Hayashida raised his eyebrows. "You don't have an idea? I have an idea. To keep you from talking about what happened when Slip Winegarden was murdered. Because I don't buy your story about not being there when he was shot. You were there, goddamn it. You were there and whether you sat on your ass and watched it or you did everything up to putting the gun against the poor bastard's head, I don't care. The point is that you know, and the Russian knows you know. He can't be too comfortable with that. So tell me now, get it off your chest, we'll see what kind of deal we can pull for you. How's that?"

"I do that," Arden said, standing up and walking away, "I'd be better off if I'd stuck my head in front of Delby's and invited Heckle to shoot me instead of him."

"So why'd the Russian ask you to go along with Slip that night? If he did, that made you a witness, right?"

"Or a fall guy." Arden stopped to look back at Hayashida. "You ever think of that?" When Hayashida said nothing Arden returned to the bar, leaned against it, and said, "Everybody at Tuffy's, all the staff, they see me leave with Slip and an hour, hour and a half later, I come back alone. The next day Slip's in the lake with a bullet in his skull. How's that look?"

"Was the Russian with you? In the car with Slip?"

Arden looked away, saying nothing.

"And was he the shooter? Khrenov?"

Still nothing from Arden.

Hayashida said, "You're staying here, right? At Tuffy's?"

Arden muttered something and started walking toward the stairs to the second floor, and Hayashida said, "What?"

Without turning around Arden said, "I've got nowhere else to go."

24

He'd been dreaming he was at a party somewhere, didn't know where, just a lot of cool people around, all being nice to him. All the women there were being nice to him, coming on to him. Especially an Asian girl he knew, she was maybe Chinese or Vietnamese. He couldn't remember her name, only that she was good-looking, telling him she had always liked him and didn't he know it before? It was good, having a girl like this come on to you, not having to pretend you were the kind of guy you think she might like, because she'd already told you you're the kind of guy she likes. Nothing makes a guy feel better than a woman, hot but friendly too, no street tramp, a girl from a good family, kind of exotic with those Asian eyes, and maybe she's gone to college, telling you that you're a special dude, and Heckle was reaching for her, just to stroke her face, when Viktor punched him in the head.

Heckle's first reaction was confusion, not knowing where he was or what woke him up, still feeling the pain but thinking maybe it was part of his dream. For a second, for one lightning-quick second, he felt sadness that it had only been a dream, that the beautiful Asian girl really had wanted to get it on with him, and then it was fear, totally enveloping shit-your-pants gut-spilling fear.

He was about to say "Hi Viktor," when Viktor bent down with his face this far from Heckle's so he was all that Heckle could see. Goose was in the room, leaning on a wall with his hands in his pockets like he was waiting for a bus. Heckle couldn't say anything. Not a word. He could only close his eyes and bring his hand to the side of his head where Viktor had clubbed him with his fist.

"You don't look good," Viktor said. He stood up and said, "Goose, turn more lights on. We see what Heckle look like, eh? See his handsome face, good-looking guy."

Goose flipped the wall switch and Viktor stepped away, the overhead lights making Heckle squint against the glare.

"Look, Goose," Viktor said, "Is this handsome guy? You think he is handsome?"

Goose shrugged. He didn't want to be here. He wanted to be somewhere else, anywhere else. Not as much as Heckle did, of course.

"He looks like shit, eh? Look at him, Goose. Take good look." Viktor reached down, grabbed the back of Heckle's shirt, pulled him off the bed and slapped him with his free hand, telling Heckle to wake up, he needed to talk, talk lots. He let go of Heckle, who swung away to sit on the edge of the bed, his hands clasped between his legs, his eyes closed, his body shaking.

"I don't know, Goose," Viktor bending to look at Heckle's face again. "He look like ugly fucker, eh? How does ugly fucker get to *yebat* pretty young girl? What, he buy her things, jewels, clothes, take her to dinners in big car? This *kusok derma,* this piece of shit? He can't buy nothing, maybe beer, maybe paper to wipe his ass. Unless he steal from me, take money from my pocket, my money out of my pocket. Is that what you do? You take money from me, use it to fuck my girl?" Viktor looked at Goose, smiling at his own words. "Smart man maybe, eh, Goose? He steal my money so he can... What?" looking down at Heckle.

"I didn't steal your money," Heckle managed to say.

"Oh, good news, good news." Viktor looked back at Goose. "You were wrong. He didn't steal my money. Only fucked my girl, woman was to be my wife."

"I didn't do that either," Heckle said, wincing and leaning away when Viktor turned back to him.

Goose stepped forward, knelt next to Viktor and looked Heckle in the eye. "Listen," he said, "Viktor needs to know what happened, that's all. You gotta tell him the truth, what you told me tonight in the car. He's not blaming you. Woman like Natalka, she comes on to a guy, young guy like you, it's gonna happen, right? How're you gonna say no to that? Viktor understands, okay? It's not your fault. It's hers. He wants to hear it from you so he can deal with Natalka later, not give her a chance to argue, make him wonder who's telling the truth. Hey," grabbing Heckle's arm, "if you think Viktor was gonna kill you over this, don't you think he'd have done it by now, soon's he walked in here? You think he'd be wasting his time? Viktor doesn't waste his time. He wants to get back and deal with Natalka, like I said. So tell him the truth. Just tell him what happened, whatever he needs to know. Then you can get the hell out of town and don't come back. You keep your mouth shut and forget about this, right? Just tell him what happened so he knows. Then we're gone, both of us, him and me. Tomorrow morning you hit the road, you're on your own. Maybe head west some-where, we don't care. Right, Viktor?", looking at the Russian who had stood up and taken a step back, saying nothing.

"Why'd you tell him?" Heckle said to Goose. "You and me, I thought we were friends."

"You and me are friends, yeah," Goose said. "Viktor and me, we're friends too. But see, I've been friends longer with Viktor than with you, right? And Viktor's the guy I work for, guy who pays me money to send to my ex-wife, cover my child support. So who'm I gonna feel loyal to? I mean, most loyal? You want a glass of water? I'll get you a glass of water," Goose standing up and going to the bathroom while Heckle stayed on the side of the bed staring at the floor and swinging his legs like he's trying to burn off his fear. Viktor standing back, his eyes on Heckle.

Goose came back and said, "Drink this," handing him the glass of water. "Then tell Viktor what you told me."

Heckle sipped the water, then said, "I'm sorry."

"Sorry doesn't cut it," Goose said. "Just tell him what he needs to know so he can take care of Natalka. Then you can go back to sleep, watch TV, we don't care."

"Her and me," Heckle said. He looked at Viktor. "We kind of loved each other. She wanted me to take her to Florida, she didn't want to spend another winter here."

"So you did it," Goose said.

Heckle looked at Goose, about to ask: Did what?, but just nodded his head.

"Where?" More of a growl than a word from Viktor.

Heckle shook his head and Goose said, "You gotta tell him, Heckle. He wants to know, you'd better tell him, then we're gone."

"In the Chrysler," Heckle said. "Couple of times."

"That's all?" Goose said, and Heckle shook his head.

"I got us a room once, motel in Scarborough. And at my place last week, my apartment. She hated it there, wouldn't go back."

"Where else?" Goose said, and when Heckle said nothing, Goose said, "Come on, there's gotta be more. You two ever go upstairs, in the apartment, Viktor's apartment?"

"Once."

It was the sound of Viktor drawing in a breath, like a man about to dive into deep water, that made Heckle look at the Russian, who said, like each word was a separate sentence, "In. My. Fucking. *Bed?*"

Heckle looked away, then back at the Russian, who reached to grab a pillow from the bed. He is going to hit me with a pillow, Heckle thought, which was silly, stupid even, but then he saw Viktor's hand go inside his jacket and come out with a gun, a black automatic pistol. Heckle raised his hands and said, "No, no, no, no, *please*," before the pillow was pressed against his face and held there by the muzzle of the Beretta and Viktor fired twice, the noise muffled enough that the shots sounded less than real and more like a movie or TV soundtrack, loud but not piercing.

Viktor held the pillow in place with the Beretta, using the other hand to pick the ejected shell casings off the bed. Goose stood back and watched blood seep from under the pillow and down the side of

Heckle's head. Both men stood listening for someone to say elsewhere in the wing of the motel "What was that?" and "Sounded like a shot," and "Call the cops," but no one did. The clock radio next to the bed said it was ten after one in the morning, late enough for most people to be sleeping, early enough for somebody to be watching a cop show on TV. Or maybe nobody cared. And if they cared, who the hell wanted to climb out of bed and go find somebody with a gun they had just fired? Or maybe they were making a phone call, a 911.

Goose had been holding his breath. Now he filled his lungs while Viktor sat back in a chair, nodded at Heckle's corpse, and told Goose to wrap it in a sheet, knot it at both ends, then bring his car around to the door, backing it up with the trunk open. Viktor knowing enough to keep his hands off things they shouldn't touch, or shouldn't have been touching.

"That place, parking garage we got started, they doing footings yet?" Viktor said.

They were driving the expressway, still a lot of traffic so late at night. Goose was careful to stay within the limit, not draw attention from cops. Goose said, "Just about. Ready to pour concrete in a few days."

"How many?"

"Days?"

"Footings," meaning the pillars of concrete sunk deep into the ground beneath the foundation of the six-story garage.

"Sixteen. I think. Maybe eighteen. I'd have to check the drawings again. Why?"

Long pause. "How many dug?"

"Three or four so far."

"How big?"

"Metre across. Three deep."

"Gravel? We got gravel there?"

"Lots of gravel."

Another pause. "We got watchman there?"

Goose slowed for the exit coming up. He knew where Viktor was going. "Yeah."

"You know him?"

"Probably."

At the office Viktor told Goose to come in and wait downstairs, not in the car. An empty car parked in a lot at this time of the night was normal. A car parked with a driver inside wasn't, whatever the reason, and the police had a habit of checking Viktor's building more often than others, looking for a reason to poke around, see who's there and what they're doing.

Upstairs, Viktor snatched a brown electric cord from a wall, about two metres long. He doubled it over a couple of times, then climbed the stairs to the penthouse condo.

She had left the kitchen light on. He walked through it, glancing at the bottle of Baileys and the empty glass on his way to the bedroom. She rolled onto her side when he entered, keeping her eyes closed, trying to get back to sleep. He unfastened his belt, dropped his pants to the floor, stepped out of them, and got on the bed.

"Doggy style," he said, taking the pillow from his side of the bed, and she turned onto her stomach, resting her head on an arm. He lifted her hips and put the pillow under it, then pushed the T-shirt out of the way.

"Help yourself," she said, her eyes still closed, her voice heavy with sleep.

He was inside her, on his knees. "Help myself, eh?" Thrusting her, making her grunt each time. "That's good, eh? I help myself, yes." He had the extension cord in two hands now, stretching it out. "Everybody help themselves to Natalka. Me and Heckle, eh?"

In the spill of light from the kitchen and from the tall windows he saw her eyes open so quickly, so abruptly that they should have made a sound, a snap perhaps, but there was no sound until the cord encircled her neck and Viktor crossed the ends and pulled. Then the sounds from Natalka were guttural and her body writhed beneath him while he rode her until she was dead.

He carried her downstairs himself, wrapped in two large plastic garbage bags.

The watchman at the building site knew Goose, but Goose didn't know him. Goose handed the guy, must've been in his fifties, not likely to call the cops, a hundred dollars. He told the guard to switch off the security cameras, open the gate, and take a hike for an hour.

"I can't go," the guy said, trying to see who was with Goose without looking directly at the man. "You know that. I get caught not here, I'm fired."

"Go get a coffee," Goose said, still offering the hundred-dollar bill.

"Thanks, but I don't need a coffee. My wife made me tea in a Thermos…"

The voice from the man next to Goose, his face still hidden, barked "Get coffee or get bullet in your ass, eh? Which you like most?"

The site was marked for eighteen footings, six across in three rows. Three had been opened, prepared for concrete, no rebar used, each opening five meters deep, a meter wide.

Viktor walked to the one furthest from the gate and nodded at it, leaving Goose to open the trunk. He carried Natalka like a groom crossing the threshold with his bride. Viktor pulled away the tarpaulin covering the hole, said "wait," as Goose approached, and removed the garbage bags. Goose looked at her face, swollen beyond recognition, blood in the open eyes, the mouth drawn back in a grimace. Viktor said, "Okay."

She seemed to take a long time to drop into the darkness. The fall ended with a splash and Goose pictured muddy water at the bottom of the hole.

He brought Heckle from the car in a fireman's carry, over his shoulder. Reaching the edge of the footings hole he looked at Viktor, who nodded and Goose dropped Heckle.

"Her on bottom, him on top," Viktor said. "What you call that?"

Goose said, "Missionary position."

"Missionary position. Why they call it that? Anyway, is good. Get shovels."

Goose figured that, together, they shovelled a cubic yard of gravel onto the bodies, about a ton and a half, before Viktor held up a hand

and tossed his shovel aside. "You be here seven, okay? You tell foreman order concrete, deliver today for sure. How many yards you think, this hole?" He jerked a thumb at Heckle and Natalka's grave.

Goose said, "Three, three and a half."

"You tell foreman change made. Put as much gravel in other two holes as here, then pour concrete tomorrow, all three holes."

"He's gonna want to know why. We're two, three days from pouring the other footings."

"Is a test," Viktor walking back to Goose's car.

"A test of what?"

Viktor stopped. "What difference, eh? What difference three filled now, rest filled later?"

Goose shrugged. "No difference, really. Maybe cost a little more, do it in two stages."

Viktor waved his words away, climbed into the car.

There would be a difference at some point, Goose thought, starting the car and backing out of the site. He looked up the street and saw the glow of a cigarette, waving until the watchman pushed off from the utility pole he had been leaning against, tossed the butt away and began walking toward the gate. Viktor's head was back, his eyes closed, waiting to arrive back at the apartment and spend the rest of the night burning Natalka's things.

Two bodies added up to two hundred and fifty, maybe three hundred pounds of flesh and bone total. A ton and a half of gravel on top of them now, about six tons of concrete added tomorrow. Then the building itself. Two tons of concrete in each cubic yard. How many cubic yards to build the parking garage? How much weight on each footing? Goose tried adding it up. Then he thought of the cars it would hold. Nearly five hundred. At maybe two tons each. All held up by the footings, with Heckle and Natalka at the bottom of one.

Jesus.

The building could stand solidly for years on seventeen footings. It could stand safely on just fifteen. So if one footing weakened because it was placed on two dead bodies, it would take how long? Ten years? Twenty years? Nothing would happen to the building. No one would notice.

No one would care what was down there. No one would ever know.

He looked at the dashboard clock. Five minutes to three. How much sleep could he get before being back at the site at seven?

Not enough. Not nearly enough.

25

Hayashida got there late in the morning, nearly ten o'clock, after going over things with Walter Freeman at Central. The telephone company had traced two calls made on Bobby Dickson's stolen cellphone to Joseph Googins. The first call made no connection. The second call was answered and the conversation lasted thirty-seven seconds. Toronto police checked Googins' address and found no one home. They had a warrant for questioning on suspicion of murder.

Hayashida didn't believe Walter was telling him everything he needed to know, but this wouldn't be the first time. Walter had spent hours with Delby when Delby arrived from Toronto, and Hayashida was sure they hadn't talked about hockey.

The rain had ended, the air turned warm, it wasn't the end of summer yet. Walking into Tuffy's, nodding to the uniformed cop at the door, his phone rang. It was Walter.

"Just got word that a motel out near the airport reported somebody named Heckle Dunne checked in last night," Freeman said. "Used his own name, paid cash. Maid came in to do the room this morning and he's not there, but there's a pillow with blood stains on it, blood splatters on the bed, a bed sheet is missing, and a couple of people thought they heard shots, middle of the night, but didn't report it. What do you make of that?"

"Somebody should speak to Khrenov," Hayashida said.

"What I know about him, his ass'll be covered."

"Get Toronto to do it. Still haven't found the weapon down here. Probably in the lake."

"The press got Delby's name last night from somebody, maybe at Tuffy's. Couple of papers dug up a picture of him, they're running it today. Reporters talked to the family early this morning, in Toronto. And for what it's worth," Freeman said, "we got word that the same prints on the kid's phone, the one this Heckle character stole, are all over that Chevy pickup."

"What do you think?" Hayashida said. "Khrenov or somebody sends Heckle over here to get this Arden character, and when Heckle does the job and gets back to Toronto he's hit to shut him up? That work for you?"

"No. Why would he come over in the middle of the day with witnesses everywhere, and get the crap kicked out of him? Then he runs away? Doesn't make sense. Doing the guy through the window with nobody around and all the rain, that works. He got the wrong guy is the way I see it. If he did, that might be enough to get him done too. Khrenov knows what kind of heat he's going to get from one of his guys shooting a cop."

"All we know is, he's Khrenov's guy, right? We don't know if Khrenov sent him or if he was freelancing."

"He'd be a stupid son of a bitch to do that on his own."

"Maybe he was," Hayashida said, stepping under the yellow plastic tape and into Tuffy's. "Stupid enough to do it on his own, I mean. It might explain why he's probably dead." Freeman said he would keep Hayashida posted and hung up.

Hayashida walked into the bar, nodding at a new team from forensics who were still there. "We found a tooth," one of them said. "Incisor, snapped off near the gum. At the base of that steel pole out back.

Must've hurt like hell."

"Anybody seen what's-his-name?" Hayashida said. "Arden, the guy who's been managing this place?"

"Officer at the beach door in the bar saw him, I think," one of the forensics team said. "I heard him mention it when he called downtown."

The cop at the door was a wiseass named Hayhurst, and he smiled at Hayashida and said, "Hell of a nice day to be at the beach, eh?"

Hayashida asked if he'd seen a guy maybe five-ten, six feet tall called Arden.

"He left," Hayhurst said. "Couple of hours ago. Said he was going to do his laundry."

Hayashida stared at him, like he was waiting for the punch line of a joke. "Do his *laundry?*"

"He had it in a bag, plastic garbage bag. I check the sheet, he's not on it, I look inside and I see his shirts, underwear, pants…"

"Where," Hayashida said, "was he going to do his laundry?"

"Laundromat, I guess. How would I know?"

"He drive?"

"Drive what?"

"Did you see him get into a car?"

"No, he walked out there," jerking a thumb over his shoulder toward the beach, "with the bag over his shoulder."

"Do you see a laundromat anywhere out on the beach strip?"

"What do I need with a laundromat? I got a wife," the cop said, trying to hide his nervousness.

Hayashida, glaring at the cop who had started shifting his weight from one foot to the other, phoned Central and gave Arden's description, called him a person of interest in the slaying of a police officer. He asked for a pickup and detention for questioning, then told Hayhurst to get the hell out and start doing something productive, like directing traffic.

Arden had left Tuffy's that morning at seven just as Hayhurst said, carrying most of his clothing in a plastic garbage bag and walking north to the bench under the willow tree where the blonde sat watching waves break on the beach. He crossed in front of her and sat on the bench, dropping the bag in front of him.

"What's in the bag?" Josie said, and Arden said, "My life."

"Is that the best you can do?"

"It's all I got."

"What happened last night?"

"Where?"

"Don't play games, please. It's all over the news that somebody got shot. One of my neighbours says she heard it was a cop. Is that right?"

Arden looked away. "I need a favour."

"So do I. A bunch of them. From maybe a hundred people. Who goes first?"

He looked at her, watching her eyes. "I need a place to stay."

"The Hilton's that way."

"I need somewhere near here. Just for a couple of days."

"May I ask you a personal question?"

"Go ahead."

She leaned toward him. "Are you out of your fucking mind?"

"I knew you'd say that. Never mind." He began hoisting the bag onto his shoulder.

She watched, then spoke with her voice softened. "What's in the bag, really?"

"My clothes. Most of them. My shaving stuff, couple of books."

"One's a dictionary, right?" Before he could answer she said, "Tell me what happened last night, at Tuffy's. Did a cop really get shot?"

"Yes. Through the office window. Once in the chest and once in the head. I was there. I saw it."

"They know who did it?"

"Heckle Dunne."

She sat back, as though avoiding a blow. "The muscle-bound creep who hung out with the tall skinhead?"

"Goose. Yeah, that's him."

"Why'd he shoot the cop?"

"He thought he was shooting at me. Trying to kill me." Arden looked around. The beach, deserted when he arrived, was beginning to fill with people spreading blankets, opening umbrellas, carrying coolers and walking along the sand, letting the water cool their feet.

"He was trying to kill you?" Josie said. "Why?"

He smiled tightly. "You sure ask a lot of questions."

"So answer them."

He rose to his feet and gripped the open end of the bag, prepared to go. "He came back to shoot me because I beat the crap out of him, then threw him against a steel pole behind Tuffy's." He tossed the bag over his shoulder. "Sorry I bothered you."

"Wait a minute, wait a minute." Josie stood up and looked around. "I owe you a coffee. You want to collect it at my place in ten minutes, fine, as long as you tell me what really happened last night. Just a coffee, okay? And if you're going to carry your clothes around like that, don't walk on the beach. You look like you're collecting bottles. Or bodies. Cut over to Beach Boulevard and walk there. You'll look like just another homeless bum that way. I'm going back along the beach."

Goose's head felt like it was filled with feathers, or that he had taken a couple of ass-kicking downers an hour before, which was pretty much the same thing. He'd slept maybe an hour in his car, not really sleeping, just drifting off now and then, before going onto the job site and pulling the foreman aside.

"You know who I am?" he said to the foreman, a guy from Croatia whose name sounded like some kind of disease.

The foreman's eyes widened and he turned his head this way and that, looking to see if Goose had brought any muscle with him, or maybe looking for a place to run in case he needed to. "Yeah, yeah, I know, I know who you are," he said. It was Saturday. Just a skeleton crew was there, cleaning up, a few carpenters checking forms, getting ready for Monday.

"Wanna change the schedule a little," Goose said, dropping an arm across the Croat's shoulders and walking him toward the open footings for the parking garage. "You see those three footings you got dug?"

The foreman panicked. "We're okay, we're on schedule," he said. "Nothing to worry about."

"That's right. Nothing to worry about. Now you see this one here, the corner footing?" He guided the foreman to the edge of the opening and felt the other man's body stiffen with fear. "You see how there's a gravel base in there already?" The foreman looking down about six feet to the level of the gravel, afraid Goose might push him in there.

"How did that get there?" he said. "Who…?" Goose turned him around and walked him away from it.

"Here's what we do today," Goose said. "We call the concrete guys, the outfit in Scarborough we're using. We tell them to gear up, we need a load today, sometime after noon. They want overtime, they get overtime, don't sweat it. This morning, before they get here, get a couple of guys down here to put in rebar, then fill the other two holes with gravel to the same level as that one, okay? Then we pour concrete just in these three footings, soon as you can, okay? Never mind rebar on that one. Fill it up to specs. On Monday we'll get back to the others and you're on schedule again."

"Why would we do that?" the foreman said. "No value there, is there? No advantage…"

Goose interrupted him. "Is it up to code? To do three now and the others later?"

The foreman blinked. "Yeah, but…"

"*Is it up to the fucking code?*" Loud enough for a sweeper across the way to look up, watching and listening.

The foreman nodded.

"Then do it. Just fucking do it. Get two guys here, weekend wages, and start shovelling. Get the concrete ordered, you've got the specs. Looks like maybe ten yards, pay whatever it takes to get it here today, and stick to your goddamn work."

Walter Freeman scheduled a press conference at noon for him and Hayashida. They would confirm that a police officer, a homicide detective actually, had been shot to death while performing his duties the previous night at a beach strip location. They would name Sergeant Weston Delby, express condolences to Delby's parents and his former wife Pamela, and announce that they were searching for one Cormac Hecla Dunne, also known as Heckle, age twenty-four, height 173 centimetres, or five feet eight inches, on suspicion of murder. Not really searching, of course. That would mean they were assuming Heckle was walking around somewhere, maybe standing with his hands in his pockets with other people, watching the traffic go by on Beach Boulevard, a traffic jam of drivers and gawkers slowing down to stare at Tuffy's as they passed, hoping to see blood stains or even bodies. But they weren't. Wherever Heckle was, Hayashida believed, he'd be weighed down with a couple of copper-jacketed bullets.

"By the way," Freeman said to Hayashida when he called, "we heard from Toronto Metro. Two of our guys talked to Khrenov this morning. He says he hadn't seen Dunne since the day before yesterday. Says he fired the kid as a driver and sent him down to do construction work at some building on Front Street. Apparently Dunne never showed up. Khrenov says he knows nothing about the guy coming around Tuffy's for any reason, and doesn't give a damn if he never sees him again, this Heckle character."

"How'd he get there?"

"How'd who get where?"

"Heckle. How'd he get to that motel last night? The truck he stole was here. What, he walked?"

"Maybe he stole something else, down there on the beach strip."

"So why wasn't it at the motel? Anybody check on that?"

Freeman said, "I'll talk to Toronto, get back to you."

"Never mind. He called Googins on that kid's phone he stole. That's how he got back to Toronto. He called and Googins came and got him."

"So you think Googins, this Goose character, you think he made the mess at the motel?"

"Why would Goose drive him there, check him in, then shoot him?"

26

Goose expected Viktor to explode, maybe throw things, kick the wall. That's what he did when he was really pissed, really upset. You never forgot seeing Viktor Khrenov let loose when he was enraged about something or somebody. This time, he seemed beyond being angry. Maybe because he had nobody to direct his anger at. Except Goose.

Goose was in Viktor's apartment. The rest of the building was empty on a Saturday. In the apartment that fewer than a dozen of the Odachni workers had ever visited, Viktor sat eating yogurt from a crystal bowl. It was the same breakfast he consumed every morning, sometimes inviting Goose in for a talk to decide what they would do that day.

"You should eat, eat," Viktor often said to Goose, thrusting a bowl and spoon toward him. Goose would say he'd wait and have bacon and eggs later; he needed grease and protein. Viktor would make a joke about Goose's eating habits, saying all that crap had cost Goose his hair and some day it would cost him his *petukh*, his cock.

Now Viktor finished his yogurt and threw the bowl across the kitchen where it shattered against the exposed brick wall, which made Goose feel better. He didn't like a silent Viktor. He preferred something he could deal with.

"He alive, I would kill him again," Viktor said. "Not so fast though, eh?" Viktor had just learned that the guy who Heckle shot at Tuffy's was no faceless uniformed cop, but Detective Sergeant Wes Delby.

"Didn't know you knew him," Goose said. He wanted to sit. He was so tired he was afraid he would fall asleep. Standing there in the kitchen, moving around a little, it kept him awake. What the hell would Viktor say if he fell asleep in the middle of one of Viktor's rants? He didn't want to know.

Viktor sat staring at the remains of his breakfast on the floor against the wall. "I help him," he said. "This Delby prick."

Goose told himself to stay cool. Viktor Khrenov helps a cop? It was all news to him.

"Last year, maybe two years, this Delby comes to me, not here, some place else," Viktor said. "'I got something on you', he says to me, and it's little bullshit stuff, on building in Brampton, you remember?" He flicked his eyes to Goose and back again to the yogurt. "Pay inspector what? Ten thousand? That's what he has got on me. Is no big deal, you know that. He says, this Delby, he says he is looking for bigger stuff, maybe I can help him, give him leads, tell him things I know but I don't testify, I stay out. So I give him some shit, okay? Union stuff at two places, big new, what you call it? Theatre on King Street, and two Irish guys fix concrete prices on apartment building. He goes in, gets what he needs, goes to court, his side wins, Delby is big man, sends me Scotch like I need it."

Goose had an idea where this was going. Maybe he should sit down. Instead he leaned against the counter, his arms folded and facing the bedroom. Are Natalka's things still in there, he wondered? Does he dare ask Viktor?

"You and me, eh?" Viktor said. "Nobody else. You and me know this. We got secrets, eh?"

"Lots of them," Goose said.

"So I give to Delby, stuff he does not know or knows, but I tell him how it happens. We meet three, four times. Then I say to Delby one day, two, three months ago, I say 'I give you lots, you give me what?

No fine, no slap on wrist for paying inspector? Okay, now you give me more that, I give you more this.' I want even deal, eh? I tell him, he gives me no more, he gets no more from me. And he tells me, he says, 'Okay, I help.' He says, 'Viktor, watch your ass with condo deal, New Bay Village.' And I know. I know who he talks to besides me."

"Had to be Slip. Only one who knew about what was going on there besides you and me."

"Delby talks to both me and Slip. Plays games, eh? Smart guy. Gets stuff from me, stuff from Slip. Can't lose."

"That's why you told me to watch him, to watch Slip." Goose nodded. "Is that why you brought Slip's buddy in, your hero, the guy named Arden? 'Cause you knew Slip would be gone?" When Viktor said nothing, Goose said, "You expected to get more from Delby? Was he gonna give you…"

The intercom from the front entrance buzzed. Khrenov pushed the button and a man's voice asked if he were Viktor Khrenov. Viktor barked "Yes," and the voice said, like it was introducing a football team or starting the Indianapolis 500, that he was Lieutenant Gary Logan from Metro Toronto Police Service and that he had a search warrant and a team of officers delegated to questioning him and searching the premises. They also had an arrest warrant for one Michael Jeremy Googins, a.k.a. Mick Googins a.k.a. Goose. Pausing long enough to take a breath he added, "You have two minutes to show yourself here at the entrance. Beyond that time, I am authorized to make a forced entry and hold everyone inside for questioning in a matter of first-degree murder."

"The fucking cellphone," Goose said when Viktor turned off the intercom. "That call Heckle made on the phone he stole from some kid. They tracked it to me." He pushed away from the counter. "I'll tell them I told Heckle to fuck off when he called. Said I wasn't going to pick him up and I never saw him."

Viktor held up a hand and shook his head. "I call you, eh?" Viktor said. "Remember? You got Heckle and I call you in your car. They trace your phone, they trace mine. They know where you are when I call. They know where I am, so you say you get him at Tuffy's, drive him to motel, leave him there. All you did. End of your story. Your car down-stairs?" and Goose said, yeah, in the lot. "Give me keys," Viktor said, stretching a hand to Goose, and Goose handed them over, admitting that Viktor was always looking two, three steps ahead, sometimes look-ing out for other people but always looking out for Viktor Khrenov first.

She looked up and down Beach Boulevard as he came in before closing the door behind him and standing against it, watching him.

"I appreciate this," Arden said, and Josie told him to save his appreci-ation, she hadn't planned on offering anything he might be obligated for.

"Leave your dirty laundry there," she said, pointing to a corner of the alcove. "You want to walk through to the kitchen, we can have some coffee. Me, I plan on mixing a Bloody Caesar."

Arden, stepping past her, knowing she wouldn't want him walking behind her, said, "Mix one for me."

He sat at Josie's kitchen table, against the window looking out at the lake, past the garden that hadn't been tended all year and past the battered Honda in the corner, weeds around it higher than the door-sills. In the other corner stood a garden shed, the padlock shining in the sun.

He had not sat like this in a private house, a place where people lived and talked about their plans and cooked meals and made love, in years. It was like being in a resort, counting the days before going back to work.

"Drink up," she said, setting a Bloody Caesar in front of him. "You get just one."

"All I want."

They drank without talking, each waiting for the other to speak. Josie spoke first. "How does it feel to see somebody get shot and know it was meant for you?"

"It's happened before."

She sat back in her chair. "Bill Winegarden?"

"I was thinking of the army. Somalia."

"What was that like?"

"Pretty bad. You get over it."

"I hear some soldiers don't ever get over it."

"They're just not as good at hiding it as other people."

"So you were pretty cool last night, watching the cop get shot."

"No." He glared at her, not wanting to hide his anger. "No, I wasn't cool…"

"Sorry, I meant…"

"You'd have to be some kind of crazy, a psychopath or something, to watch somebody being shot to death in front of you and not feel anything. I might be a little crazy, but I'm no psychopath. It bothered me, it…"

She waited for him to continue, and when he didn't she said, "I was married to a cop, a homicide detective, and I don't think it ever got easier for him, the things he saw. I just… Well, you looked pretty held together to me, kind of guy who doesn't let things get to him. Some things. I'm not making this better, am I?"

"Let's drop it."

"Okay, but just one more thing. This cop, the guy who got shot because that creep thought it was you. Was he a young guy, maybe a rookie? Because it just seems strange, you know, to be shot that way. You don't have to tell me. They're not giving anything out on the news, not the radio anyway. I was listening before you got here. They're just saying it was a police officer, and they expected to have his name at noon. One of the cops I know, guy named Hayashida who used to work with my husband, is handling the case, I hear."

"He wasn't a rookie, the guy who was shot. He wasn't a uniformed cop either. He was a detective."

"Know his name?"

"Guy called Wes Delby."

Josie sat back in her chair and stared at him, her eyes wide, before standing and walking to the side window where she leaned against the window sill, her head down, her eyes closed.

The Toronto detective who called Hayashida at Central was named Melville. The name reminded Hayashida of Moby Dick, which he thought was an appropriate connection for a homicide detective. "He's here and he's not telling us much," Melville said, meaning Goose.

Hayashida checked his watch. He had to get ready for the press conference Walter Freeman set up, telling Hayashida to take the questions. It would be a big deal, killing a cop always was, and the national press would be there along with the locals and Toronto. "He's admitting he drove Heckle Dunne to the motel, right?"

Melville said, "We had to wake him up for that," and when Hayashida asked what he meant, Melville said, "The minute he gets his ass in the back of the car, he falls asleep."

"Been up all night."

"Said he had a toothache, kept him awake."

"Didn't keep him from going to work for Khrenov this morning, obviously. So what else is he saying?"

"Nothing. That's it. Dunne called Googins, asked him for a favour…"

"Where?"

"Where what?"

"Where was Googins when he took the call?"

"With some waitress named Arlene at her apartment. Said he picked her up, she invited him back to her place. We've got somebody talking to her now."

"They in bed at the time?"

"We'll be sure to ask. Anyway, he saw the name of the kid on his phone and didn't answer the first time. It rings again, this time he answers and it's this Heckle Dunne character asking Googins to come and pick him up at some war memorial down on the beach strip, and he goes."

"Why?"

"Why what?"

"Guy's in bed or on his way there with some woman, it's a rainy night. He gets a call from some other guy saying, 'Come and get me, I'm on the beach strip,' which is seventy-five, eighty kilometres away, and the first guy puts his pants back on and drives there, leaves the woman counting her fingers, whatever? I mean, who does that?"

"Maybe they're buddies, I don't know."

"They're not buddies. Goose works for Khrenov, Heckle worked for Goose. Anyway, what's he say about Dunne, when he finds him?"

"Says somebody beat the crap out of him. Says the guy, Dunne, starts bragging about how he took care of the S.O.B. who beat him up at the bar. He takes off, comes back with a gun, Googins says he has no idea where he got it. Dunne sees the guy's shadow at the window, figures it's Arden what's-his-name, shoots him twice and takes off. Steals the phone from some kid and calls Goose."

"Didn't know he killed a cop?"

"Not until Khrenov calls Googins and tells him when they're half-way back to Toronto. That's when Googins decides he's through with Dunne, takes him to the motel, tells Dunne not to contact him again, and leaves him there."

"What happened to the weapon?"

"Googins claims he never saw it. Figures Dunne threw it in the lake."

"Did he tell Khrenov about Dunne? Did Googins tell Khrenov where he took Dunne, what he did with him?"

"He says no."

"You believe him?"

"Yeah, like I believe Madonna's a virgin."

Hayashida said, "That's good. That's a good one. Sounds like you're not holding him."

"Unless we keep him here for you to come down and do your own grilling. You want to do that?"

"Not now, probably won't learn much." Then: "Where's his car, Googins's car? You guys have it?"

"No," Melville said. "We should check it out, I guess."

"You *guess*?"

27

She wouldn't talk about her reaction to Wes Delby's name at first, just kept waving Arden's questions off. He watched to see if she would cry, but that didn't happen either. Instead, she took a deep breath and drained the last of the Bloody Caesar from her glass before saying, "The hell with it. I'm having another one."

She carried her second drink from the kitchen into the living room and sat on the sofa, looking at nothing.

Arden chose a chair facing her, thinking she knew how to dress. Too many women her age, forty years and more behind her, either tried to wear teenybopper styles that made them look desperate or slid into sensible shoes and high-necked blouses, cut their hair short and started knitting scarves. Josie did none of that. She wore her hair blonde, Arden believed, because it hid the grey, and she wore it long because men like long hair on women. She wore enough makeup to show off her eyes, a striped gold top that showed off other things, white slacks that made the most of an ass that had not yet begun to fall, and sandals with rhinestones in them, to hell with Birkenstocks.

"You enjoying the view?" she said, and he looked up to see her watching him.

"Just keeping quiet," he said. "So you knew this guy, Delby?"

"Yes. And while you're thinking about it and before you ask, no, I didn't sleep with him."

"None of my business. How'd you know him?" adding, "That's none of my business either, but…"

She took a long drink from the Caesar, made a face, set it aside. "You know Slip was talking to the police."

"Had that one figured out."

"The guy he was talking to was Delby."

"How'd that happen?"

"Delby was checking out the construction racket in Toronto. Graft, bribes, extortion. When he scored a few hits here and there they sent him looking into things on his own. That's when he started working undercover, or tried to, hoping to pick up whatever dirt he could find. The street must have spotted him pretty quick because nobody would talk to him except the Russian, Khrenov. He knew what Delby was up to and told him so, laughed at him for pretending not to be a cop. He said if Delby wanted to know what was really going on, Khrenov and him could make a deal."

"How do you know all this?"

She lowered her head and stared at him through lowered eyelids. "You want to talk or you want to listen?"

Arden nodded, folded his arms, and sat back in the chair.

The deal, Josie explained, involved a two-way street. Khrenov would feed whatever dirt he had about the guys he competed with, as long as Khrenov's company stayed clean. Delby would let Khrenov know things that might keep the Russian out of trouble, but only small stuff, no assaults, no major thefts by Khrenov or his people. They would meet a couple of times a month at a Russian restaurant downtown, a place called the Almaz. Delby let the Russian order the meal, which was always borscht and lamb stew.

"They'd set things up by sending messages to each other," she said. "Little boys playing spy games. They'd send postcards of Russia back and forth in envelopes by courier. Khrenov had a bundle of the postcards and gave some to Delby. Slip told me all this. He loved to talk about it, and I had to tell him now and then, 'Hey, be careful who you say this stuff to.' Anyway, Khrenov and Delby, they'd write crappy little notes to each other on them. 'You should take the waters here some time' and 'The women here are beautiful'. Crap like that. None of it mattered. The only important things was the date on the postcard, and that would be the day to meet.

"The Russian always came alone, arriving first and staying until after Delby left. The last time they met, Delby drives around the block, wanting to see how he got home, the Russian," Josie said. "Parks down the street and watches a big black car pull up..."

"A Chrysler."

She shrugged. "I guess. Anyway, some young woman was driving..."

"Short black hair."

She looked at him, tilting her head a little. Then: "Most of what Delby told Khrenov was useless, and Khrenov knew it," she said. "Khrenov passed the same kind of garbage on to Delby. Now and then each of them would pass along something worthwhile, just to keep it interesting. The way he put it, Delby got the better deal because he could cash in the fact that Khrenov trusted him. It gave Delby and the cops a peek into a business they knew was so damn corrupt. Things changed when Khrenov mentioned Tuffy's. Delby grew up on the beach strip, so he came down and made a contact with Slip, who figured him as a cop almost as soon as they met."

She drained her glass and set it aside.

"Delby told Slip what he was doing, checking out the construction racket in Toronto. He made the same deal with Slip he'd made with the Russian, promising to cover Slip's butt if Slip would feed him stuff. Slip agreed but told Delby that anything he knew about Khrenov was off-limits. He'd talk about what he knew in the industry, who was screwing whom in the construction business, but he wouldn't talk about Khrenov. This went on until Delby started putting pressure on Slip, told him what he knew about a couple of things on the fringe of Khrenov's operations, stuff he'd picked up from Khrenov himself. Delby told Slip how he and Khrenov would meet at the Russian restaurant, using postcards and stuff. He was trying to get Slip to trust him I guess, but it made Slip nervous, figuring Delby had more sources and connections than he expected."

"So Slip knew Delby was dealing with Khrenov, but Khrenov didn't know he was talking to Slip."

"I think Khrenov figured it out near the end. Maybe that's what got Slip killed. What do you think?"

"Delby tell you this?" Arden began folding himself into the overstuffed chair, hearing the sound of crashing waves and laughter from the beach, looking around at Josie's pictures and furniture, her woman's touch everywhere, all corn and comfort.

"A bit of it. The rest I figured out for myself."

Arden looked at her, his eyebrows raised.

"Look, the Russian and Delby had postcards and a courier," Josie said, raising her voice a little. "Delby and Slip had me. I was the contact. If Delby wanted to talk to Slip, he'd come by the bench in the morning."

"Your mother's. Thou swell and all that."

"He wouldn't stop to chat. When I showed up he'd be waiting and he'd ask me what time it was. I'd look at my watch and tell him, he'd look at his watch and say, 'Damn, mine says three o'clock,' or something like that. Then he'd say he'd better get it fixed at the watchmaker's over on Brant Street or in Aldershot, they had three or four different places. He'd say where they were without saying *what* they were. Aldershot meant a big greasy spoon on Plains Road, Waterdown meant the doughnut shop, that kind of stuff. That's how they set things up at the beginning, him and Slip. I thought it was silly, passing it back and forth that way. I think Delby did too. Thing was, nobody wanted to write anything down. No email, no text message. Nothing anybody could trace. Later on, the last couple of weeks or so, they got sloppy. Delby would come by and say, 'Tell your boyfriend to meet me at the hamburger joint,' something like that."

"Your boyfriend?" Arden said, and Josie gave him a look.

"Like I said before, we had a thing last winter," she said. "Bill and I. Nothing serious. He could be a funny guy. And a great cook, by the way. He'd show up with wine, flowers, make a pot of chili or chicken cacciatore, and it'd be good, the food. Listen, at my age, a guy who'll cook a meal, bring flowers and tell stories is a hell of a lot more appealing than some schmuck who can dance and has great hair. Most nights he'd fall asleep on the sofa, I'd throw a blanket over him, go upstairs and lock my door, and he'd be gone in the morning." Arden sat nodding, and Josie said, "What?"

"Khrenov must have found out about Delby and Slip. He's fine about playing Delby but he sure doesn't want Delby and Slip connecting behind his back. Delby could be squeezing Slip for whatever he could get that would get a conviction on the Russian."

"That's what I said. That's what I think got him killed."

"But he never told you, Winegarden didn't. He never told you what he passed on to Delby. About Khrenov."

"I didn't want to know. I just…" She shook her head, her eyes closed.

"Did you find this stuff exciting?" Arden said. "Dealing with Delby and Slip, not knowing what these guys were up to and not caring. Did you get some kind of rush from it?"

"You think my life was so boring that I needed this to add some spice to it?"

"No, just that…"

"Well, it was. As long as I wasn't too involved, as long as I wasn't doing anything illegal myself, I thought, 'What the hell? It's either this or I join the euchre club down at the community hall,' and this was better. I'd tell myself I was helping the police catch bad guys, figuring Delby might find enough to lay charges on Khrenov and I'd be kept out of it. So I went along with it. Why not?"

Arden sat waiting for her to start talking again, but she didn't. Not right away. For several minutes he watched her inspect her nails, brush back her hair, pull her legs under her, avoid his eyes.

When she spoke again, her voice had changed. It was softer, and sounded younger.

"You have to understand that my husband and I, my second husband, the detective, his name was Gabe and he and I had…" She shook her head and looked up at the ceiling. "God, this is going to sound like such a cliché, but we really had something very special. When he was shot right out there on the beach behind the house, when that happened it took every ounce of my being, every nerve, every muscle, every thought I had, to hold myself together. And when it was over, when I figured out what happened to Gabe and why, I decided I was ready to heal. That's what I tried to do for the next three years. I told myself I was healing, but I was hardening."

She spent the first year after Gabe's death helping care for her mother at the retirement home where her mother lived, and where Josie did the bookkeeping. A bisexual friend named Dewey ran a pet grooming operation. He took her to movies and sometimes dancing, and in good weather they went for drives in Dewey's sports car. Two years ago Dewey fell in love with a florist named Gary. Dewey gave up his pet grooming business, he and Gary married and honeymooned in Bermuda, and Josie hadn't heard from him since.

"In the middle of it all, Mother died," Josie said. "I was both sad and free. Only damn thing I wasn't was happy. You can probably guess the rest."

Arden said, "I don't like to guess."

She ignored him. "Met a bunch of guys. Okay, two or three guys." She held her hand up, fingers spread, looking at it while she lowered her fingers one at a time. "Maybe four. Over the two years. Including Slip."

"We all work things out one way or another," Arden said.

"A couple of them moved in, for a while. Not going to let that happen again. You see that car out in the yard, that Honda? Well, it's mine. Or used to be. I bought and paid for it new after my first husband left me. Nothing special. Just a good little car to run around, do errands, visit friends. All I needed. Anyway, this jerk I thought I was in love with borrowed it one night to go shopping, which was fine, except he went shopping at a bar in town. He came out drunk and tried driving it home. He was doing all right until he drove right past my house and didn't realize it until he got to the lift bridge, which is when a cop passed him going the other way. The cop gave him a funny look and that's when Chico…"

"Chico?"

"He was a little Spanish, what's wrong with that?"

"Nothing."

"Chico looked back at him and drove right into the bridge. Smashed up the front of the car. The cop saw it happen in his rear view mirror and turned around, going back to check on him. Chico saw him coming and didn't want to get nailed for drunk driving…"

She began first to smile, then laugh softly at the memory.

"So he figured he'd chew some gum to hide the smell of alcohol on his breath. But hitting the bridge had thrown Chico against the side of the windshield. He missed the airbag because his head was turned to look back at the cop. He broke his nose, cut his lip, he's bleeding all down his shirt, but he manages to get a box of Chiclets out of his pocket, dumps most of them into his mouth, and starts chewing them. Then he opens the door, gets out of the car, walks toward the cop who is just getting out of the cruiser behind him. Chico's mouth is bleeding and he's drunk anyway, so when he starts talking some of the white Chiclets fall out of his mouth. The cop looks at them and says, 'Holy shit, are those your *teeth*?'"

She smiled more widely, Arden smiling with her.

"The car gets towed back here, the radiator is gone, there's some work needed on the suspension, and somebody tells me it's at least a thousand dollars to get fixed. Chico tells me not to worry, just leave the car where it was. He'll find a job and pay me back as soon as he finished serving the thirty days he got for DUI, driving without a licence, all of it."

"Not a long sentence."

"Long enough. I told him not to count on me visiting him in jail and I didn't. When the thirty days were up I figured he'd be at my front door and looking for work. But he wasn't. Never saw him again. A month later I heard he was back in jail, this time for stealing car parts."

"Maybe a radiator for a Honda?"

"Cute. I don't know. He had a record I never knew about, including theft, so this time he got two years or something. Anyway, he was out of my life for good."

"And you're stuck with the car."

"I'm stuck with that poor broken down car. I kept thinking I should have a scrap dealer tow it away. I kept it there to remind me how stupid I can be, not that it's helped much. Besides, Slip liked it. Liked it so much he bought it."

"Why? Did he plan to fix it, drive it away some day?"

She sat staring out the window. Then: "I got some fishing equipment and a shotgun out of another guy."

Arden blinked. "A shotgun?"

"And a box of shells. He liked to hunt and fish. Fishing I didn't mind. Hunting bothered me. He liked to hunt ducks. Who wants to shoot a duck? I didn't like it and told him so. He took me out skeet shooting with him once, showed me how to load the thing, how to fire it. I told him to keep it to himself and said he could shoot it as many times as he wanted, I'd wait in the car. And I did."

"Bit of a yahoo, this guy?"

"Actually, he was pretty educated. He worked at the refinery down the lake. Had a good job, as I understood it. Except for him wanting to kill ducks, we got along fine. Then the refinery shut down and he said he was headed west to the oil sands. He told me he could make a hundred thousand, two hundred thousand dollars a year out there, and wanted me to come with him. He said we could live like millionaires. I said, 'Who wants to be a millionaire in Fort McMurray? That'd be like being a hockey player in Dubai.' He said it would only be for a year or so, that I could get a job there too and we'd come back with maybe a quarter of a million dollars. I told him to go alone and come back with whatever he had in his pocket."

Another cold smile.

"He wrote me one letter. One letter. Last I heard from him. I don't know if he's dead or anything else about him. Don't care either. His ugly shotgun, his fishing rod and things, a little gas stove, his hunting clothes, they're still in my basement. I should sell it all one day, I guess. The shotgun at least."

"Tough to sell guns."

"Maybe I'll just throw it out. Or give it to the police. I don't like guns. Anyway, that's about it. Just when I figure I'm not going to hear from the oilman again, Slip shows up and…" She shrugged. "If you want something to eat, I'm making myself a sandwich. You can make your own." She stood up. "There's some cold ham in the fridge and rye bread from yesterday. You want a coffee with it? And you might as well move that bag of laundry out of the foyer. Somebody might trip over it."

28

"I hate press conferences. They're like being stoned to death with popcorn."

Walter Freeman slammed the door shut and waved Hayashida into a chair. The press conference had been a half-hour zoo, four camera crews aimed at him, and a dozen reporters shouting for twenty minutes. "Can't those idiots learn to ask intelligent questions?" Walter said. "I swear, any of my kids ever said they wanted to be reporters, I'd've told them to clean septic tanks instead. They'd be doing the same kind of work and feel better about it."

Hayashida said, "Where do you think that guy from the *Sun* got the story about Dunne being in the motel, and him shooting Delby last night? And how'd he know about the bloody pillow and all?"

"I was wondering about that." Freeman tossed his jacket on the back of his chair, opened his desk drawer and withdrew a toothpick. "They gotta have people at motels, hotels, maybe maids cleaning the rooms who call it in, I don't know." He put the toothpick in his mouth, a habit left over from his attempts to quit smoking. "Walter figures he'll avoid lung cancer by chewing toothpicks instead of smoking," Hayashida once said to a couple of cops. "Now he'll probably get Dutch Elm disease."

"The *Sun*'ll run a story tomorrow about Dunne being a serial killer on the loose," Hayashida said

"Let 'em."

"Nobody's gonna see Dunne again, you figure?"

"Nobody'll care."

Freeman's telephone rang. "Some guy named Melville wants to talk to you," he said, passing the receiver to Hayashida, who told him to put it on speakerphone, they might as well listen to it together.

"Just to let you know," Melville said, "Googins got himself lawyered up, thanks to Khrenov. Heavy-duty guy from Bay Street who said Googins wouldn't give anything more than his name, rank and serial number so he's gone. Seized Googins's car, anyway, a 2017 Buick, silver, licence AZPJ280. Khrenov gave us the keys, told us to look for anything we want. First inspection shows the interior's clean, or clean enough."

"How about the trunk?" Hayashida called across Freeman's desk.

"Smells like a bleach factory. Googins says he cleaned it out last week, had some paint stains in it. The hell he did. It was washed down this morning, I'll bet no more'n two hours ago by the smell of it. We figure Khrenov might have helped. The guy smelled like a Chinese laundry. Which is a hell of an improvement."

"Where'd you find it, the car?"

"Back of the Odachni building, where we checked it out. Our people were going to drag it to our lab downtown, but what the hell would they find, right?"

"Your guys, did they look up at Khrenov's office when they were doing it, checking out the trunk?"

"I dunno. Why?"

"If they did they might've seen Khrenov up there pissing down on them and laughing."

Goose sat in Khrenov's office drinking coffee, black, trying to get the feathers out of his head, prop his eyes open. He finished telling the Russian what Melville and the other cops had started to ask him about before the lawyer arrived. He said they were asking where Heckle was, whose gun he had, and whose blood was on the bed in the motel, Heckle's or somebody else's.

"I told them, I said I didn't see no gun. Said I wouldn't've let him in the goddamn car if he had a gun, so he threw it in the water on the beach strip."

Khrenov sat watching him. "You threw gun where?"

"Off the bridge. The one in Bronte. Right over the edge, there's a creek down there."

Khrenov let out a long sigh. "You don't know if it's in water, eh?"

"It's down there somewhere. It's a damn high bridge."

"What happens, they find gun, same bullets from detective who Heckle shoots, do what you call it, testing…"

"The rifling. They look at the rifling marks, match it to the bullets."

"They do and they say, 'Hey, this gun shoot Delby, but not in lake like Googins said'? What happens then?"

"My prints aren't on it, Viktor. I used a rag. I'm not that stupid. I say I don't know, only knew what Heckle told me. You told me yourself, you got your guy, who was it? Lewicki? Little guy downstairs who always wanted Heckle's job, the guy who cleaned out the trunk? Anyway, he did a hell of a job. There's nothing connecting us. The cops push me, I'll say Heckle got out of the car to take a leak, maybe that's when he threw it over, whatever." When he saw Khrenov nodding he said, "And what're we going to do about the other guy, your hero?"

"You think maybe he's clean?"

"I think maybe we should make sure. You still think Winegarden had something to give Delby, what we haven't found?"

"Maybe."

"This Arden, the new guy, he's had time to look around, maybe hear things. Winegarden's gone and now so is Delby. People're gonna be spooked over there. He could be ready to talk to whoever puts pressure on him. They'll probably talk about sending him back to Millhaven. We still don't know nothin' about what he took, what Winegarden had. I mean, whatever he took, whatever he had, shouldn't we check it out and get our hands on it, get rid of it?"

"How?"

"I'd start with your hero, see what I can pick up. I'll go tomorrow. I'm so fucking tired now, I can hardly talk."

Viktor sat staring at him. Then he said, "Go upstairs and get sleep. Don't go back where you live, your apartment, eh? Not for few days."

Goose was already on his feet, stumbling for the stairs, saying, "Trust me, Viktor. I never intended to."

She told him to relax, she would do the dishes herself. Doing the dishes was comforting to her. "My sister and I, her name's Tina, she lives in Vancouver with her rich husband. Tina and I used to do the dishes with my mother." Josie was drying cups and saucers, washing a butcher knife and sliding it into a wooden block with the others like it. Arden sat at the table by the window.

"Back when we were kids and Mom could still talk, Tina and I loved hearing her tell stories, always looking for a moral or some lesson for us. My father was alive and we lived down near the steel plants. Mother would talk to us when we were doing the dishes, tell us stories that meant something or made us laugh. She would wash, Tina and I would dry. You look back…" She set the dried cup aside, staring at it as she spoke. "You look back and you think, 'Why didn't I realize how happy I was?'"

"Somebody told me, a long time ago," Arden said, "that we only know happiness when we look back at it. When you're remembering things, like you did just now, you don't remember maybe that you didn't have a lot of money or somebody was really screwing you over or you were worried about this or that. None of that must've mattered because you've forgotten about it. You just remember being happy."

She turned to look over her shoulder at him, seeing him at the table wearing a golf shirt and jeans, penny loafers on his feet, still no socks, his hair shining in reflected sunlight off the lake, his hands clasped in front of him. Big hands. They were the first thing she looked at when she met a guy, his hands. Arden had large soft hands.

She turned back to the sink, put her own hands in the warm soapy water. "Or maybe it just seems that way before all the crap happened, before my dad was run over by a train when I was twelve years old, and things started falling apart. I flunked out of pre-med and married the wrong man. Tina was smart. She married for money and moved out to British Columbia. Mother had a stroke that took away her voice, my first husband turned into a class A jerk, my second husband was shot practically in our own back yard… God, what a mess," looking down into the sink as she spoke. "Sometimes I think if we knew what was coming in our lives, if we had any idea about what was going to happen to us…" She shook her head.

"What would we do?"

"I don't know. I guess it's better that way, don't you think?" She pulled the plug in the sink, watched the water drain out, and said, "Gabe always wanted us to get a dishwasher, but I refused. I think because standing here, doing the dishes, reminded me of Mother and made me feel safe. I haven't felt really safe since he and Mom died." She took a tea towel from the rack, turned to face Arden, and said, drying her hands, "And here I am alone in my house with a guy who went to prison for breaking a man's neck. Makes me wonder how stupid I am."

"Or trusting."

"Same thing."

"I don't think so." He sat back in the chair, stretched his legs in front of him, and looked around at the pictures on the wall, watercolours of houses in the country, and landscapes with mountains on the horizon. African violets bloomed in earthenware pots near the window, a large green ceramic frog sitting among them. The colours of the house were relaxing, tones of beige and pale blue, and everything was spotless. How long had it been since he'd sat in a room like this? He couldn't remember. He thought briefly of winter, what it must be like when the lake isn't blue and warm but grey and frozen, when the beach is deserted and wind whistles across the bay and under the bridges. It would be a haven, he believed. A place to read and listen to music, watch flames from the fireplace, sleep under duvets and wake in the morning to the aroma of coffee.

"Do you want to hear the story?" he said, "about what happened to the guy, the one whose neck I broke? Because there's more to it than people know."

"Isn't there always?" she said, leaning against the sink, her arms folded.

He told her about his sister Donna Lee, how it was always Donna Lee with her and not just Donna, how she was fifteen years younger than him, "a surprise baby" who his mother treated like she was a doll to dress and put to bed, not a daughter, not a real person.

"My mother got Alzheimer's in her fifties," he said, "and I took over getting Donna Lee out of her teenage years safely without seeing her fall in with druggies and other people."

His sister turned to Arden for everything she needed. Their mother eventually didn't know who her children were or who she was herself, and she died in a nursing home on Donna Lee's twentieth birthday. Their father—"our old man," was the way Arden referred to him—had always been distant, and he stayed that way. After his wife died he mortgaged the house and spent the next few months gambling it away. When the money was gone, so was he. Neither Arden nor Donna Lee saw him again, nor did they care.

"I didn't see Donna Lee for a while after my marriage fell apart. I was trying to keep myself together and she'd been working at various jobs, just getting by, doing her best to survive. Then one night, I'm living in an apartment over a butcher shop on James Street, working with a security outfit and trying to stay sober, and she calls me. She's crying and nearly hysterical. She tells me this guy had raped and beaten her. She thought she'd been in love with him and now her life was a mess and she just wants to die."

Arden rushed over to her little walk-up. She'd been waitressing, hoping to get back into university. She had always wanted to become a teacher, and maybe work part-time at a dance studio. She'd been a good dancer, taking ballet when she was a kid, even though the family could barely afford it. When she opened the door he saw the cut over her eye and the bruise on her arm. She couldn't stop crying. Arden told her they would call the police, but she begged him not to. She had heard stories of girls reporting rape, how they'd been so often humiliated by the police, and the rapist got off anyway. Besides, there was something else.

"This guy's name was Kottmeier, Jason Kottmeier. You know that name?"

Josie nodded. "Sounds familiar."

"Kottmeier and McCann. Biggest law firm in town. Her boyfriend's grandfather started it fifty, sixty years ago. He makes a big deal about it, as if it's a title he inherited, like royalty. The family's still in it, the offices fill three floors of a building downtown."

Donna Lee had met Jason Kottmeier at a dance contest just as he was about to finish law school. They dated a few times, dinners, movies, parties with friends. She never met his parents and never expected to. The family was too rich and powerful for their son to get involved with a truck driver's daughter. It would be a fling, a romance, nothing serious.

"They'd gone out and had a few drinks," Arden said. "They come back to Donna Lee's place, which isn't much, especially for a guy living in one of those big estates down the lake. But Donna Lee, you know, she's attractive and she's got this little girl thing going that a lot of guys like. She's just basically a good-natured soul who thinks everybody else is as trusting as she is, or should be. Some people might call her naïve but she's, uh…" He smiled in embarrassment and looked away, blinked, and lowered his head.

"Sweet?" Josie said.

"I guess. Anyway, I needed to do something besides tell her she should cheer up, things would get better. I had an idea what she was going through. I'd just discovered a couple of months earlier that my wife, my second wife, had been screwing around on me for years, me working a lot of night shifts. So I kind of lost it. I decided to hell with doing things the right way, whatever that was. There's something pure about physical violence, you know?"

"Pure?"

"When it's justified. You know what Mike Tyson said once?"

"The boxer? Not sure if I care."

"He said, 'Everybody has a plan until they get punched in the face.' So you can sit around talking about things, and count on the law to do something, but that's all talk, all bullshit until something happens."

"Like punching somebody in the face? What kind of guy are you?"

"I'm not that kind. Really. I'm not that kind of guy at all."

"So you just broke his neck, this Kottmeier guy."

Arden looked away, said, "Maybe this wasn't such a good idea, telling you this."

"Hey, it's all right. If you offered to break the neck of some guy who beat me up and raped me, I'd wave flags, do cartwheels, whatever." Her voice softened. "It was your sister. I understand."

Arden called Kottmeier's cellphone, told Kottmeier who he was, said he knew what happened, and asked Kottmeier what the hell he had to say for himself. Kottmeier denied attacking Donna Lee, told Arden he could go to hell, said he didn't know what Arden was talking about, and promised that if Arden spread those lies around, to the police or anybody else, he'd see that Arden's ass got a good kicking and his family would sue him into poverty.

"I remember that line," Arden said. "'We'll sue you into poverty.' Which was funny because I wouldn't've had far to go at that point."

Then Kottmeier got confident, saying he was coming over to Donna Lee's place to straighten things out and make sure she got the same message. Donna Lee became hysterical, begging Arden not to let Kottmeier anywhere near her. Kottmeier arrived anyway, and Arden went outside to meet him, the night mild and rainy, the street deserted.

"He nearly fell down when he got out of his car, he was so drunk," Arden said. "He'd gone home and started drinking after what Donna Lee said he'd done. I told him to go back home, that I would talk her into letting the police handle it or I'd go to the police myself. He tried pushing past me. When I grabbed his arm to stop him, he took a swing at me, which is when I swung him around and…"

"You broke his neck."

"It's not as simple as that."

"*Somebody* broke his neck, right?"

"I grabbed him from behind, his neck in the crook of my arm. It was a move we learned in the parachute regiment, special forces. I wanted him to calm down and just go home, but he wouldn't stop moving. He kept screaming, swearing at me and Donna Lee, calling her a bitch and a skank and other things. I told him if he didn't stop struggling I'd break his neck. He didn't, and I did."

"It's that easy?"

"If you know how. You put your knee against the small of the back and…" He shook his head. "Never mind. It wasn't a full break, by the way. It was a severe dislocation. That's what the doctors, what the courts called it. But it messed up his spinal cord and he hasn't walked since."

"And you still feel guilty about it. Why?"

He looked at her, smiled, ducked his head. "Because that's only half the story."

Josie pushed away from the sink to sit at the table across from him. She stretched her hands toward his without touching them. "Let me guess. It wasn't really rape."

"You got it."

"And you've been beating yourself up ever since."

"No." He shook his head. "You don't beat yourself up when you're sitting in a prison cell. You can't bother. You just try to save your own ass. Other people do the beating up."

29

Forensics told Hayashida they had gotten everything out of Tuffy's they could expect to get where Delby's murder was concerned, and Hayashida could release it back to the owner.

Which gave Hayashida an idea.

The guy who answered the phone at Odachni, an accountant who came in on weekends, told Viktor about the police officer who wanted to talk to him, calling from the beach strip. "I told him, I said you're really busy," the accountant half muttered, leaning into Viktor's office, "but he said whatever you were doing I should get you on the phone, it was that important."

Viktor glared at the telephone before waving the guy away and reaching for the receiver.

"How are you today, Mr. Khrenov?" Hayashida said when Viktor spoke his name into the telephone.

"I am fine, and why do you need to know?" Viktor said.

"You're good to travel?"

"What, you are sending me back to Russia?"

"Not that far. We need to talk, you and me."

"So talk." Viktor leaned back and put his feet on the desk, admiring his new loafers, brown calfskin, made in Italy, six hundred a pair.

"Face to face."

"What time you coming?" Viktor leaned forward to rub a scuff mark from the toe of one loafer.

"Now, see, you've got something wrong already," Hayashida said. "I'm not coming into Toronto. You are coming here to see me at your dump on the beach strip."

"You are funny man," Viktor said. "I need you to tell me when to laugh."

"No laughs. You have a car, I understand you have a driver, and you have a property that is a crime scene. That's your place, Tuffy's. I hate driving into Toronto, sitting in traffic for an hour or so. And when I get there people're rushing around, too busy to talk. Some people like the place, I understand that. My brother, for example, loves being there but he's a lawyer so you gotta take that into consideration."

Viktor sat in silence, half listening to the detective. Hayashida had said something about Viktor having a driver and Viktor's instincts, always sharply honed, spiked at the comment. They'd checked Goose's car, did they want to check the Chrysler? Did this detective with a Japanese name know about Natalka? Viktor had a brief flashback, picturing Natalka naked in the kitchen and hearing her squeal with excitement when he bought her a gift. "You are telling me what?" he said, interrupting Hayashida.

"I'm telling you that if I drive over to see you I'll bring a couple of uniforms plus a carful of Toronto gorillas from 42 Division and a warrant saying we'll put your ass in jail for at least forty-eight hours while we check you out on suspicion of a murder charge. How does that sound?"

Viktor sat up straight. "Maybe," he said, "I call your lawyer brother, pay him to keep me away from you, eh?"

"Go ahead. He's a tax lawyer. Look, Mister Khrenov, I don't know what you plan to do with this place, Tuffy's, but we're getting ready to hand it back to you, maybe in a day or two. Before that, we need some answers, and I can get them in one of three places. Your place, which

I won't like. Out at the Toronto West Detention Centre, which *you* won't like. Or here on the beach strip, which I'll like so much that I'll buy you a jug of your own beer if you come over. How's that sound?"

"I drink no beer. What time?" Viktor ran it together in one thought.

"How about four o'clock?"

Viktor's answer was a grunt of agreement before hanging up, swinging his Italian loafers from the desk and walking to the door leading up to the apartment. He shouted up the stairs, "Goose, wake up. You are driving me somewhere."

He had to scream Goose's name three times before Goose answered, asking did he have time to get a cup of coffee and where were they going in such a damn hurry. Viktor said, "Beach strip," and kicked the door shut, putting another scuff on the loafers and almost breaking his *proklyatyy* toe.

Josie sat shaking her head, her eyes closed. "So you're telling me," she said, "that you break this guy's neck, the guy your sister told you had beaten up and raped her..."

Arden said, "Like I said, it wasn't broken. I severely dislocated the vertebrae between C five and C six resulting in trauma-based ischemia. That's how the doctors put it." He smiled tightly. "You remember stuff like that, you hear it yelled at you in court."

"Okay, my mistake. Either way the guy can't walk now..."

"He can with crutches."

"And you get charged with grievous bodily, which gets you a bunch of years in prison, and then your sister says maybe it wasn't rape after all? How's that happen? I mean, I can imagine things getting a little rough between them, which makes her pissed at him so she throws him out and then she calls you to say she's been beaten and raped?"

"She was a little drunk."

"And after you dislocate his neck and screw up his spinal column, she tells you the truth? I mean, what the hell?"

"You want to hear the weird part?"

"Didn't I just hear it?"

"They're married."

"Who's married?"

"Donna Lee and Jason. Just had their second kid a couple months ago. So I guess he's not as crippled as everybody thought." Arden was smiling. Hell, you had to smile.

"Aw, Jesus." Josie looked away, shaking her head, then back at him. "You're serious? She cries rape, you break the guy's neck, never mind that stuff about dislocating it, he winds up in a wheelchair, you go to prison, and now they're Mr. and Mrs. whatever?"

"Kottmeier. That's how it turned out."

"And you're damn calm about it."

"It happened a long time ago. I did it, and I said I was guilty. The court said it wouldn't matter whether the rape happened or not, I was still guilty. Anyway, while I'm in Millhaven they get married. He's working for the family law firm, they've got a big country place, and they're rich and content. They said they've forgiven me, which impressed the parole board enough that I got released soon as my chance came up."

"You ever talk to her, your sister?"

"She sent some letters, cards at Christmas and my birthday, stuff like that when I was in prison. She feels pretty guilty about everything."

"I hope to hell she does. She lies about getting raped, which puts her boyfriend in a wheelchair and you in Millhaven? I mean, talk about screwing up people's lives. And you're not angry?"

He thought about that for a moment, although he didn't need to. He had spent two years and a bit thinking about it. "No," he said. "If I stayed angry I would lose control over my life, and who wants to do that? But the story about me breaking the neck of my sister's rapist got me respect in prison. Kept a lot of rough guys away from me. So." He shrugged, finished with talking about it.

"It got you here on the beach strip too," Josie said. "Mixed up with Slip Winegarden and Viktor Khrenov, and now with Heckle Dunne."

He gave a lot of thought to his reply, believing the words he was about to say. He just needed a push to say them out loud. Looking at her across the table, Josie watching him with something more than

JOHN LAWRENCE REYNOLDS

concern and sympathy, he didn't want to define it any more than that, so he said, "And it got me here with you."

"You nearly hit him," Viktor said, meaning the truck that Goose cut off on the highway. He said it calmly, like telling Goose he had left his fly open.

"I need some crank," Goose said, wiping his hand across his eyes. "I'm so goddamn tired."

They were in Goose's Buick. Viktor wasn't ready to ride in the Chrysler yet. He didn't want to picture Natalka driving it, remember sitting next to her and reaching over to pull the hem of her dress up her thighs while she giggled and kept looking straight ahead, Viktor pulling it up until her panties were showing and he could put his hand in the warmth of her there, both of them sitting in traffic, making her smile, making *him* smile.

He wasn't smiling now. "No drugs when with me," Viktor said to Goose. "You know that. You want to be awake, you stop, get more coffee."

"I drink any more coffee, I'll be pulling over every five minutes to take a leak," Goose said. "My damn prostate. Doctor says I've got the prostate of a man thirty years older than me. What's that mean?"

Viktor said nothing. He was trying not to think of Natalka. He had forgotten Heckle.

They caught a photographer from one of the Toronto papers on the roof of Tuffy's, looking for a different angle on the place. How he got there Hayashida didn't know, but he wouldn't have given a rat's ass if the idiot had fallen off and broken his leg. There had to be a dozen other reporters and people with cameras outside, wandering up and down the beach strip looking for something new to say about the place. They already had lots to say. First Tuffy's manager is found shot in his car at the bottom of the lake, then a detective is shot through the window of the place by some freak who stole a kid's iPhone. Somehow the shooter gets himself to Toronto and checks into a motel, where somebody leaves a mess of blood in his room but nobody knows whose it is. If it's the shooter's at

Tuffy's, who did it and where was whatever was left of him? And if it's not his blood, he could be roaming the streets with the same gun he already used to kill two people. You want twists? Hell, this story had more twists and turns than six miles on a roller coaster.

And there were more to come. Hayashida didn't believe for a minute that anybody except Heckle Dunne was shot in the motel near the airport. Melville had called to say they checked out Dunne's apartment and took DNA samples to look for a match with the blood in the motel room. Hayashida expected it to be Dunne's. Heckle was probably killed because he screwed up and shot Delby instead of Arden. So who killed Heckle? Goose? Didn't fit. Goose was too smart to do Dunne after checking him into the motel and with his cellphone records putting Dunne in Goose's car half an hour earlier.

The team Walter Freeman put together to work with Hayashida kept calling him, most of them with damn little. So far they had a couple of guys in the North End, who hung out with dealers and bangers and didn't mind scoring a point or two with the law, saying some guy who sounded like Heckle Dunne had come around looking to buy a gun. "Beat up real bad," one of them said. "We figured he wanted to dish out some ass-kicking of his own to whoever did it to him." Neither of them sold him a gun, of course, and they didn't know where he had gone to get one. Hayashida didn't believe it. You get the word out among the right people and they know you've got the cash, you'll end up with somebody who'll sell you whatever you need if you put the cash in his hand.

It all told Hayashida that Heckle Dunne hadn't shown up at Tuffy's intent on shooting somebody. He'd gone for a gun only after Arden, a guy with time in the Special Forces and a couple of years at Millhaven, gave Heckle a good ass-kicking. Which reminded him. He considered calling Central, putting out an APB on Arden and getting him back to Tuffy's, maybe squeeze him some. Instead, he decided to catch up on things from people who might know something they hadn't talked about yet. Especially people on the beach strip, and he knew where to start. He had at least an hour to kill until Viktor Khrenov arrived from Toronto. Khrenov, he was sure, wouldn't be early. He would take his damn time.

30

She turned her head away at first when Arden tried to kiss her, but then she let his lips find hers and it was a good kiss, not a kiss that would lead to the sack but one that hinted it might happen some other time.

"You're one damn interesting guy," Josie said. She reached her hand to touch his face, him bending over her, their eyes locked.

"I'd trade whatever's interesting for something dull, like having a steady job and a wife and kids, mowing the lawn on Saturday mornings, drinking beer with buddies." He stood and looked around for a place to sit, feeling he'd pushed her too far, too fast.

"Yeah, well." Josie patted the sofa next to her. "Sit down here. What the hell. I fed you, gave you a couple of drinks, listened to how you put some guy in a wheelchair and spent a couple years in prison because your sister had second thoughts or something. We're practically old friends. You might as well stay for dinner."

He sat beside her. "How about breakfast too?"

"You're pushing it."

He smiled, stretched his legs in front of him and stared at the opposite wall, waiting for the moment to pass. The smile faded and he looked out the window to the beach and the lake beyond. "You want to know what I really am? I'm worried. Worried that a week from now I'll be back at Millhaven, locked up for another year, year and a half. They'll revoke my parole. They'll do it on suspicion, nothing more. All they have to say is that I was working alongside another parolee, which they knew, and that my name's been mentioned in two murders, his being one of them."

"You had nothing to do with either, right?"

"I was there, I saw…" He shook his head.

She leaned back, crossed her arms. Her mood had changed, just like that. "You were there when Slip was killed? You didn't tell me that before. You said you knew what was going on, but…"

"I was in the back seat. The Russian was beside him in the front. He told Slip where to park, then started riding him, saying Slip had been stealing from him, money and other stuff."

"So the Russian shot him."

"Twice. The first time in the arm when Slip raised his hand. The second time in the head. Slip was pleading with him, saying Viktor owed him. Jesus. I wished I'd never seen it. I thought he was going to turn around and shoot me too. Then I realized I was his cover. Everybody knew I was with Slip, or should've been. I'd been seen leaving Tuffy's with him, Slip telling them we were going to check out this vacant lot on the shoreline. Nobody could place Viktor there. He even called himself from Slip's cellphone back in Toronto. The phone records would place Slip where he was shot, and Viktor in his office. Nobody knew there was anybody but me with Slip when it happened, except the girl who picked us up on the highway in Viktor's big black Chrysler. She knew."

"You can always find her."

"I can always find gold up my ass too, I guess. Same chance."

They sat quiet for a while, Josie feeling something more than sympathy for him, Arden feeling embarrassed about admitting to this woman that he was frightened about being sent back to prison. He had done nothing to deserve it, yet his life was about to turn into the same damn unfair exercise that had sent him there in the first place.

Josie said, "The Russian was right, you know."

"About what?"

"About Slip stealing from him. He took lots. Not just money. Stuff that could put Viktor away for ten years easy."

"How do you know this? Did you see it?"

"Once. I told him I didn't want to see it again. Slip had started skimming cash within a couple of weeks after he started. Not enough for Viktor to notice at first, but…"

"How much did he take?"

"He didn't know himself. Said it was maybe fifteen thousand. You have nice hair."

"What else?"

She dropped her eyes from his hair. "I really wanted to stay out of this."

"How hard'd you try?"

Long pause. "He'd been making notes. Slip bought one of those notebooks that school kids use. A red one with wire binding. He wrote in it."

"What'd he write?"

"What he knew that Viktor was doing, him and Goose and the rest of them. All of them crooked, Viktor an animal sometimes. They like to talk, he said. Among themselves, Viktor especially. He bragged about how he ripped people off, wanting people to know what a clever guy he was. He figured they were all so intimidated by him that they'd never say anything, and even if they did, they'd have no proof, just stories from a bunch of ex-cons."

"So Slip started writing down everything he heard."

"Dates, names. Who Viktor bought off, who he took with him to places where they could raise hell. Inspectors, bankers, anybody he could hustle, anybody who could help him get things done. They'd stay away from places like Vegas, which were too obvious. They'd say they were going fishing, and sometimes they did. Viktor had a friend with a salmon fishing camp in Labrador. It was deep in the bush. Slip went along once to provide a little muscle, Viktor told him. They fly to Goose Bay in a corporate jet, where a couple of helicopters take them maybe a hundred miles inland, nothing around until they get to this fishing camp that's like a hotel in the middle of nowhere. It's all guys who went, of course. The place was stocked with beer, liquor, steaks and hookers."

"How often did he do this, Viktor I mean?"

"Whenever he had to. Whenever there was something big enough that he could make an extra million off it. There was more too. Other stuff he'd do."

"Graft? Payoffs?"

She nodded, lowered her head to her hand. "Beatings. Murders." She lifted her head and rested her chin on her hand. "Slip said he was sure Viktor had killed at least three people. I don't…"

She covered her eyes with her hand and started shaking her head from side to side.

"I don't understand all the killing that goes on in the world, all the hatred. Neither did Gabe, my husband. He spent every working day in the middle of it, and he never understood it either. I would say to him, 'Ask for a transfer to something else, robbery, fraud, even traffic.' But he wouldn't. Or couldn't. I think seeing all the ways that people hurt others, kill them and not even think about it sometimes, I think it was an endless train wreck to him and he couldn't stop watching it. From up close."

Arden waited a moment. Then: "What did Slip do with the money and his notebook? And why did he do it anyway? I mean, I can understand skimming the cash, but keeping all those notes? Why bother? And how long did it go on?"

"Since before you got here. He wanted out some day, but Viktor wouldn't have let him go. Slip had seen enough, heard enough. He was no angel, but… He'd need cash to go away, far away. He used to talk to me about it. He'd say soon we would have enough, him and I, to go away for a year or so, get lost somewhere while the police used his notes to investigate things and eventually shut Viktor down, get Viktor off the streets. He would talk about all the stuff he had that the police would fall over themselves to get. He'd hint about it to them, the police. Probably to Delby as well. I think he was looking for protection down the road, I don't know. He trusted Delby at first, but I think… I think Delby might have turned on him, looking for something to really hang Viktor with, put him away for years. All the risk would be Slip's, not the cop's. Or maybe Slip just wanted to cover his butt in case it all came down on Viktor and everybody with him."

"I heard Viktor say Slip had taken something besides money from him. He must've meant whatever was in the notes."

"He had some documents too. Stuff Slip picked up to prove what he'd been saying about Viktor." She looked at him abruptly. "How would he have known? How would Viktor know about them?"

"From Delby, who else? Delby was playing both ends, talking to both Viktor and Slip. He didn't give a damn about Slip. He probably got Slip to pass something along to him, something that would back up whatever Slip had been saying about Viktor. Then he'd use it to put pressure on Viktor, who'd figure that it could only have come from Slip. Where do you…"

He stopped, raised his hand. They listened to sounds from the beach for a moment. Waves crashing, children laughing, lake boats sounding whistles before entering the canal into the bay, then the ringing of Josie's doorbell. She stood to look through the window facing the front porch and said, "Oh, hell."

If there was one thing Harold Hayashida would believe for the rest of his life, the thing that he would be prepared to bet his career, his house and his pension on, it was this about women: They were not only more perceptive than men; they were more honest too.

"It's because we're more sensitive than you guys," Hayashida's wife explained to him. "More intuitive too," she added, which went along with being more sensitive, so it didn't add up to a lot. He just knew that when he needed a new angle on things, something to get the blinkers away from his eyes, it helped to discuss them with a woman.

"Yeah, it works," Walter Freeman said when Hayashida talked to him about it. "The way I see it, you talk to them and you start wondering what they look like naked, how they'd be in the sack. But you gotta pull yourself back to reality, and when you do, when you come back to dealing with serious stuff, things look different. You don't need a shrink to explain that. You'd get the same effect taking a break from trying to figure out quantum physics and try to imagine the Leafs winning the Stanley Cup. When you come back to reality, you see something you didn't see before."

Still, Freeman wasn't interested in bringing more women into the force, especially into homicide. "Remember that redhead we had here, two, three years ago?" he said. "Not bad looking, nice legs…"

"Sylvia," Hayashida had said, knowing where this was going.

"Remember what happened to her? She's on the job for what? Six months? And gets herself knocked up. Terrific. Then, after she costs us six months maternity leave, she says she's not coming back because now that she's a mother she can't deal with the stuff we handle. That was a hell of a lesson, wasn't it? She's okay wiping brains off a car until she gets preggo, and then she can't stand the idea of even wiping a nose anymore, unless it belongs to one of her own brats."

"Women change when they get kids," Hayashida tried to explain. "Makes them, I don't know, softer, more protective."

"Shoulda told that to my mother," Freeman said, draining his beer. "Softer? Listen, when I was fourteen years old I weighed a hundred and seventy-five, hundred and eighty pounds, and my old lady could still swat me across the head hard enough to detach my fuckin' ear. And even if they do change," pausing long enough to release a belch that sounded like a burst of machine gun fire, "even if they do change, that's my point. Men *don't* change. You and I are the same dumb bastards we were when got into this job. Nothin' to be proud of, okay, but we're predictable, right? Predictable's good. When you're building a team, predictable's damn good."

Like most homicide cops, Hayashida wouldn't discuss his work with his wife. General stuff, sure. He'd mention the idiots he encountered during the day, a few characters, sometimes the suspects they were running down. But not often. And not in detail. And never with the idea of asking her opinion of things, how he should act, what he should do when he was up against something he couldn't solve. Sometimes when he and everybody else at Central were getting headaches from banging their skulls against the wall, talking to a woman might have helped them find some other way of dealing with things. Trouble was, there were no women in Homicide, and other guys' wives were off limits.

But there was always Josie Marshall.

She took her time opening the door, but it was worth it. Tight white pants, knitted top, sandals with rhinestones, and he liked the blonde hair, who wouldn't? He said, "How you doing?" and she said she was fine and was there something he wanted? He said, "Just a chance to talk to a smart woman for a few minutes, somebody who could help me with what's been happening over at Tuffy's."

"Probably with a cup of tea thrown in too, right?" she said, stepping away from the door, leaving room for him to enter, so he did.

31

Hayashida had done this before, after Josie's husband was murdered on the beach outside her door. He had led the investigation into Gabe Marshall's murder, just about the only guy in homicide who found it difficult to believe that Gabe had shot himself in the head with his own weapon. Since then, he had found a reason to drop by now and then, see how Josie was doing and sometimes meet the current man in her life. He knew of two before Slip Winegarden, but Hayashida didn't believe Winegarden had moved in with her. Not like the Spaniard or Mexican, whatever he was, the guy called Chico. And some other guy who seemed pretty straight but was long gone and Josie wouldn't talk about him.

If he admitted it, and why the hell should he?, Hayashida's interest in Josie grew at least a little sexual after Gabe was murdered. Just a little, he told himself. Fantasy sexual. Like, just holding on to the feeling that you could if you tried, and that she would let you if you played things correctly. The fantasy was enough, he could settle for that. He didn't know if he would ever leave his wife for another woman, because he had yet to meet that woman. But if he did, she would be a whole lot like Josie, he was sure of that.

"I've got nothing to go with the tea," she said, leading him through the living room and into the kitchen.

"Tea isn't necessary," Hayashida said. He sat at the small table and looked around. Somebody had been here recently. Talk about women's intuition all you want, but his wasn't bad either. "Just need to talk about what's been happening at Tuffy's."

She sat opposite him. "God, I can't believe it. First Slip and now this."

"You knew him, right? You knew Wes Delby, didn't you?"

"Look…"

"You were his link with Winegarden. I figured it out. When Delby needed to meet Slip, you were the one who got the message and passed it on."

"Leave me out of this, okay?"

"How the hell do I do that?"

"Okay. He'd meet me, Delby would, on the beach."

"Where on the beach?"

"A bench down the way. Early in the morning. He didn't want to go into Tuffy's, didn't want people to see him there with Slip. They'd meet at other places. Hidden Valley Park, a place on Plains Road. I was never there and I never visited any of the places. I was just trying to do a favour."

"So you don't know what they talked about."

"I assume it was about the Russian."

"Delby mentioned the bench. It was the last place he met Slip."

"That's when I knew it was going to fall apart. When I got there that morning, Slip told me to go home. He said he'd meet Delby there himself, he didn't want to wait."

"Must've been desperate."

"He was scared shitless."

"About what?"

"About who. The Russian. Khrenov."

"He'd been feeding stuff to Delby, right? Things he picked up along the way, maybe notes, receipts? Probably skimming cash from Tuffy's too. Working the bar, not ringing everything up, just a few bucks now and then. You could hide eighty, a hundred on a good night." When she said nothing, just kept avoiding his eyes, he said, "Where is it?"

"Where's what?"

"Whatever Slip had on Khrenov. I don't give a damn about the money, but I need whatever Slip had that can put the Russian out of business."

"I don't know."

"Come on, Josie…"

She stood up and walked away to lean against the pantry. "I don't know and I didn't want to know. When I found out what he was doing I told him he couldn't come in this house any more, not for a visit, not even to use the john. I told him he was definitely not to hide any of the stuff he was taking from the Russian here. Then he asked me to keep it here and I told him not a chance. I said I wouldn't let him in here again, and I didn't." She looked away, then back at him. "He kept notes. In a red spiral-bound book like kids used in school before they got iPads and things. He wanted to show it to me once, what he had on Viktor, but I wouldn't even look at it. The less I knew, the better. That's when I told him to stay out of my house."

"So you'd go to Tuffy's to see him, maybe have a drink."

"Bacardi and Coke on the house. All I got from him. Almost all. He bought me a couple of things in the beginning, cheap jewellery. He'd pick up the tab for dinner at Tuffy's, and he gave me five hundred bucks for my old car out back, the one Chico bashed up, the little bastard."

Hayashida looked out the window at the wreck. "What'd he want with it?"

"Said he'd get it towed away and sold for scrap. Said the engine was probably still good, people would pay for the parts. Whatever he got over five hundred he would split with me fifty-fifty."

"What do you know about Arden, the guy who took Slip's place at Tuffy's?"

"Not much." She sat down again. "Do you think he had anything to do with Slip's murder?"

"Probably not. I think he was set up by Viktor as a patsy, somebody he could send us after if he needed to. This Arden guy, he's not the kind who should be running with Khrenov and the rest of them. Do you know about how he almost broke a guy's neck, turned him into a paraplegic after he'd heard the guy had raped and beat up his sister? Then he finds out the sister marries the same guy while her brother's in prison for it? I mean, Jesus, talk about being handed a bad deal. Anyway, I don't think he had anything to do with Delby being shot last night either. Except for beating the crap out of Heckle Dunne."

"Where is he, this Dunne guy?"

He thought about that for a moment. "Never mind him. Where's this Arden guy?"

"I don't know."

"And if I ask if I can look around the place, you'll say no."

"I'd just say you can't without a warrant."

Hayashida stood up. "I'm not suggesting Arden's a bad guy. I don't think he is. But if he doesn't contact us by tomorrow, I'll report him in violation of his parole and he knows what that means. You tell him that, okay?"

Josie stood up to follow him through the living room to the front door. "If I see him."

Hayashida left without looking back, without saying more.

"I took my stuff down there with me," Arden said when she opened the basement door. He was holding the black plastic garbage bag he had brought from Tuffy's. "It was sitting right there on the floor in the living room. I grabbed it and took it with me. Good thing too. And I saw that shotgun and all the fishing tackle that guy left. Remington pump action. Nice gun, but maybe you should lock it up or…"

She turned and walked away.

"I was below you when the two of you were talking in the kitchen," he said, following her. "I heard every word, like I was up here with you. What'd he want, anyway? Just to see if I was here, right?"

"I guess." She started filling the kettle, then set it aside. To hell with tea. She opened a cupboard, pulled out her bottle of brandy, poured some in a glass and drank it, wincing as it went down.

"What's wrong?" Arden walking toward her but she turned away, shaking her head.

"You know when you were talking about happiness?" she said.

"And you said that we only realize we were happy when we can look back and say 'I was really happy then'? Well, I keep looking back to living here with Gabe, and don't tell me we should all keep looking ahead instead of backwards. I've heard all that and it's probably true. But I can't help it. I look at what I am now and where I am and who I've got, which is hardly anybody at all, and…"

She didn't turn away this time when he came to her. He put his arms around her and she folded herself into them, her face against his shoulder. They stood that way, Josie letting tears flow, Arden staring out at the garden, beyond the forlorn wrecked car to the lake, listening to the sounds of water and people.

When she lifted her face from his shoulder she found his mouth and kissed him openly. One of them, it didn't matter which, began moving toward the living room and the stairs, up to the bedroom, Josie making sure the front door was locked and then, in her bedroom, closing the blinds.

A hundred years ago, wealthy families from the city built homes on the beach strip for the sand and the water, but mostly for the breezes off the lake that cooled their bedrooms at night, gentle and reliable natural air conditioning. They lived there from June to September, bringing servants and gardeners with them, inspiring the café and dining room christened Tiffany's, which evolved into Tuffy's.

So much had changed and the summer residents were long gone, but the onshore breezes remained on hot afternoons like this one, pushing the lowered blinds aside to enter through open windows of the second floor and into the bedroom where Arden undressed her, pulling the knitted top over her head and unfastening the white pants, each watching the others' eyes.

When she lay with her head on his chest, listening to his heart regain its normal beat and his breathing slow to a more gentle rhythm, he said, "I really didn't expect this to happen."

She said, "Surprise, surprise."

"Two surprises? What's the other one?"

She smiled and closed her eyes.

Goose counted the hours of sleep he'd had since yesterday morning, and it added up to two and a half, maybe three. He needed something to help him keep moving, keep his head clear. Was a time, ten years ago, when he'd be able to go all night, with or without drugs, just keep his ass in gear and his eyes open, and now...

Viktor should be driving, not him. Viktor didn't like to drive himself. Viktor preferred to be driven, mostly by young girls wearing short skirts, sitting beside him so he could reach them with his catcher's-mitt hands, the two of them grinning and staring straight ahead, nobody knowing what they were doing.

Goose had seen it, riding in the back of the Chrysler and in Viktor's Escalade. One time in the Escalade, the girl before Natalka had been driving, the one with long hair and great legs, the hell was her name? They were stuck in heavy traffic on the expressway, moving at walking speed, the Russian's left hand inside her panties and the girl biting her lip so she wouldn't laugh. Goose was in the back, knowing what was happening and he looked up through the open sunroof to see a bus alongside them full of tourists riding into Toronto for their first taste of Canadian life. They were looking right down into the Escalade on the driver's side, watching Viktor and the girl, what was her name, Tanya, Terry, something like that. Twenty, thirty men and women, crawling over each other to look into the Escalade and see the Russian's hand up the girl's skirt.

Goose had said, "Viktor, there's a bus beside us and a bunch of Chinese are watching everything you guys are doing," which made Viktor laugh like hell and made Tanya, or whatever her name was, close her legs so fast and tight that Viktor claimed later, telling about it and laughing, that she nearly broke two of his fingers...

"Slow down, slow down...," he heard Viktor say now, and Goose let his foot off the accelerator. He was driving down Beach Boulevard on the beach strip, not remembering that he had turned off the highway and crossed the lift bridge over the canal. How the hell did that happen?

He drove more slowly to Tuffy's, swinging into the parking lot and turning off the engine. Viktor had been looking around as they approached, like it was the first time he'd come here.

"Early," Viktor said, looking at his watch. "Not four o'clock yet." Through the front windows of the dining room he saw Harold Hayashida staring out at him.

"Listen," Goose said. "You don't need me in this, whatever the cop's gonna talk about. Why don't I crawl in the back seat and grab some sleep, okay? I mean, I'm nearly falling over here."

Viktor already had his door open and one foot on the ground. "Don't be pussy," he said. "Come in, sleep later."

Goose rested his hands on the steering wheel and his head on his hands. He'd never been so tired in his life. When this was over, when all the crap of this day had ended, he would find a place to hide and sleep for a week, and to hell with the Russian.

32

Viktor was headed for the bar but Hayashida cut him off, saying they should talk in the kitchen where they could close the doors and have some privacy. "Be better if we didn't have anybody with us," he said. "Unless you've got a lawyer," quickly adding, "but you won't need one."

Looking around, counting four uniformed officers he could see, Viktor shrugged and tilted his head, signalling Goose to stay in the dining room, which was fine with Goose.

"Prefer to do it in the office," Hayashida said over his shoulder, "but forensics wants it left untouched for another day maybe. I'll go in there later and get you a receipt for the money." He pushed the door open and stepped aside, extending an arm to the Russian.

"What money?" Viktor said, walking past him. "For what?"

"Your money. In your safe from last week. I used a warrant to open it. You want to see the warrant, I'll get it for you. Your guy Arden put the money there like he's supposed to. Have you seen him lately, by the way?"

Viktor grunted and shook his head, sitting down at a table near the stainless steel counter where the dishes were prepared before being carried into the dining room.

Hayashida walked to the doors leading in and out of the kitchen, making sure both were closed. "We got the combination of the safe from Miss Darby, who seems to know everything going on around here. Good worker, I'll bet. You get this place going again and if your man Arden heads back to prison, maybe you should make her the manager." He pulled his chair closer to the Russian, able to look him straight in the eye.

"I will sell," Viktor said, looking around the kitchen. "This place, gives me nothing but headache. Let somebody else have headache, not me."

"Up to you." Hayashida took his notebook from an inside pocket of his jacket. "Anyway, I need you to tell me what Cormac Hecla Dunne was doing here yesterday. That was his real name, Heckle's. In case you weren't aware of it. Why was he here?"

Viktor stared back as though deciding whether to answer. Then: "I do not know."

"Some people say he was here to take money from the safe in the office."

"He wants to rob me, why does he shoot police detective?"

"We understand it was a case of mistaken identity."

Viktor smiled, looked around. "Maybe he thinks detective is me, shoots me to get my money?"

"Viktor."

"What?" Looking at the detective.

"The reason I asked you in here alone wasn't to keep other people from hearing what you said. It was to keep other people from hearing what *I'm* going to say."

Which got the Russian's attention. "Tell me what you want to say."

Hayashida pulled his chair closer to Viktor's, close enough that the Russian leaned away. "You might think you are one smart Cossack," Hayashida said, "but I'm telling you that you are a fucking dirt bag, and I am going to put your fat hairy ass in prison as soon as I possibly can. We've got Delby's notes, okay? We know what he told you and what you told him, we know that you and Delby got together to trade information, and we know that somewhere along the line Winegarden got his balls caught up in all the stuff you were talking about, the stuff in Delby's notes. Delby must have spilled something to you, something you'd know he could only get from Winegarden. That's why Winegarden was killed, for passing along details from Delby, stuff he probably squeezed from Slip, stuff you knew would put your ass in a sling if Delby passed it on to us. And there's the money we suspect Winegarden had been skimming from you. Must have pissed you off royally."

Viktor smiled, looked away.

Which made Hayashida almost lose it, his voice getting louder. "Then Heckle Dunne tries to steal your money. He winds up killing a cop, and you know that's going to bring a ton of crap down on you from us, the stupid bastard thinking he can do something like that, which is why the blood on the pillow in that motel room near the airport is Heckle's and nobody else's, *sit the fuck down!*" He put a hand on the Russian's shoulder, saying it so loud that Viktor closed his eyes and turned his head away.

"This I don't need to hear," Viktor said, sitting straighter in the chair. "You bring me here, all this way, to tell me lies about myself? You are nothing to me."

"Where's Heckle Dunne?"

"I do not know. You tell me he is dead. How do you know that?"

"How about your guy Arden? He disappeared this morning. Where'd he go?"

"I do not know about him. You say he's dead too maybe?"

"Who shot Slip Winegarden?"

"You are detective. I am not."

"What would you think if I brought Goose in for questioning about this stuff?"

"I think you would be wasting time." Viktor actually smiled a little, feeling better now. "You say you know what I know, about Heckle and Slip, okay? We are both, what? We are both dummies about these things. Slip, he was in bad way, sad man, no friends. Heckle, he was murderer, you tell me that. Somebody shoot Heckle maybe? I think so. I am without him and I am without Slip. So now I sell this place, save my money, it is headache for somebody else, okay? Arden, hero man, he is out of job now for sure. And you talk of money," holding up his index finger. "Give it now and I go. Keep talking to me, I call lawyer and we wait, okay? No matter to me."

Hayashida stood up. "Let's get your money for you to count. I'll give you a receipt. When the case is settled you can have your money. Maybe."

Viktor followed the detective out of the kitchen on their way to the office. Goose, who had planned to sleep in one of the booths near the window, had yet to close his eyes. Seeing the Russian now, Goose called his name softly.

"What?" Viktor said, walking behind the detective.

Goose glanced at Hayashida. "I need to talk to you," he said, holding a folded newspaper in his hand for Viktor to see.

"You coming?" Hayashida stopped and turned back to Viktor. "I can dump the cash in the evidence file and you'll need an injunction to get it back. If we'll let you. Otherwise, you better move your ass."

Viktor waved Goose away and followed the detective into the office. "You gotta see this," Goose called to Viktor's back.

The window that Heckle had fired through to shoot Delby was covered with heavy plywood, and much of the room was black with fingerprint powder.

Hayashida knelt in front of the safe, turning the knob while reading the combination that Charm had given him. "I'd advise you to have the combination changed, you plan to keep using this thing," he said, not looking up. "But that's up to you." He turned the lever, pulled the door open and removed a tin box from an inner shelf. He stood up, placed the metal box on the desk and opened it. Inside, covering the money, most of it tens and twenties, were several sheets of paper.

"Here's your receipt." He held the sheets of paper up, began to read them. "It's for the exact amount opened by our people during the investigation yesterday and this morning. You want to count it and you agree with the figure, sign each copy of the receipt. Maybe someday you'll get the money. Maybe not. It's up to you."

"Don't need to count," Viktor said. "Leave it here, Goose picks up tomorrow maybe." He looked into the open safe. "What's other stuff?"

Hayashida looked at the papers in his hand again. "Says you've got staff names and addresses, account numbers with suppliers, tax information, deed, other crap you need or don't need in there, in the safe. We're seizing it under a warrant linked to Delby's killing. You sign where it says, agree that nobody in the investigation took something that wasn't yours, and you're on your way." Hayashida smiled at Viktor. "And you know, you just gotta *know*, that this isn't where it ends. We'll be back at you, either here or in Toronto, with or without a warrant. You need a pen?"

The cooling breeze on naked sweaty skin. Looking around at the female touches in the room, flowers and pictures and small porcelain animals. The sounds of people on a beach in summer, none of them sad or threatening. The feel of her body against him. Her voice.

"You never told me what you're going to do." Lazy, her eyes on the ceiling.

"About what?"

"About the rest of your life. You tell me your parole officer is ready to send you back to prison if you don't quit your job at Tuffy's, and you said Hayashida wants you to keep working there."

"You forgot the Russian."

"What's he going to do?"

"I don't know."

"Why did you throw all your stuff into the plastic bag, your clothes and things?"

He smiled at that, turned to her and said, "I was running away from home, like I did when I was eight years old."

"How far did you get when you were eight years old?"

"About two blocks."

"That's as far from here to Tuffy's."

"You know, I think you're right."

"What happened? When you ran away from home the first time?"

"I went back. On my own."

"And this time?"

He laid his arm across his eyes. "I don't know." When she said nothing, when she didn't invite him to stay with her beyond this moment, he stood and walked naked to the window, pulling the blind aside to look out at the lake and down at the garden. "Slip really gave you five hundred dollars for that car?"

"Should I have asked for more?"

"Why?"

"To get more money for it."

"I mean why did he buy it from you?"

"I told you. He said he'd sell it for parts and scrap or whatever they do with cars that don't work anymore, and we'd split the profit."

"Did he try to sell it?"

"I don't know. What difference does it make?"

"Is it locked?"

"Slip got the keys when I sold it to him. I think it's locked. I tried to get in it once, just to sit behind the wheel and remember what it was like to drive my own car, but Slip locked it up."

"He ever use them, the keys?"

"For what?"

"To get into the car." He walked to the chair where his clothes were.

"I saw him unlock the door a couple of times, after I wouldn't let him into the house. Once I saw him sitting behind the wheel, his head down. I thought he was sleeping. I was in my bedroom, getting dressed. A few minutes later he was gone. Didn't come to the house, which was fine with me. Where are you going?"

He was pulling his pants on. "I saw a sledge hammer in the basement. Mind if I use it?"

"Answer me, I have question," Viktor said, walking out of the office ahead of Hayashida.

"If you're wondering about the safe, I'm the only one who has the combination besides Miss Darby," Hayashida said. "And your hero Arden. We'll lock the place up when we leave and keep it that way, until the court tells us to hand it back to you."

Viktor shook his head. "Why am I here? You bring me here, say I should hurry, and for what? To sign paper, count little bit of money?"

"Kind of rattled your cage, did I? Good." Hayashida looked around. The closest person was Goose, standing at the entrance to the dining room, a folded copy of the newspaper in his hand, staring at Viktor. Hayashida lowered his voice. "I know you did Slip Winegarden, and I'm pretty sure I know why. And I don't believe for a minute that the blood in that motel belongs to anybody but Heckle Dunne, which means you're involved in that too, all right? I'm just letting you know what I know, Viktor."

"Stupid man." Viktor smiled and looked away, through the windows toward the beach.

"You're telling me I'm wrong?"

"For saying what you think. I already know what you think and I do not care, but I thank you for telling me."

"You know I'm right, and now you'll need to take some risks. That's why I got you over here. To remind you what I know and what I'll do."

Viktor turned his back and walked away, toward Goose who had been shifting from foot to foot as though waiting outside a locked bathroom. Goose let Viktor walk past him, then stepped in front and opened the newspaper. The front page shouted COP MURDERED ON BEACH STRIP above a picture of Wes Delby. "I've seen this guy," he hissed at Viktor, shoving the newspaper toward him. "On the beach strip, with that blonde Slip was banging. I saw them talking together, him and her. She *knew* him, this Delby cop, and she sure as hell knew Slip. He used to be there lots, at her place. She's the one that's gotta be holding whatever Slip had on us, I'll bet my ass on it."

Viktor looked over the top of the newspaper in his hand to see Hayashida climb into his car and drive away.

Arden hadn't noticed the spare tire before. It was leaning against the fence almost hidden behind uncut grass. It belonged, he was sure, in the Honda, and seeing it there, out of the Honda for some time, grass growing around it, told him where to look.

It took three swings with the sledgehammer to break the glass on the driver's side door. Arden reached in and unlocked it, climbed in and sat in the driver's seat, looking around. The car smelled of dust and age and the murky aroma that trapped air gets when heated in the summer. He found the release handle beside the driver's seat, pulled it up and stepped outside again, walking to the back of the car where the trunk lid sat partially open.

Inside were two cheap suitcases. He lifted one, feeling the weight within it and told himself, no, it's too easy, opening the suitcase anyway, pulling the zipper to look inside and seeing bundled yellowed newspapers. He opened the other luggage as well. Inside were more newspapers, and riffling through them he found no documents. Putting the luggage on the grass he lifted the carpet from the floor of the trunk, opened the cover of the spare tire compartment, looked inside and said aloud, "Slip, you sly son of a bitch."

33

Charm Darby's telephone number was on the list in the safe, the one with the names and addresses of Tuffy's employees. Viktor told Goose to call her, Goose knew her, she wouldn't be afraid to talk to him maybe.

When she answered the phone and Goose gave his name, he could tell right away that Charm was upset, scared to say anything until Goose calmed her down, saying he was at Tuffy's with Viktor and they were offering her the job of managing Tuffy's when it opened again in two, three weeks.

"I can't," she said, and when Goose asked why she said she just couldn't, that's all.

"You're thinking that one guy, who was the manager, offed himself and the next guy's disappeared and a cop was shot in the manager's office last night, right?" Goose said. "Listen, I understand. That's not good. It scares the hell out of you. Well, guess what? It scares the hell out of *me*."

"I've got two kids," Charm said, her voice shaking. "You know, it's nice of Viktor to offer and all that, but I can't, I just can't."

"You're right, sweetheart," Goose said, looking at Viktor, waiting for Viktor's nod of approval. "We understand, Viktor and me. He's with me now, nodding his head. He knows what you mean. He likes you for that. You got kids, they come first, you can't take chances. By the way," Goose raised his eyebrows while watching Viktor, "you're still on salary and will be for a month, maybe more, okay?" Viktor nodded, agreeing. "So don't worry about making the rent for a few weeks, 'cause you're covered."

Charm said, "Thank you," and Goose said, "And when you're looking for another job, you list Viktor and me, we'll give you the best damn reference you'll ever have, good enough to get you a job running a resort back in Jamaica. Isn't that right, Viktor?" Another nod, another "Thank you" from Charm.

"Listen, you know that blonde from around here, used to come in and have a drink with Slip now and then?" Charm said nothing, so Goose went on, "Josie something? Marsh, Marshall? You know her? Where can we find her, talk to her?"

"Why…" Charm began. "Why would you want to see her?"

"Offer her a job. I mean, Viktor needs to find somebody to run the bar here when all the shit settles and he can get the place up and running, and I thought she'd be good at it, if she's interested."

"She wouldn't want it."

"Well, maybe you can let her decide after Viktor and me talk to her. Where's she live? I mean, I know it's down here on the strip and you know practically everybody here. What's her address, telephone number?"

"I don't know."

"Aw hell, Charm. Don't give me that. Look, we just want to offer her a job. She says she doesn't want it, that's cool. We go back to Toronto, run some want ads, Viktor'll find a dozen people. We'd rather have somebody from the beach strip who knows everybody, knows the place. So just give us the address. You don't know the address, I'll bet you can tell us where the house is, what it looks like."

Goose could hear Charm breathing through the receiver.

"Charm, sweetie, you going to talk to me or are you going to sit there pretending we're not on the other end of the line, Viktor and me?"

"She's a good person." Charm sounded on the edge of tears, like she was going to fall apart and Goose would be able to hear every piece of her drop off. "Josie's good, she wouldn't want ..."

Goose figured she was about to say Josie wouldn't want anything to do with him and Viktor. He said, "Just a minute," put his hand over the receiver and watched Viktor, whose face was a furrowed mask, before removing his hand and saying, "Viktor wants to know the names of your kids and maybe how old they are, maybe he'll send them a present, okay? You're still in the east end, down on Kenilworth?"

The tears started. Through them, Charm said, "Please, Goose..."

"Where's she live, Charm?"

"A two-storey house down near the canal, a block from it. On the lake. Yellow with brown trim. There's a big brown fence between the yard and the beach. Goose, Josie's got nothing to do with Slip or anything else. Not anymore. She just drops in for a drink maybe once a week..."

"Good," Goose said. "We'll thank her for her patronage," and hung up.

When he gave Viktor the description of Josie's house, Viktor stood and said "Let's go."

Goose remained sitting for a moment, trying to remember when he had ever felt so tired and so dirty.

"That's the book," Josie said. The red wire-bound notebook sat on top of the heavy waxed cardboard box Arden brought in from the old Honda. He set both on the kitchen table. The words WADMAN FRESH ATLANTIC LOBSTER were printed on the sides of the box.

"We'd get a couple of these at Tuffy's every week, on Fridays," Arden said, meaning the waxed cardboard box. "Dozen live lobsters inside, flown in from Newfoundland," unfolding the cardboard flaps. "Now what do you suppose this is?" He pulled a handful of fat white business envelopes from the box, set them aside and opened one, removing a stack of twenty-dollar bills before putting it back and flipping open the other envelopes.

"That's what he was putting in the car," Josie said. "Cash from the bar register."

"Probably from other places too. You see cash, you don't ring it up or you ring up part of it, twenty dollars, forty dollars less, and keep the difference. Nobody knows. What's in the book?"

"Some stuff he told me." Josie was turning pages. "In the beginning. A lot of stuff he didn't." She closed it and handed the notebook back to him. "Copies of emails. Don't know where he got them. Looks like dates and names and money Viktor passed around to get supplier kickbacks."

Arden opened the book, ran his eyes down Slip's neat writing in a range of ink colours. "Where'd he learn all this stuff?"

"He'd go to Toronto once a week for meetings." Josie sat at the table, staring out the window at the garden. "They'd have meals, drinks, sometimes women. A big boy's club. He said they'd talk about what they were doing or going to do. Goose, Viktor, couple of guys managing the construction projects, their accountant and a bunch of others would be there. They'd sit and brag about it. Slip said they couldn't help bragging how they were paying off all kinds of people in the business, some of them union guys. He'd listen and laugh along with them. Then he'd come back here and write down everything he'd heard about what happened, what was going to happen…"

"He really planned to use this stuff, didn't he? Figured he'd put Viktor away, keep the money…"

"Shhhh." She stood up. "Viktor's here."

He looked to see Viktor Khrenov in the back yard, walking along the line of the fence, his eyes on the Honda, Goose tottering a few steps behind. Arden said, "Jesus."

"Should I call the police?"

Arden, holding up a hand and watching, said, "What'll they do? Charge them with trespassing? Stay here. I can talk to Viktor. He's got no reason to be upset with me." He walked to the door, then turned. "Quick," he said, pointing at the lobster box and the booklet, "hide that stuff somewhere."

"You see what I tell you?" Viktor was standing at the back of the Honda, looking into the trunk, the newspapers from the luggage tossed aside,

"You watch for little things. You say, 'Why Winegarden keep keys to Honda when he doesn't drive Honda, eh?' You did that before, we save lot of time. Look in his room, everywhere, and here it is." Then, looking up, "And here is famous hero, tell us everything."

"What's up, Viktor?" Arden said, looking around as he walked toward them.

"He is very cool, eh?" Viktor said, looking at Goose, who moved to one side, blocking Arden's path to the gate leading to the beach. "Where you been, hero? People looking for you. Popular guy, eh? Policemen, women, Goose and me, want to know where you are, nobody knows."

"Only been gone a day."

"Good day for you, eh?" Viktor leaned against the Honda. "Yesterday you beat up Heckle, he comes back to shoot you, shoots cop instead, now you have new home, good looking blonde lady inside."

"What do you guys need?" Arden said.

"We need what you got," Goose said. "Out of there," pointing at the open trunk of the Honda.

"What, that old spare tire? You guys can have it. Hell, you can have the whole car." Arden took a step toward the tire leaning against the fence, and Viktor kicked him on the side of the knee, hard and perfectly aimed. Arden collapsed on the grass, pulling his injured knee to his chest, grimacing in pain.

"In Russia, we shoot knees," Viktor said. He drew his foot back and kicked Arden's ribs, rolling him onto his side. Arden managed to open his eyes and through a cloud of red he saw Viktor standing over him with an automatic pistol in his hand, pointing it at Arden's head. "No more kicks," Viktor said. "Not good for shoes. Nice shoes, eh?" He raised one of his Italian loafers over Arden's head and Arden raised his hands to his face.

"We're going inside," Goose said. "Look for what was in the car. You come with us or you stay here with both kneecaps shot off. Your choice."

Arden said, "Help me up," and Viktor turned his back, looking around, making sure nobody was watching while Goose bent from the waist and extended a hand.

They heard the sound as soon as Arden opened the door into the kitchen, footsteps going upstairs and a door slamming.

"Who's here?" Goose said.

Arden closed his eyes, wondered how it had come to this.

"Hello," Viktor barked, closing the kitchen door and locking it behind him. "Come down and we talk, okay?"

"Is it the blonde?" Goose asked.

Arden said nothing.

Goose said to Viktor, "We'd better get her. She could be on the phone up there."

Viktor, who had been looking around the kitchen, handed Goose the automatic and walked past him. "Shoot him, you need," he said, and reached to pull one of the knives from the wooden block, a carving knife, dropping it to choose another, this one a broad-bladed butcher's knife, a German-made Henckel with a long stainless steel blade.

"You know where the shit is," Goose said to Arden when Viktor began climbing the steps to the second floor. "You tell us now and I'll call Viktor back. We'll take it and get the hell out of here."

"No, you won't," Arden said. When he finds her, Arden kept asking himself, what'll Viktor do to her?

"Look, I'm tired of this crap, okay?" Goose was saying. "Truth is, I'm tired as hell totally. I just want to get back to Toronto and get a good night's sleep."

"You kill Heckle?"

"I ain't never killed anybody," Goose said, and he looked up at the sound of Viktor's voice above them, the Russian on the upper floor calling out, "Lady, come see me, okay? Come talk to me, pretty lady," followed by a sudden crash.

Viktor had kicked in the door of the front bedroom, lifting his foot to the level of the latch and splintering the door jam. They listened to his footsteps cross to the far wall and a closet door being yanked open, then more footsteps, faster now, to the rear of the house, overlooking the beach, Josie's room. Arden pictured the room, the window open and the breeze off the lake toying with the drawn blinds, the unmade bed, the strewn clothing, the tilted lampshade. "You are here, eh?"

Viktor called, and the closet door in the larger bedroom opened and slammed shut again.

"If you don't want to kill anybody," Arden said, "get the hell out while you can."

Goose said, "Fuck you," looking back at the ceiling to follow Viktor's footsteps as they walked back through the upstairs hall. When they stopped the rattle of a doorknob could be heard, followed by loud knocking on a door.

"Hey, Goose," Viktor shouted, talking more to Josie behind the bathroom door than to Goose. "She is having pee or maybe shower. You shoot hero and then maybe come join us, okay? You, me and blonde. Shower wake you up, you will feel good, eh? Okay with you, Miss? Two big men, give you a good time, eh? Make you feel young again. Open door now, we get started. You don't open door, makes no difference. No difference to me, big difference to you, eh?" Then, after a beat, Viktor called, "Okay."

Then two nightmarish sounds.

The first was familiar—Viktor kicking in another door with his foot, breaking the latch and shattering the door jam. A heartbeat later, the house shook with the next sound, this one louder and sharper. Goose and Arden both knew what it was, Goose not believing it.

34

Had Goose not been so deprived of sleep he might have acted differently, quicker and more wisely. The second sound from upstairs, the one that followed Viktor's shattering the bathroom door with his foot, told him all he needed to know, because he had heard that sound before. Now he stood listening to new sounds from above, different sounds, human sounds.

Josie's screams were the loudest, a stream of staccato screams, short and piercing. She was screaming not just from fear but from something else as well. Arden counted five screams. When they stopped he and Goose could hear other sounds, softer and falling in pitch, sounds that could only have been made by Viktor.

Goose stood half-turned from Arden, trying to understand what the sounds meant. He knew what they were. He just couldn't understand why he was hearing them.

With Goose turned away, Arden reached to wrap his arm around Goose's neck from behind, his arm under Goose's chin and Goose's neck in the crook of his elbow. Placing his knee against the small of Goose's back he prepared to pull and turn, pressuring the fifth vertebrae, twisting it until it snapped. But pain stopped him, the pain from the knee holding his weight and from the ribs on his left side, where Viktor had kicked him as Arden lay on the ground. His knee began giving away when he shifted his weight and his ribs felt like somebody had planted a knife between them. Arden tried to tell Goose he could break Goose's neck right there and then, do it with one move, he'd done it before. Instead he groaned, and when his arm dropped away Goose twisted and turned to look at Arden, annoyed and confused.

"The hell are you doing?" he said. "Are you nuts?" The Beretta was still in his hand, held at his side. All he had to do was raise it and point it at Arden, which is what he started to do as Arden backed away, stepping out of the Beretta's line.

"Look, you can still go," Arden said.

"Like hell I will," Goose said, and when a woman's voice behind him said "Hey," he turned to see Josie at the bottom of the stairs with the Remington in her hands, the muzzle aimed at Goose's stomach but wavering, just like Josie was wavering, standing there with blood splatters on her face and on the open toes of her sandals.

Arden said, "Tell him to drop the damn gun."

Josie said, "Drop the damn gun."

Goose let go of the Beretta and Arden stepped around him, kicking the small black gun across the floor.

Arden said, "Now tell him to get the hell out."

Josie said, "Get the hell out."

Goose might have argued, might have challenged Josie, might have done almost anything except what he did, hearing the gurgling sounds from upstairs and seeing the shotgun in Josie's steadying hands. What he did was hang his head, turn, and walk to the door leading to the garden, Arden following him until Goose, without speaking or looking back, let himself out the door and started walking through the garden toward the beach, just a guy taking a walk on a pleasant late summer's day.

Arden slammed the door and slid the dead bolt in place.

Josie put the gun on the table and stood with one hand on a chair, her head down, her eyes closed. Arden walked to her, preparing to hug her but she raised her hands to hold him off and said, "Don't," then changed her mind and reached out to him. "Thank god it worked," she said in his ear, and he asked "The gun?" and she said, "Scaring him off. I only had time to take one shell upstairs with me. The gun's empty."

He told her to sit down, and said she'd been wonderful before turning for the old landline telephone on the counter near the refrigerator. She gripped the sleeve of his shirt. "I didn't know what to do," she said. Her voice was steady now. "I was going to call 911 when I saw them out there kicking you, and Viktor holding the gun. I knew they wouldn't stay out there with you, they'd come in here, and calling 911 wouldn't stop them in time, they would kill both of us or at least you, out there by the car. I remembered the shotgun downstairs. I ran down and got it and grabbed some shells out of the box. I was going to load it down there, but I was so nervous I dropped most of them, and when I came up I only had one in my hand, and they were nearly coming in the door so I went upstairs and locked myself in the bathroom and loaded it in there, just the one shell."

He kissed her hair, got the telephone and brought it to her. "Call them now, 911," he said. "I'm going upstairs."

"Don't," she said. "Don't go up there. It's… My god, it's…"

"I'll dial it for you," he said, and took the phone from her and pressed the three buttons before handing it back.

His foot on the first step of the stairs, he heard her tell someone that she needed help, two men had come into her house and tried to kill her and she had shot one of the men and he was upstairs, probably dead and, yes, she would stay on the line but she wanted them to hurry.

Josie had been sitting on the toilet with the cover down when Viktor kicked the bathroom door open. She had managed to push the lone shell into the chamber, pumped it into position and sat there, the gun aimed at the door, listening to Viktor come up the stairs and kick doors open, inviting her to come out and join him and Goose. She knew what she would do when he kicked open the bathroom door in front of her. She didn't know what would happen, but she knew what she would do, as if she had a choice.

When the door flew open she saw the butcher knife in Viktor's hand and the smile on his face that was still there when she closed her eyes and pulled the trigger. The recoil twisted her elbow and she shouted in pain. When she opened her eyes she began screaming in horror at what she had done. Seated as she was, the gun had been aimed just below Viktor's waist. He had been unbalanced when she fired, the foot he had used to kick open the door not yet back on the floor. The shotgun blast that almost dislocated Josie's arm knocked the Russian onto his back, which is where Arden found him now, rolling his head from side to side, the blood pooling around and under him. Josie's bloody footprints traced a path down the short hall to the stairs.

"They're coming," she called up from the kitchen. "They're on their way," and Arden stood looking into Viktor's eyes, keeping his own away from the mess of blood and flesh between Viktor's legs. Viktor's head stopped moving long enough for him to fix his eyes on Arden's and they looked at each other until Josie called again, asking Arden to come downstairs and be with her, to please come down, which is when she finally began to cry.

Viktor was still alive when Arden turned and went down the stairs, steadying himself on the bannister.

It was nearly dusk by the time Hayashida arrived, whispering to one of the uniformed cops while watching Arden and Josie sitting at the kitchen table where they had been since the 911 response, drinking coffee and speaking in monosyllables. He followed the cop upstairs to look at Viktor's body and came down within a few minutes.

"You aim to do that?" he said when he sat at the table with them. He was wearing a golf shirt, jeans and sneakers. "I mean, there's self defence and then there's, I don't know, vengeance or something."

"I didn't aim," Josie said. "I was sitting there, he kicked open the door, I closed my eyes and pulled the trigger."

"She told that to the first cops who got here," Arden said, and Josie said, "Two or three times."

"You said he was after something, a notebook?"

"It was in the car," Arden said.

"What car?"

"The Honda," and Arden nodded toward the wreck at the back

of the garden, its trunk lid still open.

"What was it doing in there?"

"Slip Winegarden hid it there. He'd write down everything he heard from Viktor and Goose, anybody who talked about what was happening."

Hayashida said, "He told Delby he had a ticket away from the Russian, something to buy his way into witness protection or whatever. Where's the note book now?"

Josie said, "In the refrigerator," and Arden said, "Really?"

Hayashida opened the refrigerator. The red notebook was leaning against a carton of milk, propped up by an open jar of pickles.

Arden threw Josie a look, his eyebrows raised.

Hayashida began flipping through the notebook, walking back to the table. "Delby knew about this, but he never saw it," he said. He stopped, still standing, running his finger down one of the pages and thrusting out a bottom lip. "Lot of good stuff here," he said.

A uniformed cop came in from the garden, nodded at Arden and Josie, and whispered to Hayashida for some time before leaving.

"We found Goose," he said. "Sleeping on a hammock in somebody's backyard down the strip. What's with that guy? He on drugs or something? Anyway, he's giving up, getting smart. Even before he was told about the charges he'll be facing, first-degree murder for sure, he said he never killed anybody but he was around when stuff happened and he'll tell us about it. Wants a lawyer in the morning, probably do a plea deal and that's okay. Apparently we asked if he knew where Heckle was and he said yeah, he did, and he'd tell us where, and there was somebody else with him, some other body, but he didn't want to be around when we found them. The hell do you suppose that means?"

They carted Viktor's body out in a bag half an hour later, and one by one the cops and the photographer and forensics left the house. Arden and Josie remained sitting near the window, Arden nibbling at a muffin someone had brought them.

"You're not gonna want to stay here tonight, even if I could let you," Hayashida said. "You have any place to go?" Then, looking at Arden, he said, "Tuffy's is still out, by the way."

Both shook their heads and Hayashida said, "Why don't you head across the canal to the hotel on Lakeshore for the night? You can come back and get your personal things tomorrow, give you time to find a new place for each of you to live until everything shakes out. I can call and book a couple of rooms," and Josie said, without lifting her eyes from the table, "One will do."

Arden wasn't asleep, hadn't been asleep yet, when he sat up in bed and reached to shake Josie's shoulder.

"I'm awake," she said.

"Where's the money?" he said. "What'd you do with it?"

"I hid it."

"Where?"

"In the oven."

"Why?"

"Because it wouldn't fit in the refrigerator."

"Why didn't you tell Hayashida about it?"

"He didn't ask."

"Do you think he knows about it, about Slip skimming cash all these years?"

She sat up in bed, brought her knees close to her chest, wrapped her arms around them. "I don't know. What do you think?"

"I think we should tell him about it."

"Why?"

"Because it's not ours."

"Whose is it?" When he didn't answer she nudged him with her elbow. "Come on. Whose money is it? Slip's? He stole it remember? And he's dead."

"I get your point."

"Viktor's? Fat lot of good it'll do him. Besides, he was hiding loads of money from the tax collectors and using it to launder other money. Aside from the fact that he's dead too."

"I guess we give it to Hayashida."

"For what? Evidence? They don't need evidence."

"Maybe they need the money."

"Yeah, sure."

Arden thought for a while, shaping his words. "Look, I know what you're thinking, but you have to remember that I'm still on parole and the guy I report to, Renton, is a mean bastard."

Josie lay back and he settled beside her.

Josie said, "Hayashida told you he'd give the guy a detailed report, your parole officer, and get you off the hook."

"Okay, but if the word gets back to him that I took money that doesn't belong to me…"

"Whose money?"

"Don't start that again."

"I'm serious. Nobody knows it exists. Nobody knows who it belongs to. And nobody will be able to track it to you anyway. It was in my car, in my house, and if I'm caught spending it on anything, it won't affect you at all. But we won't be caught."

"Pretty sure of yourself."

"I'm not sure of a lot of things but I'm sure of that. I'm getting pretty sure of you too," placing her hand on his stomach. "God, I can't believe what I did tonight, killing a man." She reached to wrap him in her arm and he turned to her.

"You saved your life is what you did," he said. "Mine too." When he realized she had begun to cry he said, "Are you going to be all right?" and when she said she was, he said, "Do you want to talk about it some more?"

She shook her head and said that she would speak to a trauma counsellor, somebody one of the people who arrived with the 911 response team mentioned. "I'll work this through. I won't let this ruin my life. I promise."

"Who're you promising?"

"Myself. And you," sliding her arms up behind his neck and pulling him to her so she could kiss him.

Afterward they lay in silence, Arden's arm around her, listening to each other's breathing.

"Maybe we'll just take a little bit of the money," she said. "How much did you say might be there?"

"I'm guessing fifteen thousand, more or less"

"What if we… Okay, what if I took five to start. Maybe later I could tell them I found the box in the basement, Slip just put it there before I locked him out. I can get back in the house tomorrow, to pick up our clothes and things, and when nobody's looking I'll carry out the lobster box. Who's going to question me? How's that sound?"

"What would you do with it, the five thousand?"

"This is the good part. The house won't be ready to move back in for a couple of weeks, so where'll we go?" When he said nothing, she said, "I'd like to go to one of those resorts on a lake up north, a fancy place where you can order eggs Benedict for breakfast and there are chairs and lounges where you can sit on the pier or on the lawn and read books and order drinks, and at night you hear the loons when you're lying in bed, waiting to fall asleep. And the duvet covers are filled with down, so you leave the windows open for the cold fresh air. Maybe get one with a fireplace. The leaves'll be changing colour soon. Probably already started. Doesn't that sound good?"

"You want me to come with you?"

She said, "Yes. Yes, I do."

He lay quiet for a few moments, then said, "I think you'll need more than five thousand," which made her laugh and snuggle closer to him.

Another few moments of silence before Josie said, "I just thought of something."

"What?"

"All this time, even before I met you, when Slip told me you were coming, he called you Arden, the hero. That's what he said. 'You're gonna meet Arden the hero.' Even Viktor, that's what he called you. 'Arden hero,' he said. That's the name the people at Tuffy's gave you too. That and Arden what's-his-name."

"I'm not a hero, and please don't say I am."

"That's not the point."

"What's the point?"

"I've never heard anybody use your last name. Ever."

"You want to know my last name."

"Considering what we've been through and what we're talking about doing, don't you think I should know it?"

"You want to know my last name?"

"I insist."

So he told her.

THE END

BEACH BLUES

JOHN LAWRENCE REYNOLDS

The following is a special preview of *Beach Blues*, the third book in the acclaimed 'Beach' series.

1.

It took Bobby Blaine half an hour to walk down the beach from Josie's house to *Tuffy's*, including fifteen minutes spent on a bench facing the lake while he admired the view.

It was a lovely view. Three in the morning, the beach deserted, the water like glass, and a full moon low on the horizon. It looked even better thanks to the residual high Bobby had picked up from the weed he'd consumed in Josie's garden. She wouldn't let him smoke it in the house, wasn't even happy about having him toke up in her garden. *It ain't illegal anymore*, he reminded her, *they won't bust either of us for it*, but Josie told him if he wanted to get high around her he'd have to stick to margaritas. If he wanted to get high on grass, he'd better do it outside.

So he'd finished the joint sitting alone in her garden. He went back inside to say goodnight and maybe talk her into sharing her brass bed with him, but she was zonked out on her sofa. Bobby remembered when a margarita used to be the best pantie-remover next to a diamond ring or a bottle of Chanel. Maybe they still worked with younger honeys, but for women in their forties it seemed that alcohol just didn't cut it anymore.

He'd thought about kissing her goodbye while she slept, but that wouldn't do much. He decided to leave her there and tease her the next time they met, make her think something happened between them and she'd been too drunk to remember.

He turned out her lights, set the door latch to lock behind him, climbed the steps from the garden to the beach, and stood in the moonlight saying *Wow!*, first to himself, then aloud.

Later he'd tell himself if the view hadn't been so damn dreamy, if the night had been chilly instead of tropical, if Josie had been cooperative, if he hadn't been riding the high from the grass he'd copped, if all or any of this had happened, he wouldn't have been lost in the bullshit romanticism of the moon rising over the lake, standing there alone with no alibi and *Jesus!*, things would have changed so much for so many. Especially for Abbie.

Damn.

But he'd walked for a while in the sand, the moon so big and clear you could count the craters on it. Halfway back to Tuffy's he reached the bench Josie had paid for as a memoriam to her mother, and he sat on it, telling himself that making it with Josie would make this the best damn summer of his life, all thirty-seven years.

It was pretty damn good already. He'd gotten over Doris dumping him after nearly four years together in Montreal, worked out some new tunes, got a producer saying nice things about doing another recording session in the fall, and picked up this summer gig at Tuffy's, room and meals and three hundred cash a week plus tips. Hell, even his playing was getting better. He could just about make that bitch of a change from F-sharp to D Minor on the Dylan tune Josie liked to hear him play. He'd keep working on it and surprise her with it sometime. For now, he just wanted to sprawl on Josie's bench with the beach strip and the rising moon all to himself, just lie back and close his eyes.

He woke maybe ten minutes later to laughter, sitting up to see a couple silhouetted in moonlight at the water's edge, the girl giggling while the guy tried to pull her into the water. She kept holding back until he succeeded, screaming as she fell with a splash, the guy falling in with her then pulling her up and wrapping his arms around her. Bobby watched them hug in water waist-high, watched them kiss, and heard them speak to each other softly. Bobby could probably guess the words. They came out of the water arm in arm, and began walking back toward the canal, the way he had come.

What the heck was he doing on the bench? He had a room back in Tuffy's. He rose and resumed walking south, the moon shining impossibly bright on his shoulder. Reaching Tuffy's he expected to encounter Rollie the night watchman, but there was no one around. Light spilled from the kitchen. Maybe Rollie was in there making a coffee, or sipping a beer he'd heisted from the cooler.

Bobby pulled his room key out of his pocket, slipped it into the door marked STAFF ONLY, made sure it was locked behind him, and climbed the steps to the next floor, stumbling once and telling himself if he slipped and fell he'd just curl up and stay there, he was so damn sleepy.

His room was the second door on the right, a waterfront suite they'd told him, because it had a private bathroom and a picture window facing the lake. The bed was positioned to face the lake. A small upholstered chair and a simple pine set of drawers, left over from the time when Tuffy's had been a small hotel on the beach strip, eighteen rooms on three floors. Inside the room he considered raising the blind to let in the moonlight but he'd seen enough of it. He kicked off his shoes, stripped down to his shorts, tossed his clothes toward the chair, slipped under the thin top sheet and closed his eyes.

He had no dreams and heard nothing until a key slipped into the lock on his door and Maggie's voice said, *Well, aren't you the early riser?* as she entered to clean his room.

Bobby grunted and rolled over. Good thing he'd pulled the sheet over him. Maggie was a sweet old gal, and she'd probably not appreciate seeing his flabby body out in the open.

"You want me to open your blind, get the sun to wake you up?" He heard her cross the room to the foot of the bed. "Or you gonna sleep until you have to get up and play your gee-tar this afternoon?"

"Yeah, sure," Bobby said, which could've meant anything.

The window blind snapped up. Sunlight snuck its way under his eyelids, and he closed them tighter.

"You know, you might…" Maggie said, turning to look at him from the window side of his bed. He heard her take in a long breath, as though she were about to dive into deep water. He heard her shout "Bobby!" loud enough to make him open his eyes, sunshine or not.

"What have you done? *Lord Jesus, what have you done?*"

He sat up to see Maggie standing in her blue outfit, her hands alongside her head, staring at the floor in front of the pine cabinet on the other side of his bed. Bobby turned, leaning on an elbow to follow the line of her sight but seeing only Maggie's ass as she bent from the waist in front of him. She stumbled up, turned and ran to the door, saying *O my god, O my god,* opening the door and shouting *Help, help, somebody get up here, room two oh four, and call a doctor, somebody call a doctor!*

Bobby watched her run out of the room, thinking *Has Maggie gone nuts?* Then he rolled on his side again, to look down at the floor and stared into Abbie Bergen's open eyes, still blue but no longer shining. Her mouth, her pretty, rosebud mouth, was open wide enough for the tip of her tongue to emerge. A wire had been twisted so tightly around her neck that it had cut into her flesh, carving a necklace of blood that had spilled on the floor beneath her head.

Scrambling footsteps and voices began gathering in the hall outside his room, Maggie's voice stuttering *My god, my god, I can't believe it!* Bobby remained staring at the wire, which wasn't a wire at all but a *D'Addario* phosphor bronze standard weight E-string, the same ones he used on his battered Martin D40 that had been owned by Neil Young. Bobby had broken an E-string like it last night near the end of his final set on the patio, taking it off the Martin and tossing it aside, finishing his set without it. He'd collected his tips, shut down the stand, put his equipment away, and come to his room, this room, where people were leaning inside and saying *Holy shit!* and *What the hell?* He had placed the Martin in its case on top of the dresser, tossed the broken E-string in the wastebasket next to the chest of drawers and left for Josie's, who had promised him nachos and margaritas and intelligent conversation when he finished his gig, tossing the broken E-string in the wastebasket next to the chest of drawers.

Somebody had used the E-string as a garrote, a goddamn garrote, to choke the life out of pretty little Abbie, and what the hell was she doing in his room dead?

2.

"Cute little rascal, wasn't she?"

Drew Deforest stood in the hall outside room 204 watching the forensic team at work, three of them moving carefully around the body of Abbie Bergen. The guitar string remained in place. One of the team members shot close-up pics of the deep incision it had made in the young woman's neck. Others dusted the pine dresser and windowsills for fingerprints.

Standing on tiptoes, Deforest looked beyond the body and the bed, through the window that opened onto the beach. A dozen or so people stood behind the yellow plastic tape surrounding Tuffy's — some, ankle-deep in water, staring up at the building, pointing and talking.

"Sure as hell can eliminate rape as a motive." Deforest was watching the people on the beach but speaking to Charu Majumdar, the medical examiner who had formally declared the young woman dead and now stood next to Deforest, scanning the room and frowning. "But you'll check anyway, right Charlie?"

"I will, but yes, it's not likely." Majumdar shook his head. "Terrible thing. Terrible."

"Like you haven't seen worse." Deforest turned and stepped into the hall. "Where's the Polack?" he said to one of the uniformed cops.

"Downstairs with the bearded guy," the cop replied. "Want me to bring him up?"

Instead of answering, Deforest turned to look back into the room. "How long're you guys going to be?"

Without looking up one of the forensic team members said, "Ten, maybe fifteen minutes." She was kneeling, carefully removing the guitar string from the girl's neck.

"Let me know when you're leaving," he said to Majumder. "I'll be downstairs with the beard."

Two uniformed cops, including Sergeant Ken Katchanoski, who'd first responded to the call almost an hour ago, stood next to a booth at a window facing the lake. Bobby Blaine sat alone in the far corner, a glass of water in front of him. He was shaking, clutching a tissue in his hands and dabbing his eyes with it.

"What's he been saying?" Deforest said to Katchanoski.

"Not much." Katchanoski, tall and dark with a killer black mustache, turned to looked over at Bobby "Pretty upset."

"You check his hands?" Deforest keeping his voice low, his eyes on Bobby.

"They're clean. If he pulled the string on that girl he must've been wearing gloves." Katchanoski looked back at the detective. "Who the hell would do that and leave her there, in his own room?"

Deforest nodded. "Where's the staff? Anybody else show up?"

"They're in the kitchen. About eight of them. Three guys from Central're with them. Four more outside, securing the place."

"Charlie's coming down when they take the body out." Deforest began walking toward Bobby. "Let me know when he gets here. I want to talk to him."

"Yachetti and Kraftcheck are on their way," Katchanoski said.

"Send them into the kitchen to get statements," Deforest said over his shoulder. "And seize the security cameras. Let's get everything from ten last night on."

You thought you knew what it was like to be alone. That's what Bobby was thinking, scrunched as tightly as he could be in the corner of the booth, his head in his hands. He'd written blues songs about being alone and lonely, put a couple of them on CDs years ago. *On My Own In Okotoks*. That was kinda fun. And *The Last of the Love in Her Eyes*. It got some air play. Like he knew what being alone meant.

Thinking of the songs he'd written and recorded made it easier to deal with the nightmare he'd been living for the last hour. He'd been too stunned to scream, too horrified to do anything but stare at the body on the floor where it had been, it *had* to have been, on the other side of the bed when he came back from Josie's six, seven hours ago. He had been standing over Abbie with one arm outstretched, leaning against the wall for support, trying to convince himself he was dreaming, that this was a grass-inspired hangover dream, when Charm arrived and screamed *Bobby, what the hell have you done?* Somebody else, it had to be Carter from the kitchen, muttered *You son of a bitch!* Somebody screamed, *Get away from her!* when he began to kneel beside Abbie and somebody else warned from the hall, *The cops are on the way*.

He'd stood to put on his jeans and everybody in the hall made room for him when he left, watching him walk to the back steps, crying and shaking his head, saying *It wasn't me, it wasn't me*. No one spoke to him. When he sat on the landing alone, no one approached him.

The first cop to arrive, the sergeant with the black mustache, nudged Bobby with his toe and asked if he was the guy who'd slept in the room with the body, as though it was some kind of kinky act, some kind of, what's the word? Necrophilia or something. Kill a beautiful girl like Abbie and fall asleep with her on the floor beside him. Who the hell does that? Bobby had said *Yeah, he was*, and the mustache had taken him by the arm and marched him downstairs, almost shoving him into the bar and telling him to wait there, saying he could have a glass of water and warning him to keep his goddamn mouth shut until he was asked some questions. Bobby's face was wet with tears that wouldn't stop and his body wouldn't stop shaking.

Now he looked up to see some new guy walking toward him, and you'd have to be deaf, dumb and blind not to know he was a detective. The guy's head was a little too large for his body, a square face under fair hair cut short and standing up, a brush cut they used to call it, and he was smiling, a tight smile that had nothing to do with being happy.

Wearing a sharp suit, beige over a plain blue shirt, a lump under the jacket up near the left armpit.e waited form

"Your name's Bobby Blaine?" The detective sat opposite Bobby, who nodded and drew his arm across his eyes.

"My name's Deforest. Anything you need?"

Bobby shook his head.

"How long you had that beard?"

Bobby stared back, thinking *He wants to talk about the beard?* "I don't know." Bobby shrugged and looked away. "Since I was about twenty, I guess."

"Looks good." Deforest sat back, looked around. "You work here, right?"

Bobby nodded. He still felt sick, still felt like he would throw up.

"Hear you're a musician, singer. When do you do your number?"

"Weeknights. Do two sets outside on the patio." Talking to the floor, not looking at the cop. "Downstairs in the bar if it's raining. Four on Saturdays and Sundays. Afternoons, evenings."

"Get paid, and they give you room and board too? Sounds like a good gig. I got a cousin does the same thing out in Winnipeg. Plays nice finger-style guitar. Scuffles around like everybody else in the music business. Name's Keith Barnes. Ever heard of him? Part Indian. Mother was from some place up near Kenora. First Nations I guess you gotta say now, but he's still Indian to the family. So what do you know?"

Bobby blinked. "About what?"

Deforest stared back for a moment, then leaned forward and lowered his voice like he didn't want anybody else to hear. "About the pretty little girl strangled with a goddamn guitar string in your room, you dumb shit. The hell do you think I'm talking about?"

"I didn't know she was there. I had no idea."

"You spend the night with a corpse in the same room with you and you never notice her?"

"I got back here late…"

"Back from where?"

"Visiting a friend…"

"What friend?"

Bobby sat back in the booth. "Aren't…" He frowned, looked away. "Aren't you supposed to tell me I've got a right to… maybe not talk to you, ask for a lawyer?"

"Your rights?" Deforest sat back and spread his arms. "Yeah, you've got rights. A whole fucking book of them. Now look around. Who else is here with us?"

"I don't get…"

"How many goddamn rights do you think you've got, just you and me, nobody else around? You want to play dummy with me, go ahead. We'll stop now, I'll cuff you up, and your ass'll be downtown in an eye-blink. But you know what? I don't think you're dumb enough to kill a sweet little honey like that and just flake out in your bed like you'd just finished banging her. I may be wrong. You want to tell me I'm right, I'll listen. You want to play legal with me, I'm not your friend, okay?"

Bobby lowered his head, folded his hands in his lap. "After the gig last night…"

"What time are we talking about?"

"Midnight. I finish at midnight. I put my gear away…"

"What gear?"

"Amplifier, effects box, that stuff. I keep it in a room off the kitchen…"

"Your guitar too?"

"No, I lock it in my room. So I go up, put the guitar in its case in my room, and I leave it on top of the dresser."

"It's still there."

Bobby looked at him confused.

"Your guitar. It's still there. Had the forensics people open the case and look into it. They said it was a nice guitar. Kind of old and beat up, but what do I know about guitars? Anyway, it's missing a string."

Bobby nodded. "I broke the E string last night…"

"What's that look like?"

"The bottom string. The heaviest one. It's copper wound."

"Like the one used to choke the girl. What'd you do with it, the broken string?"

"I guess I brought it upstairs with me…"

"You guess?"

Bobby shrugged. "I think…"

"What good's a broken guitar string? I mean, what else can you use the damn thing for?"

"Nothing, really…"

"Except maybe to practically cut off a girl's head, right? Did you see what that thing did to her? Did you get a good look? Or maybe you saw it last night. Show me your hands."

Bobby raised his hands, palms out. "The police officer upstairs already looked at them…"

Deforest glanced at Bobby's hands. "You keep all your broken guitar strings?"

"I don't keep them…"

"So what do you do with them?"

"I… sometimes I…"

The door to the bar opened. Katchanoski took two steps into the room and stopped, a sheet of paper in his hand.

Bobby looked at him, then began again. "I don't know. I mean, I don't leave them lying around. I usually take them… I take them with me."

"Why? You just said they're no good, the broken ones."

"I don't like to litter, I guess."

"Litter? Jesus Christ!" Deforest stood up. "You're facing the tightest first-degree murder charge I've seen and you're afraid of being called a fucking *litterbug*?"

Bobby began shaking again. "I didn't… you said…"

Deforest waved his words away and turned to face Katchanoski walking toward him, extending the paper. "Forensics did a quick search," Katchanoski said, his eyes on Bobby. "Here's the list. They're on their way and Majumdar's getting the body ready to move."

"I want to see him before he goes," Deforest said, scanning the paper. He looked back at Bobby. "Bunch of interesting stuff in the dresser. You've got, what? A box of twelve condoms, five left. And what looks like maybe fifty grams of grass…"

"I bought that legally," Bobby said.

"Like I care. Sounds like you're having a hell of a good summer. Play your guitar, get laid, smoke a little dope when you feel like it. You're a lucky guy, you know that? You ever use one on that girl in your room?"

"No." Bobby shook his head, looking away. "No, we never… She was…" Still shaking his head.

"Was what?"

"She just wanted to talk with me sometimes. She liked talking with me…"

"About what?"

"Anything. Music, books… She'd had a rough life. Her parents were killed in a car accident back in February. It crushed her. She liked talking to me because I listened to her and she knew I didn't… I wouldn't…"

"Wouldn't what?"

"Make a move on her."

"Why not?"

"Because I liked her. She trusted me. I mean, I would, you know, if she'd ever said anything, done anything to say she wanted to, but we kind of connected as friends, sorta. We had a connection. My mother died last year and it took me months to get over it, so we had that in common."

"Smoke weed with her?"

"Couple of times."

Deforest stared at Bobby. Then: "How'd she get into your room?"

Bobby breathed deeply, looked away. "She had a key."

"A *key*? To your room? Now where the hell did she get that?"

"I gave it to her. I had a copy made for her."

"Didn't she have her own room?"

"Yeah…"

"Where is it, her room?"

"On the top floor…"

"You ever in there?"

Bobby shook his head.

"She'd rather be in your room than her own, just so the two of you could talk about what? Politics? The weather? That's what you're telling me?"

"It's complicated…"

Katchanoski pulled a stool from the bar and sat on it. When Deforest turned to look at him he said, "You want me to go?"

Deforest said no, he might as well stay for the rest. He turned back to Bobby. "Where'd you go after you finished last night?"

"Like I told you. I took my guitar up to the room and left it on the dresser."

"Then what?"

"I went to visit somebody…"

"Who?"

"A woman who lives down the beach, near the canal."

"This woman invites you back to her place after midnight? Who is she?"

"An older woman. She's smart and funny. Comes here a lot… To Tuffy's. Everybody knows her."

"She got a name?"

"Josie. Josie Marshall. She used to be…"

But Deforest had turned to look at Katchanoski again. "You hear that, Katch? He spends the night with Josie Marshall. Jesus. Here we go. Here we goddamn go."

This concludes our special preview of *Beach Blues*, available in hardcover in the Fall, 2022, wherever At Bay Press books are sold.